Painting Kisses

OTHER BOOKS AND AUDIO BOOKS

BY MELANIE JACOBSON

Painting Kisses

A NOVEL

· MELANIE JACOBSON ·

Covenant Communications, Inc.

Cover image by Covenant Communications, Inc and *Painted watercolor background* © donatas1205, courtesy istockphoto.com

Cover design copyright © 2014 by Covenant Communications, Inc.

Published by Covenant Communications, Inc.
American Fork, Utah

Printed in the United States of America
First Printing: October 2014

20 19 18 17 16 15 14   10 9 8 7 6 5 4 3 2 1

ISBN 978-1-62108-851-6

For my parents, who I know would have been proud.
That really is its own gift.

Acknowledgments

My husband is incredibly supportive. I couldn't have done any of this, any books before this one or since, without him. I know because I never even had it in me to try before he came along. Thank you to my children and their patience with my general air of distraction. Thank you to Amy Lou, who reads first and often last and who babysat so I could write. Thank you to Kristine Tate and Brittany Larsen for their patient weekly feedback. Thank you to my beta readers, who offered encouragement, praise, and honest criticism: Rachel Gillie and Susan Auten (whose book you should read if you haven't yet). Thank you to Jana Parkin and Krista Jensen, who fact-checked my art details. Thanks, as always, to my editor, Samantha Millburn, for her eagle eye. Thank you to my extended family and my family by marriage, who are both full of adopted aunts on either side who cheer for me and are proud of me, and that matters. And I apologize to anyone I missed: I promise it's because I'm thinking I made you read one of the other projects I have waiting in the wings, and I get it all jumbled up in my head. It happens a lot. Thanks to everyone for their regular patience with that too.

Chapter 1

Hell was full of either coffee or dried bits of omelet.

Maybe both.

Definitely both, I decided as I wiped up the spillover from the twentieth breakfast I'd served since starting my shift. These construction guys made a bigger mess than my niece Chloe did. Then again, Chloe was probably the world's only three-year-old who ate with the table manners of the Queen of England . . . when she wanted to.

I swept the plates into a plastic bin and pocketed the five-dollar bill tucked under the salt shaker. It was more than fair for a fifteen-dollar ticket. I minded the clean up a little bit less. A very little bit less.

"Lady? Lady, I need a refill."

I put on a smile and scooped up the coffeepot on the counter. "Coming, Mr. Benny." It had taken me only a couple of weeks to memorize the regular orders for a dozen different customers, including this raisin of a man's, but he still hadn't learned my name after almost a year of coming here. Was it such a jump from "lady" to "Lia"? For someone who shorted my tip three times a week, apparently yes.

The diner's door swished open, and Aidan stuck his head in. A happy sigh tried to sneak out of me, but I didn't let it. I barked at him instead. "You're confused. It's not Saturday."

"Is it clear?"

Clear like your lake-blue eyes? Yes. Desirable for you to be here in the middle of the week unexpectedly? Yes. Acceptable for me to be all schoolgirly about it? Nope.

"Ramona isn't here. It's clear." Ramona was the *R* of the T&R Diner, co-owned with her husband, Tom, who was a killer short-order cook.

Aidan made his way to the only open table, with Chief, his Australian shepherd, at his heels. He folded his long body into the corner booth, and Chief settled down beneath the table with a faint jingle of his tags.

"Did I hear Chief?" Tom hollered through the pass-through window. "Ramona's going to catch us one day."

"Not us," I hollered back. "You. You let that dog in. Not me."

"You know you love him," Aidan said. "Also, I just heard his stomach growl."

"*His* stomach?" I repeated. "Better be, because I know you wouldn't try telling me how to do my job with that lame hint."

"Of course not," he said, grinning. "But I'm not going to stop you if you want to come take my order." He couldn't be that much older than me, but crow's-feet already framed his eyes. Too much working in the sun, probably. Not that they looked bad. Not that anything about him looked bad.

"Don't care what *you* want, but Chief's is done." I darted to the window and scooped up a plate of breakfast sausage, then made my way to Aidan's table.

One of the other regulars protested. "That's supposed to be my sausage. I ordered first."

Tom grunted. "It's time I told you the truth, Hogan. I like that dog better than you. You can wait." He slapped his spatula against the griddle for emphasis while several of the other men chuckled.

I set Chief's plate down in front of the dog before crossing my arms to brace for Aidan. "What are we on today?"

"We? I like that you're showing team spirit."

"You're making me. This is a stupid goal."

"You're full of . . . energy this morning. What are you on? And can you give me some?"

"Sleep," I said and held up my hand to cut him off when I saw the glint in his eye. "Whatever joke you're about to make, don't. You, me, and the word *sleep* have no business in the same sentence, so don't go there."

He put on a wounded look. "I can't believe you'd even think I'd make that joke."

I rolled my eyes. "You're right. Sorry."

"I mean, it's way too easy. I like a joke I have to work for."

"Why are you even here on a weekday?"

"School's out. I'm on a summer schedule now."

He went to school? A lot of the blue-collar guys who came into T&R would never consider trying to start college in their late twenties. Most of them were focused on working their way up in their unions or getting themselves foreman jobs, from what I'd overheard in their conversations. They weren't academics, just down-to-earth guys who had wives and kids and who were trying to pay the bills. And that was exactly why I'd chosen a dive like T&R to work at and not one of the high-end breakfast cafés farther up Big Cottonwood Canyon. Down-to-earthiness. For the rest of my life, I could never get too much of it.

"Summer schedule?" I asked. "Does that mean I have to put up with you on more than Saturdays?" I didn't know if I wanted him to say yes or no.

"Probably. You're on the way to my jobsite. And by you, I don't mean you, Tom!" he called. "Especially not on number twelve day. You can bet that when I get the number twelve, I'm just here to see Lia."

"Get a room!" a guy in a red hat said.

"At least get her digits," another guy yelled out.

"I try every time I'm in here. No dice."

"If it works, give them to me," Red Hat said. "She always tells me no too."

"Liar," I said to Red Hat, trying to act like having the whole diner's eyes on me didn't fluster me, even though my cheeks had warmed. "You haven't asked me for anything but breakfast."

"Can I have your number?" he asked.

"No." I hadn't meant to be funny, but laughter rolled across the diner, along with a catcall. Mr. Benny scowled and clapped his hands over his ears.

"How come I can't have your number either?" Aidan asked.

"Because you can't order me off the menu like you do a chicken-fried steak." More laughter from the other guys. Aidan took it all in with a smile—that one I'd actually been trying to earn.

"How come you're not like this every day?" Hogan asked, grinning despite still not having his sausage.

"Don't know what you're talking about," I growled and stared pointedly at my order pad. But I did know. In the three years I'd worked at the diner, I'd made a point of meeting every flirtatious customer remark with a polite smile that discouraged any follow-up. If it didn't work, I went with pretending I couldn't hear the comments. The regulars knew they could expect friendly, quiet service. I didn't have the knack for the patter and teasing that the other girls had. First-timers came in and tried to flirt with me from time to time, but I couldn't do it. I wished I could wave a wand and make them think of me as an invisible food-delivering robot.

I couldn't be clever with anyone I didn't know well. Only the other employees got jokes out of me. Other employees . . . and Aidan.

He'd startled them out of me the first time. He always had *The New York Times* on his iPad when I dropped food by his table. After a while, I'd maybe, sort of, definitely spied to see what kind of stuff he was reading. Current events, arts, sports, business. He read it all.

One day he'd been reading a review of an artist I'd known and loathed ever since I'd met him at a joint show we'd done. He called himself Zhaday, which sounded stupid on a middle-aged white guy from Delaware. I read about this band once who insisted on a huge bowl of M&M's in their dressing room with all the brown ones picked out because they were rock stars and they could. This guy was like that. But worse was that Zhaday's art had no soul. His earlier work did—I'd studied it and liked his sense of form and color—but he'd lost that somewhere along the way.

The piece on Aidan's screen had shown Zhaday's interpretation of the Museum of Modern Art in Manhattan as a decaying monument, rotting almost organically. "Disturbing View of New York's Place on the International Art Stage," I read the headline aloud. "Disturbing? Sure, if we're talking about the pandering he's doing with that painting."

Aidan choked on his coffee, spluttering and laughing at the same time. It was kind of cute. "That was perfect. I'm buying you a drink."

I shook my head, embarrassed at outing myself for reading over his shoulder. "I don't drink."

"Sure you do. Coffee? Orange juice?"

And I reddened even further because I thought he meant meeting me for a drink, date-style. "Orange juice is great."

"Tom?" he called. "Can you get Lia here a glass of orange juice on me when it's convenient?"

"Don't hurt yourself, big spender," Tom grumbled, but that only made Aidan laugh again.

And somehow a tradition had been born—whichever one of us made the other one laugh first when Aidan came in got treated to a glass of OJ.

"Speaking of chicken-fried steak," Tom said, tapping the bell and derailing my memory train. The bell was supposed to let the servers know a meal was done. He never actually used it for that. It was more like a punctuation mark. *Ding, ding, ding, ding.* "Get that joker's order, and maybe I can cook him something that'll keep him too busy eating to talk."

"You're a genius, Tom," I said. He waved a spatula and bent over the grill again. I whipped out my notepad and gave Aidan an expectant look. "What can I get for you?"

"Your last name."

"You're like a bad movie. I already told you—I'm not on the menu."

"What did I get last time?"

"You think I remember that kind of thing? That I'm sitting around memorizing what you get every time you come in here?" Even though I had my eyes narrowed at him, I had to fight a smile at the easy way we fell into this routine. Not having to wait until Saturday for this felt like eating dessert first.

"You don't remember?" he asked, faking a hurt face.

"Yes. But you shouldn't assume it."

"Oh, come on. Tell me I'm special, that you only remember for me."

I gave him the look my sister Dani used to give me when we were kids and I said something she thought was stupid. I pointed to Mr. Benny. "Two cups of coffee, fifteen minutes apart, with a plate of scrambled eggs and a side of hash browns in between. Red Hat over there? Short stack with a side of bacon and two glasses of OJ. Guy coming in from the parking lot? Three eggs over easy, hash browns, and two cups of coffee, black." I tapped my pencil on the order pad. "This is a prop so I don't intimidate the rest of you with my gigantic brain. Also, you're not special."

His grin broke out. "Why ask me when you know what I'm getting?"

"I like to give you the illusion of choice. You're on number eleven, chicken-fried steak. It's not too late to back out."

"Should I?"

"Have you regretted anything yet?" Tom asked from the pass-through.

"No," Aidan admitted. "But I'm worried that at some point you'll make me pay for mouthing off."

Tom snatched the next ticket down from the window. "I might spit in it, but I won't screw it up. You gotta—"

"Respect the grill," I finished. "You've mentioned that a time or two."

"You're worse than him," Tom said, slapping a piece of steak into the flour and dredging it like he was trying to kill the beef again.

Aidan winced. "You should take that personally, Lia. Very personally. Worse than me is pretty bad."

"You win," I said, losing the fight against a laugh. "You *are* bad. Orange juice is on me today."

Aidan pumped his fist in victory. "That's ten to seven. I'm pulling ahead."

"Don't be so impressed with yourself." I lowered my voice. "Mr. Benny makes me laugh first every single day."

"But is it on purpose?"

I grinned. "No. And today I get the last laugh on you because next time you come in, it's the number twelve." Number twelve was liver.

Aidan sighed.

"No one's making you do it. You can skip to thirteen."

"No, I can't, and it's your fault. When I came in that first day and asked you what the best thing on the menu was, you should have told me. Then I wouldn't have to try it all myself."

"I did tell you."

"You said it's all good. Twenty-five things can't all be the best thing."

"Why not?" Tom interrupted. "You think I haven't figured out a thing or two after owning this grill for nine years?"

"Don't worry, boss. Aidan only means about half of what he says. I'll buy your orange juice today too if it makes you feel better."

Tom snorted. "Why would it make me feel better to have you buy me something I have to make if I want to drink it? And don't you have other tables to serve?"

I rolled my eyes at Aidan, making him laugh, and made my way over to the guy at table three and poured his coffee without even asking. "Three eggs over easy with a side of hash browns?"

He nodded, bleary-eyed.

I turned to Aidan and stuck my tongue out.

He shook his head and turned his attention to his iPad. Must be something good. I'd sneak a peek when I dropped his chicken-fried steak off.

The next table was a new face. Dirt-crusted boots and a tan face this early in May meant he was probably one of the construction guys working on the new ski resort. "What can I get for you?" I asked.

"Hey, beautiful. Straight to business with no foreplay? I like it."

I heard someone snort into their coffee cup. It sounded suspiciously like Mr. Benny. I didn't look around to check. I could handle stuff like this only if I convinced myself that no one was watching. I drew out my order pad and lifted my eyebrows slightly without acknowledging the guy's come on. "Would you like to hear the specials?"

His eyes brightened like I'd issued a challenge, and I struggled to keep my face blank. Great. The challenge guys were the worst. I'd gotten used to customers who ranged from teen snow junkies to old men flirting with me, even though, at first, I couldn't figure out why they did it. I wasn't a knockout. When my life-drawing instructor had assigned us to do self-portraits in art school, I'd titled mine *The Median*.

Medium brown hair, longish. Medium height. Brown eyes. Not pasty white skin, not tan. Kind of scrawny. Nice mouth, maybe, but lips always chapped from biting them. I was nothing to object to. I also wasn't anything to stop and take notice of. I was the middle, which is why I figured out pretty fast that the reason customers flirted with me was that I was here. They flirted with all the waitresses, even Dot, who was older than my grandma.

Most of them backed off after I ignored their passes a time or two, but not the challenge guys. They made it some kind of personal mission to get an acknowledgment of their pickup skills. It was weird. They didn't even want a date out of it. They wanted to force you into playing along or snapping at them.

They hated when I ignored them, which left me one option: run away.

"Why would I want to hear the specials when I already see something special?" he said in a silky voice that I wanted to believe, for the sake of self-respecting women everywhere, had never worked on any woman, ever.

"The corned-beef-hash plate? Yeah, it's great. I'll bring it to you with a side of home potatoes."

I tore off his order sheet and fled to the kitchen.

"That's not what I want," he called after me.

"Son, it's what you're getting," Mr. Benny said. "You'd best eat it."

"But—"

Aidan cleared his throat, and I glanced out at him through the pass-through window in time to see him cross his arms over his chest. The construction guy's eyes widened, and he started to say something, but Aidan nodded once, and just like that, the guy shut up and fiddled with some sweetener packets instead.

What in the world? Were crossed arms some kind of bro code I didn't know about? Either way, I was glad New Guy was done with his challenge. I poured some fresh orange juice and swung by Aidan's table to deliver it.

"I could have handled it, but thank you," I said, setting the glass down in front of him.

"I didn't do anything."

"Accept the gratitude."

"I'll take whatever you're willing to give me," he said in resignation.

I fought a grin. I *had* shut him down about a billion times already, but he'd been a good sport about it.

He lifted the glass like he was toasting me and took a swallow. I watched his neck muscles for about two seconds before I realized how weird it was to stare at his throat and find his juice drinking sexy.

That's why Aidan was harder to put the brakes on, because he had an elusive, dangerous charm. He'd taken my rejections as a challenge too, but each time I shut him down, he sat back with a smile on his face, as if he were looking forward to seeing what I would come up with next, not trying to wear me down into submission. It was the same mixture of humor and confidence my ex-husband, Donovan, had charmed me with. Unfortunately, Donovan's charm had hidden dark, spiny secrets.

I turned on my heel and fetched the coffeepot so I could busy myself at other tables, topping off drinks and checking on customers so I wouldn't get drawn into any more schoolgirl staring at Aidan. I knew exactly what to expect each of them to tip, and even with Mr. Benny's miserly dollar, I was happy with the total. If tomorrow was about the same, I could trade away my Friday shift.

"Order up," Tom said.

I scooped up the chicken-fried steak and set it in front of Aidan. "What are you going to do when you've tried everything on the menu?" I asked. Move on? I'd miss . . . Chief.

Aidan leaned back in the booth. "If you're worried I'll quit coming around, you can say so. Try, 'Aidan, I'd love to see you sometime, not at the diner.'"

I stuck a hand on my hip, and he nodded like it was the reaction he'd expected. "Aidan, I'd love for you to not come to the diner."

"That's not what I said."

"But it's what I meant. Eat your steak, and go away."

"I don't want you to miss me. Come on, Lia. I'm not cold enough to leave you hanging like that, wishing for me to show up."

"Not wishing for you. For him." I pointed at Chief.

Aidan reached down to scratch behind the dog's ears. "Chief might be the only reason I ever even get dates. Do you get tired of women using you to get to me, boy?"

"I'm going to refill your coffee now, but you should know it's the second time today I've considered serving a drink over someone's head."

"Sounds like you could use a break. How about you take one with me, like later today over dinner?"

"Do you ever give up?"

"Nope. I'm kind of relentless in a nonstalker way."

"If by relentless you mean annoying, I guess I can't argue." I rested my hand on his table and leaned toward him, lowering my voice in my best guess of what sultry-voice was supposed to sound like. His eyes darkened, and I smirked. "I'll tell you what. I won't give you a date, but I'll give you something even better." I turned. "Tom?"

"Yeah?"

I straightened. "Get Aidan an extra side of bacon, please." I patted the table as Aidan laughed. "Don't you feel better already?"

"You seem to. Better than last week, anyway. What's the secret?"

You showing up when it's not Saturday. But I wasn't going to say that, so I gave him another true answer. "Daffodils."

"Your secret is daffodils?"

I nodded at the window, where the bright-yellow heads of daffodils peered over the ledge from the window boxes Ramona insisted on keeping there. Ours at home had bloomed two days before, and Chloe and I had spotted them in several neighbors' yards on our walk yesterday evening. "Haven't you been seeing them everywhere you go?"

"Yeah, I've seen them, but they're not mood altering."

"Then you're broken."

"No, I depend on a different substance: bacon. Didn't you promise me some?"

"Don't get all demanding about free bacon," Tom warned from the grill. "Order's up."

I deposited it in front of Aidan. "I'm going to ignore you for the rest of your breakfast. I have work to do."

He tapped his iPad. Yep, he was reading the *Times*. "I'll entertain myself."

I made the next circuit of tables on autopilot, more interested in the daffodils than the customers. The flowers were beautiful, especially against the weathered wood of the window boxes Tom refused to repaint. The urge to capture the blossoms, pushy upstarts glowing against their banged-up backdrop, squeezed me like an ache, and I caught my breath as the painting formed in my mind. It was a quiet picture, unlike any of the work the New York galleries had flipped out over when I'd been married to Donovan Beckman, the artsy novelty in my in-laws' circle of socialites and power brokers.

The feeling pushed against my stomach like hunger in the morning and out to my fingers and toes like a good stretch after a run. Muscle memory made my right hand twitch in anticipation of touching my brushes.

Except I had none. I'd sold or donated every last bit of my supplies when I'd run away from New York. And suddenly that was Shakespeare-level tragic.

So now what?

Chapter 2

I counted my tips. Twenty dollars more than usual, thanks to Aidan. Guess he liked free bacon. I could take Friday morning off if I needed to. But as I passed the window box on the way to my car, I checked my watch. I could squeeze in a trip to McGill's Art and Frame if I hurried.

I slid my phone out of my pocket and hesitated before pushing my sister's number. Did I really want this? I'd passed McGill's going home hundreds of times in the last three years and had never once felt the urge to stop and check it out. Now, suddenly, I was Juliet to its Romeo, irresistibly drawn to it despite knowing how badly painting had ended for me last time. How did this make sense? But I kind of didn't care.

I tapped out a quick text. *Need to do errand. 1:30 ok?*

I pulled out onto the road when Dani's reply came back. *No prob.*

All the way to McGill's, I thought about the daffodils. If this were five years ago, I'd have painted them pushing up through the broken concrete of a Manhattan sidewalk, stalks nearly the size of trees serving as a commentary on the inability of cities to pave over nature no matter how hard they tried. It would have been a huge canvas, saturated in color and priced at the Van Exel gallery in the low five figures, maybe more.

My hands clenched the steering wheel like it was trying to escape me. Even though I'd been happy with twenty unexpected bucks in tip money after lunch, I couldn't make myself miss the ten thousand–dollar paydays on those pieces from my old life. Every stupid cent I'd earned from my work had come to me tied up in strings.

I'd been over it all way before I'd actually gotten myself together to walk out. I didn't want to make that art anymore. I hadn't wanted anything to do with art, period, since I'd left. Yet here I sat, wanting to make something so badly that my car was trying to drive itself to the paints for me.

Six months ago the thought of trying to paint had squeezed my chest so tightly it had strangled my breath. Today a ticklish excitement fluttered inside me instead. The daffodils appeared in my mind's eye exactly as they were, perfect in their imperfect planters.

I pulled into the parking lot and separated fifty dollars from my tip money before stepping out of my car. When I opened McGill's door, it broke open the dam of memory, and I grabbed the doorframe to keep my balance in the flood of scents that carried me right back to being young, stupid, poor, and utterly happy to even wander the aisles of the art store near school.

A deep breath helped, and I followed the signs to the paint aisle. If I could have hugged the tubes of paint without scaring the middle-aged man examining the acrylics, I might have.

I stopped in front of the oils and took another deep breath, not to steady myself, but to absorb the experience through more of my senses. The tubes of pigment were slick and familiar beneath my fingertips. Cadmium yellow, ultramarine blue, viridian green.

I picked up the burnt sienna and turned it over and over. I'd created countless mountains out of this color mixed with violet, built them up and then carved windows into their sides with ivory black and titanium white. That had been my most popular motif, the idea that the man-made towers of commerce dotting the Manhattan skyline were urban mountains, precisely engineered modern versions of what God had made forever ago. I loved staring up at the skyscrapers, from the Chrysler Building to the Empire State Building, but they didn't move me inside—reach in and hollow me out and leave me bigger—the way a hike through the Uintas did.

I touched the yellow. It was a tube of daffodils if I added some white. I pictured it on the canvas. I'd need to carve through it with my palette knife to get the right texture on the petals.

I dropped my hand. The picture was wrong. I moved farther down the aisle, assessing the selection. Nothing could beat my favorite SoHo art supply store in New York, but McGill's understood quality; all the best brands were represented here. They had everything I needed.

Not oils.

The thought thrummed through me, and I stepped back from the shelf. Not oils? I'd made a small fortune over a four-year period by working in oils, had retreated into the astringent smell of linseed oil and turpentine.

The sharp scents were as comforting to me as the smell of rising bread. When things had fallen apart with Donovan, the bite of the linseed oil was one of the few things that had cut through the gray haze in my head and snapped the world into sharp, painful focus. Which was why I'd gotten rid of it all. I hadn't needed clarity that demanded more from me than I'd had to give.

I stood six feet from the end of the aisle, and I should have been smart enough to take the three steps toward that exit.

When I'd given everything up, the hunger to splash all I had inside me across a canvas, to give visual shape to the chaos in my brain . . . had disappeared. Died. Faded. I didn't know. I just hadn't wanted to paint. But the chaos itself had disappeared too. And that had been good. And I hadn't missed any of it. The constant hum of ideas *or* the painting.

Until the daffodils. And for them, I didn't want oils.

The facing shelf housed all the watercolors. I hadn't done watercolors since my first year in art school. I'd done plenty in high school before I'd had the cash—or confidence—to invest in oils. Some of my truly wretched early work had hung in my parents' house before they'd packed it all to move to Saudi Arabia for my dad's job. But now I itched to try again, to see if I could do something more than portraits of our family cat. The oils overwhelmed me—they were staring a hole into my back—but the challenge of doing a crazy, bright daffodil in delicate watercolors and still making it shine? I couldn't resist.

I fingered the fifty dollars in my pocket and laughed. The other man in the aisle didn't even look up. He was obviously used to artists. I knew better than to think my extra tip money would be enough to get me out the door with even the basics to do a simple watercolor. I should have cared more about blowing the cash. But I didn't. I'd been squeezing pennies until they screamed, and my biggest splurge in a year had been premium chocolate. Every week. Twice. Twice every week.

Besides, this went beyond a splurge. This wasn't an indulgence. The itch was so bad that the urge to paint had ballooned from want to need; there was no other way to stop it except to do it.

A basic color kit from the brand I'd seen in the studios at the art school found its way into my hands. I'd have to start with cheap synthetic brushes, but they'd get the job done. It wasn't like my daffodils would be going into Van Exel's. I picked up the nicest watercolor paper. Couldn't skimp there.

I flinched when the cashier read off my total, but as I settled into my car with my bag of new supplies riding shotgun, I didn't care. It would be worth it.

Chapter 3

I smiled all the way home, and it only grew bigger when the front door to the condo flew open and Chloe barreled out, a crown of dandelions hanging halfway off her head. I braced myself for impact, and she threw her arms around my legs.

"I wuv you so much, Wia!"

"I love you too, sweet pea. How was your day?"

"Great!" Chloe hollered before taking off at a run for the house again.

"Get your errand done?" Dani asked, leaning against the doorway. She still had two classes and a shift at work to get through, but her eyeliner had already smudged faintly under her eyes. Or maybe those were circles of exhaustion. I wished I could mix up some yellow ochre and rose madder and paint them away, eliminate her constant tiredness with a few strokes.

"I got it done," I said. "Hope it didn't stress you out."

She grimaced and pushed herself upright. "If anything, it made me feel better. You shouldn't—"

"Nope." I held up both hands to stop the words about to come out of her mouth. "I'm not having this conversation again. I'm doing exactly what I want to. Stop with the stressing." That almost got a smile. When it didn't come, I got my chest knot. It was hard, dark, and fist-sized and lodged itself behind my sternum every time something bad was about to go down. As harbingers of doom go, it was painfully accurate and therefore handy. I exhaled like I did every time I got the knot, always in the hope that it would loosen up enough that I could breathe. It never helped. "What's wrong?"

She almost told me. Her mouth opened to say the words, but she paused and smiled. It would have eased the knot if it hadn't looked like a superhuman effort had gone into making the corner of her lips turn up. "Nothing's wrong. Just tired. We can't all have glamorous jobs in roadside diners."

"Shut up. I'll make you a sandwich before class." Maybe I could weasel the truth out of her with food.

I herded her into the kitchen and pressed her down into a chair before pulling together the fixings for her favorite turkey-and-avocado sandwich. She took a bite, and the chest fist loosened the tiniest bit, even though I was never convinced she was eating as much as she should. She caught me staring, and I flicked my gaze out to watch Chloe run around the tiny backyard. "What's she doing?"

"Chasing a butterfly." Dani set her sandwich down. "I hate leaving her."

I pushed her plate closer. "Eat. And she's fine. I swear I keep a good eye on her other than most of the time when I leave her to forage for wild plants in the backyard while I lock myself in my room for *Real Housewives* marathons."

She nudged my foot. "Stop. You know I'm glad I can leave her with you, but I don't like being away from her."

"You're doing the right thing."

"I guess."

"I *know.* Nursing school would be hard for anyone, but for a single, working mom? You're my hero."

"You're going to make me puke."

"Don't. It took me almost two minutes to make that sandwich."

She didn't laugh. "She'll start preschool in the fall. It'll free up more time for you." She teared up.

The fist tightened so fast I had to stifle a gasp. Dani didn't cry. Tendrils of dread spread out from my chest, creeping down toward my stomach. I shoved the plate out of the way and took her hands, careful not to let the weight of my worry squeeze them too tightly. "Talk to me."

"We were at the park this morning. The other moms were talking about preschool, where their kids are going, which teachers to try to get. I can't afford any of the private ones around here. And because my schedule is as tight as it is, Chloe either has to attend right by the house or right by work. But that would make you have to drive so far out of your way to get her. I don't know what to do. Move?" That sent her tears over the brink, and she pressed the heels of her hands into her eyes to stop them.

"I'm sure there are a ton of programs to help moms like you," I said. Dani had refused any kind of public assistance for herself beyond loans to pay for her tuition at the U, but she'd been fierce in giving Chloe every advantage she could. Dani wouldn't reject a handout if it meant taking care of her daughter.

"Sure. But none of them are for any of the private schools around here. And that was the whole point of being here—to give her a good start."

We'd found a condo on the border of the elementary school district with the highest test scores in the state. When I'd threatened Donovan's parents with going public about exactly how much money their son had stolen from the sales of my work, they'd written a check to cover a massive down payment on the condo without blinking. I could have probably wrangled a check five times the size and bought a McMansion, but I hadn't wanted to be under their thumb.

I squeezed Dani's hands. "I'm sure we'll find something great for her. We still have three months before preschool will even start, right?"

She pulled her hands from mine and wiped her cheeks, but more tears fell. "Sorry," she said on a shaky sigh. "This is what I've been so scared of ever since I had her. I know I'm never going to dress her in Janie and Jack, but I thought I could give her the important things. Like a good school."

"You can still give her a good school. She'll be at Aspen Heights, starting in kindergarten, and we'll stay in this condo as long as you guys want. I promise you, there's nothing to worry about."

"There's everything to worry about," she said, dropping her head to her hands. "All the kids starting at Aspen Heights will already have two years together at schools where the teachers smell like lilacs and all their snacks are prepared fresh by stuck-up chefs."

"They smell like lilacs?" I repeated, trying not to laugh when her distress was as thick as tar.

"The point is that the preschools by my work probably smell like asbestos and desperation." The defeat in her expression killed my amusement. "This is the first major thing I was determined to do for her, and I can't. How am I supposed to get anything else right if I can't do this? Did you know most of these people put their kids on the waiting lists for these places when the kids were babies? I'm in over my head, and Chloe's going to pay for it."

Dani was already holding herself together with only sheer grit and lots of cheap coffee, but I pushed at her as gently as I could to see if I could break through her panic. "Public schools don't require preschool. She'll go to Aspen, same as the other kids, and I'm sure by the end of kindergarten you won't see a difference in her preparation versus anyone else's."

"That's the thing!" she burst out. "I already do. Haven't you noticed how different Chloe is from other kids at the park?"

The anxiety in her voice startled me, but worse was the familiar stir of not-rightness that prickled my stomach whenever I watched Chloe play— or more like not play—with other kids. "I mean, she's a little shy. And I know I'm not an expert, but I'd bet my entire pathetic bank account that she doesn't have any developmental delays."

"She has social ones," Dani said, her voice quieter. "And the more I watch her, the more sure I am that they're outside of normal. She needs a private program with a low teacher-to-student ratio so she can't disappear."

"I think state law limits how high the ratios can be, same as elementary classrooms," I said, trying to calm her.

"But they can't pay the teachers enough to guarantee they care like the private preschool academies can. And the private schools do have smaller teacher-student ratios. The other moms are always talking about that. I just need someone to see Chloe and love her and send her into kindergarten feeling confident. Otherwise I'm afraid she'll . . ." She trailed off, and more tears fell.

"I think you're not giving the public preschools enough credit. But if you really believe that, let me homeschool her. I'll be the best private preschool teacher ever."

"I love you," Dani said, her smile watery. "But how does that overcome her social delays? She needs to learn how to be around other kids."

She had me there. "I really think you're stressing about this more than you need to, and that's because you're a good mom," I hurried to add when her jaw hardened. "This? How worried you are? This is why you were made to be Chloe's mom. It proves you're doing the most important stuff right. Don't stress. Stuff always has a way of working out." And it would this time because I'd make it, for Chloe and Dani.

She gave me a watered-down smile. "Yeah. You. You're the way it works out. You do too much, and I can't thank you enough for it."

"Shut up. You thank me too much. Go wash your face, try again with your mascara, and get out of here."

This time her real smile showed up. "You want to lick your finger and rub at my smudges? Or maybe tuck my shirt in?"

"Fine. Ignore me. You look fantastic, and you shouldn't change a thing."

She pushed up from the table and checked her reflection in the microwave. "Holy cow. I'm going to go wash my face and fix my mascara."

"Told you."

She rolled her eyes but returned from the bathroom a few minutes later minus the tragic raccoon look. On the deck, she called for Chloe, wrapping her tiny daughter up in a long hug. Some days Chloe made it harder for her to leave than others, clinging to her and crying, but today was a brave day, and Chloe smoothed Dani's hair back to kiss her on the cheek before wiggling loose in pursuit of her butterfly again.

Dani came back in and scooped up her purse and backpack. "She needs to go to bed on time tonight."

"Of course."

Her eyes narrowed. "I mean it. No *Dora* marathons."

"But I love it so much."

"You just like being Chloe's favorite."

"Guilty. Now get out of here."

She smiled, another real one, and left.

I poked my head out the sliding door. "Chloe! Come in for a minute." She veered toward me, still running, and I braced myself again and scooped her up. "Want to draw?"

"Piwates?" she asked, her eyes lighting up.

"You can draw pirates. I'm thinking about daffodils."

"Those?" Chloe pointed to the planter, and I nodded. She let go of me and clapped. "Yes, Wia! Draw them!" She scrambled down to fetch her pile of scratch paper in her toy chest behind the sofa, then ran back out and thrust the crinkled sheets at me. "I get my colors." And she ran off again.

I set the papers on her plastic easel, the closest I'd come to the real thing since New York. "Why don't you work here, and I'll use my own colors," I said when she returned with a box of crayons.

That made her giggle again. "You not have any colors, silly Wia."

"I got some Lia colors today. I'll show you."

"Okay," she said, already more interested in putting a finer point on her pink crayon in the box's sharpener. I retrieved my supplies and sat down to work, capturing the lines of the daffodils in a few easy pencil strokes. I'd sketched so many things for Chloe that it was easy to translate the flowers into graphite, but for the first time in a long time, I wanted to give them more life and color.

Chloe showed me a pink scribble with a green line poking out of it.

"Beautiful flower, sweet pea. What do you think of mine?"

Chloe's eyes widened. "Bootiful. Color it," she said, plucking the yellow crayon from her box, which made me laugh.

I held the sketch away and studied it. "Maybe I should use these," I said, showing her the watercolors.

Chloe stared at the tubes behind the plastic window. "That not crayons."

"No, those are paint."

Chloe wiggled her fingers. "Paint!"

I hugged her because I couldn't resist squeezing the cuteness. "Not fingerpaint. Watch this."

I laid down a piece of watercolor paper on the tabletop, opened the cap on the yellow cadmium, and squirted it onto a plastic plate, then picked up an inexpensive synthetic brush and swirled it through the yellow, mixing it with water, loving the resistance as the paint slowed it down. Chloe watched in silence, and I drew a deep breath before touching my brush to the paper. The yellow blossomed on the page, and with a couple of quick strokes, the petals of the daffodil appeared.

"Wia," Chloe breathed. "Dat like magic."

The place that had cracked open inside me when I'd first imagined the daffodil painting widened even further, this time like a full-body stretch on the inside. It *was* like magic. The chest fist had disappeared with the flick of a paintbrush.

I pressed my forehead against Chloe's. "Would you like me to finish this?"

"Yes, pwease."

I pressed a kiss against her brow. "Then I will. What will you work on?"

"I make flowers too. Outside!" She raced back to her easel and dragged it toward the door.

I loved her determination and gave her a hand with the other side, helping her carry it out and set it up in the late-afternoon sunshine. She plopped herself down with her yellow crayon in hand and attempted a careful, crooked petal.

It took a few minutes to get my own paper set up properly on a thick piece of cardboard at the patio table before I could focus on capturing the way the light played on the stem differently than the blossom itself. Peace washed over me. It would be worth a hundred extra shifts to buy more supplies and chase that feeling.

I had no idea how long I'd worked when I heard the neighbor's sliding door open. Chloe had wandered out to the grass at the edge of the deck to weave a daisy chain when Griff stepped out and waved. "Ladies. Always good to see you out here."

"Also good to get the weather that lets us be out here," I said. I was proud it came out louder than a mumble. That was progress.

"Yeah. Too bad about all the sunshine," he said, making me grin. Griff was happiest if the clouds were hinting at snow conditions. He always skied until the last possible day of the season, and days on the slopes were numbered.

"What are you ladies up to?" he asked, surveying our deck.

"Hi, Gwiff," Chloe said, her voice soft. She kept her eyes on her daisies.

"Sweet pea," Griff said, his voice a gentle invitation for her to look. He'd been doing that for a while now. At first it had bugged me that he borrowed my nickname for Chloe, but when it had actually gotten him past her debilitating shyness enough for her to talk to him, I forgave him for the theft.

He leaned across his railing and peered at Chloe's easel. "Did you draw your flowers?" he asked. "That's really good."

"Thank you," Chloe said, her expression proud. "Mine is as pretty as Wia's." She ducked her head again.

"You're drawing too?" he asked me, his eyebrows lifting.

My cheeks heated. I wished I could mix up some ochre to cover the red creeping across them. The other colors I would need flashed through my head: aureolin yellow, alizarin crimson, cobalt blue. "Kind of. I'm painting."

"Can I see?"

I hesitated. I'd never been shy about my work before, but I hadn't worked in watercolor to mastery the way I had in oils. I could see all the flaws in the daffodils I'd committed to the paper, but I could also see how to fix them. The objective part of my brain that had been one of my greatest assets as a critic of my own work told me I had nothing to be embarrassed about. Still, I hesitated. I couldn't decide if showing my first work in years to a casual acquaintance like my neighbor was a good or bad way to start. When the pause after his question had grown awkward to the point that he looked as if I would need to paint the growing pink out of his cheeks too, I cleared my throat with a mumbled apology and stepped out of the way so he could see.

He pushed his sandy blond bangs out of his eyes and squinted, their startling light green appearing even brighter against his skin. He always looked sun-fresh thanks to the time he spent on the slopes, and even though it had deepened the lines around his eyes, I liked the character it gave his otherwise boyish face. I couldn't believe a dozen women hadn't already tried to snatch him up. Or maybe they had. I'd seen a date or two of his drop by over the last two years but never more than once. Someone would wise up and drag him to the altar eventually.

Griff studied the picture for a long, quiet minute. "How come I didn't know you could do this?" he finally asked, his voice tinged with awe. "Because that's not the first time you've ever painted flowers."

"I haven't done it in a long time."

"It's so good it's hard to believe you haven't been locked away in your condo doing this all day, every day."

I surprised myself by telling him more of the truth than I'd given anyone since I left New York. "I used to." I left it at that, and Griff let it drop, which is one of the things I liked about him.

"I feel inadequate soaking up all the talent out here like a freeloader. Chloe, I'm no good at painting. Is there anything I can do that would make me part of the club?"

"What a talent?" Chloe asked, her brow furrowed.

"Something you're good at," I said. "What could Griff do for a talent while we draw?"

"Music," Chloe whispered. "Guitar."

"Do you think that would work?" Griff asked, his face serious. "I want to do my part to belong."

Chloe nodded, the third victim of blushing cheeks.

Griff nodded. "If you're sure, then I'll be right back." He disappeared into his house and emerged a couple minutes later with his guitar. He took a seat, propping his feet up on the rail while he picked out the opening strains of a Spanish piece that immediately made my hips want to twitch. Instead, I picked up my paint and considered how to approach the stem. I squeezed the green tube and laughed at myself. Had I really thought a handful of paints would be enough? It had never been enough before, and at the same moment my head released the painting inside it, and it flowed out through my fingertips, the creeping frustration of not having everything I needed to make it exactly what I saw tried to crowd it out. I needed a deeper green, and it would take mixing in its opposite, a red I didn't have, to give me the right shade.

I'd go back to McGill's tomorrow to get some other colors.

The thought stopped me cold, the crescendo of the song swelling under Griff's skillful playing with a reality that broke me out of my painting high.

There wasn't money for this. There wasn't money for this any more than there was money for a dozen other things looming, and all of them, until an hour ago, had mattered more than watercolor supplies.

I set the brush down and stared out past the top of the fence to the Salt Lake valley spread out below. Maybe it was time to sell this place. The market was decent. We could move into an apartment with rent cheaper than my mortgage, and maybe the difference would be enough to pay for the preschool Dani wanted. And something simple like paint wouldn't feel so far out of reach.

Once the idea took root, I couldn't shake it. It would tick Dani off if I interfered, but too bad. I watched Chloe bent over her newest drawing, with her tongue sticking out as she concentrated on trying to make a petal. That girl was my heart, and I hated the idea of her sitting in some overcrowded preschool in a crumbly building downtown while Dani tried to make her life work. And I hated even more the stress carving lines around my sister's mouth far too early. She was younger than me. She shouldn't already be carrying the weight of the world on her shoulders, but she was. It was the weight of Chloe's world, and I could maybe do something about that.

"I'll be back in a second," I told Griff and slipped into the house to retrieve my laptop from my room, then returned and went on a Google hunt with his guitar as my sound track, something more bluegrass now. I pulled up all the preschools in town to see if I could figure out which ones Dani was thinking of. All of them looked like places I'd quit adulthood to play in for a few hours a day, but I guessed that was standard for a community where poverty was a foreign concept. After six years in New York, I missed the diversity like an ache, but there was no denying that sticking well-to-do people all in one place produced some high-caliber schools.

I descended into the world of local mommy bloggers, and in between braiding tutorials and a million soft-focus pictures of darling kids in hand-knit beanies, the same name kept coming up: the Bethwell Academy. Thirty minutes later, I had an appointment to check it out in two days. I wouldn't tell Dani because the director was clear over the phone that they had no openings for fall, but I had a plan. If it worked, I'd tell Dani, but I didn't want to let her down if I failed. But I wouldn't. I watched Chloe's blonde head bobbing in time to Griff's music. I couldn't fail.

Griff had drifted into something more folksy. That was one of my favorite things about listening to him play, that he never stayed in a box. I scraped together some courage and tried small talk. "Griff?"

"Hm?"

"Do you ever play at Leifson's?" That was the restaurant he managed at the Snowtop Lodge. I'd never been there because the filet mignon prices way outstripped my hamburger budget. But maybe someday I'd go. I'd taken for granted all the upscale restaurants and fine dining during my marriage to Donovan. It was literally the only thing I missed.

At first, the whole concept of wealth had fascinated me. Donovan had taken me to parties in homes luxurious beyond anything imaginable and paid for dinners that cost more than my groceries for a month. It had been intoxicating, and he'd done it all without thinking about it, like it was no big deal. And it never was—for someone who'd come from money.

Somewhere, something had gone wrong though. We'd dated for a year and married. I had to strike a compromise with his mother to get a low-key wedding, but in return, she threw us an elaborate reception. The first year after that had been good. But work got hard for Donovan, and he came home tense and frustrated more and more often.

The tension it introduced into our comfortable Tribeca apartment made it hard to paint, and most times when I tried to pick up a brush, I pictured disinterested friends of the Beckmans checking the paintings out for size and writing thoughtless checks to purchase them. So I painted less.

Donovan freaked out when my work trailed off, and that broke the thing between us that had already begun to crumble. I tried for a few more months to get him to talk to me; I got us a counselor—I tried everything to pull us out of the spiral we'd dived into. None of it worked.

I finally told him I was going on a retreat with a teacher from art school who had invited a handful of her students to join her for a month on Martha's Vineyard. It would cost about two thousand for the month to cover all travel, board, and food expenses, but when I tried to send the money, my payment was declined for lack of funds.

That's how I discovered Donovan had stolen several hundred thousand dollars from me, and there was nothing left. He'd been fired from his job as an investment banker six months before, and he'd been using my money to support his lifestyle and keep up appearances.

It was a huge web of lies. He'd been leaving our apartment every day but not going to work. He'd blown a huge chunk of the money he'd stolen on illegal prescription painkillers—an addiction that had led to his termination in the first place. And by the time it had all shaken out, I'd left New York with a check from his parents to pay for my silence, and I'd had no desire to ever look back.

Griff's mellow voice returned me to the present. "Leifson's isn't a live-music kind of place," he said, but the tiny upturn of his lips said he was pleased that I thought he should play there.

"I'd think anywhere is a live-music kind of place if the music is good like yours." Ooooh, *bold*.

He patted the guitar. "This is just for fun. Just for me."

"And us," Chloe said, looking up from her painting. She'd moved on to butterflies. Happiness spread through me like it did every time I saw the evidence that she'd gotten the same art gene I had. She made some pretty amazing stuff for a three-year-old.

"And you," Griff agreed. He leaned over the rail again, and Chloe, knowing what he wanted, leaned the tiniest bit his way so he could ruffle her hair and then smooth it again.

"I wish I had a daddy like you," she mumbled, looking down.

Griff looked at me for help.

I froze. Chloe had never talked about a daddy before. I blinked, my lashes flapping like one of Chloe's butterflies had come to life, and I processed a useless answer with every blink. I couldn't wrap my mind around the fact that not only had Chloe noticed the lack of a father, but she had also put some thought into what she wanted in one. Another stress for Dani. Dang.

Griff cleared his throat while I sat silent, overcome by eye tics. "That's lucky," he said to Chloe. "Because someday I hope to have a girl like you."

"Why you don't?" Chloe asked.

"That's not something we ask people," I said, finding my voice and keeping it gentle.

"Why?"

Griff's expression looked about what I imagined a fly in a spiderweb looked like while it was figuring out escape. I wished him the best because this was all kind of awkward to explain while he sat there, if "kind of" meant "excruciatingly."

I did it anyway. "We don't ask because the details of why people's families are the way they are aren't for us to know. People will tell us if they want us to know."

"But Griff don't tell us."

"Maybe Griff doesn't want to," I said, trying to shoot him my best *I'm sorry* with my eyes.

"I guess I haven't found the right person, sweet pea," Griff said.

Chloe leaned toward him again, her eyes full of worry at this news. "You can be daddy here. You can come to my house and play with my dolls whenever you want."

As much as I wanted to leap from the deck and run away with Chloe thrown over my shoulder, never to face Griff again, I couldn't help pulling her in to squeeze every bone of her tiny, generous body. "That's the bravest offer she could ever make, just so you know."

Griff smiled despite his reddened cheeks. "I'm honored."

"You welcome," Chloe said quietly and bent back to her work.

"Sorry," I said. "She doesn't propose fatherhood to a lot of people."

"It's okay. I kind of feel like a rock star now."

"Which is exactly what I think you should be, the way you play."

He shook his head to dismiss the compliment. "I'll tell you what. When you get your stuff in the Guggenheim, I'll come play at the exhibit opening."

I swallowed and struggled to give him a normal smile. I'd shown in the Guggenheim already, but I didn't want to explain. "Deal," I said and left it at that.

Griff glanced down at his watch. "I'm about to fire up the grill. Can I throw some extra on for you guys?"

It was an offer he'd made a few times before to be polite, and I'd always declined and then disappeared into the house so it wouldn't be weird with me sitting there ignoring the smell of the food he'd offered, but I wanted to stay out and paint longer. "Sure. But let me make a salad."

He grinned. "Perfect. I'll be out in a minute."

And somehow it worked okay. He grilled, and we chatted. I had a couple of false starts, but I reminded myself to think of it as talking to Dani or Tom, and the conversation got easier. When I went in to make the salad I'd promised, I didn't dread going back out to find more things to say. And when I had to put Chloe to bed, I was sorry to bring that part of the night to an end.

Once she fell asleep, I spent more time researching Bethwell Academy and plotting how to crack it. I was torn between excitement that I had a solution to get Chloe in and stress about how we could pay for it. Even with tuition so high it made me dizzy to think of it, every now and then, a flashback to the evening with Griff surfaced, and a tiny burst of endorphins pushed the stress back, making me smile even though no one was there to see it.

Chapter 4

212. The numbers in my phone display were enough to summon the chest fist, this time with a helping of nausea. If my phone had suddenly morphed into a rattlesnake, it still would have spiked my adrenaline less than the Manhattan area code flashing at me.

Who was it? I rejected each guess as soon as I thought of it. None of those people would call me. Unless it was . . .

The alert on my phone announced a voice mail.

"Leandra, it's Victoria." I flinched at the use of my old-life name. "I know we haven't talked in a while, but I've got an offer I don't think you can refuse. Call me. And before you delete this message, remember you owe me. I fought for you, girl. Do me the courtesy of giving me a call back."

I deleted the message. It had taken me way longer than it should have to figure out that exploding onto the New York art scene had everything to do with Donovan and the creepy tendrils of his Beckman family connections and not with my talent.

But Victoria had truly loved my work or had done a good job of convincing me she did. And I'd call her back infinity times for that alone, only . . . later. I wasn't ready for a conversation with her.

Hm. *Dramatic, much?* Time to get over myself before I had to punch myself in the face. I hopped up to change into my running clothes, hollered at Dani that I was leaving, and hit my favorite trail at a slow jog. It was as empty as I'd hoped it would be for my late-morning start time. This was what had sent me straight back to Utah after working so hard to escape—these trails at the base of mountains that touched the sky. I grew bigger inside simply by looking at them, the view somehow making it easier to breathe, to put everything in my head in perspective.

I'd grown up as the artsy outsider, my hands always stained with whatever paint or pastel or drawing pencil I was experimenting with at the moment. The girls at school could all dance and sing or act. They knew how to dress and flirt. And I wandered around with strange pictures in my head that itched to come out of my fingertips. I never could figure out where I fit here with the girls and their Miss America talents. The only two times I felt like I belonged were when I had a sketchpad in my hand or when I was in the mountains. Being in New York had taken one of those things from me, which was probably why most of my work there had referenced the mountains here.

I slipped my phone out of my armband and called Dani. "Why'd I ever move away from here?" I demanded when she answered.

There was a long pause. "I still don't know why you came back. New York has to be big enough for Donovan *and* you, right?"

"If it didn't have you and Chloe in it, it would always be too empty. Be home soon. Love you, bye," I said, hanging up before she could answer. I attacked the trail again. I'd escaped to New York and art school with the velocity of a human cannonball two days after high school graduation. I'd wanted to leave the loneliness behind.

I pushed that thought away and focused on the trail, pouring on speed. I ran for an hour before I found a head space where I could call Victoria.

I went home and showered and wondered what I would say. *No,* mainly. Over and over and over again.

Fresh out of art school, I wouldn't have dreamed of telling the owner of the Van Exel gallery no. Given her ability to launch careers with a single show, *no* was a word *she* said a lot but rarely heard. But that had quit mattering to me three years ago, and the idea of telling her no now filled me with a sense of immature glee, like the satisfaction I saw on Chloe's face every time she threw a shirt she didn't like to the floor. I understood why she did it; it was a total rejection of someone else's control—a hard feeling to resist.

I settled into my deck chair and pulled up my caller ID, staring at it for a long moment to remind myself the digits were a phone number and not the combination to unlock a demon portal. I was done with my demons. This was just a phone call.

The phone only rang twice before Victoria answered with my name. "Leandra."

"It's Lia now. Leandra's gone."

"You better find her," Victoria said, sounding unperturbed. "Because I'm about to make her a lot of money."

I drew in a deep breath and spit out the word I'd practiced on my run. "No."

"No?" She made it sound foreign.

"I meant no, thank you."

"You don't know what you're turning down."

"The specifics don't matter," I said. That thing that had driven me to paint before, to layer color after emotion after thought in thick oil paint across the huge canvases I'd loved, had burned out of me. I didn't need to work out my place in New York through my paintings, didn't need to solve the tension of having my roots deep in the Rockies while I reached up for the validation of the people who moved like absurdly powerful ants in the skyscrapers and penthouses around me. I didn't belong there. I had nothing left to say about it with my brushes.

"Leandra—"

"Lia."

"Lia," she said, and her tone held a note I never thought I'd hear from her. It was the tone I used on Chloe to get her to abandon her toys for bedtime, a tone I'd heard Victoria use on other artists who were "difficult." And that was the kindest description I could think of.

I sighed. I didn't want to be one of *them*, the artists who took themselves so seriously that they lost touch with reality without knowing or caring. "Yes, Victoria?"

"The International Man of Mystery is back."

I drew a sharp breath. That was her name for him. I'd called him Daddy Warbucks, like the billionaire in *Annie*, and if I'd had anything close to a patron, he was it. He'd bought over a dozen of my most expensive pieces over the four years Van Exel had carried my work. He'd done it anonymously, and since he worked through an assistant to buy the work, even Victoria didn't know who he was. We'd spent a few idle lunches together speculating about his secret identity, but Victoria wasn't interested in digging too deep as long he kept the checks coming, especially when they ended in a row of juicy zeros.

"I'm not painting anymore," I said, pulling myself together. "Sorry to disappoint you both, but it's not my thing."

"Why not?" she asked, and I didn't hear judgment in her voice. "Help me understand, Lia."

If she had said Leandra, I probably would have ended the call. If she had sounded like she was looking for an explanation so she could pick apart its flaws and sell me on doing more work, I would have given her a polite good-bye and pushed the whole call out of my mind. But I heard concern, the same concern I'd heard in Dani's voice when she'd coaxed Chloe into explaining why she didn't want to go to her dance class when the kid loved dancing more than she loved Lucky Charms and cartoons combined. Relief had radiated from Chloe once she'd let the truth flood out: the other girls had sparkle leotards and satin tutus, and her plain black ones left her wanting fancier dance clothes like a housefly among fairies.

Dani had spent the next three nights embellishing Chloe's outfits so they wouldn't embarrass her. Chloe had lit up brighter than her newly bedazzled leotards when she'd seen them, but I suspected it was telling the truth to her mom that had made her feel better.

So I told Victoria the truth. She wouldn't be able to fix what was wrong with me, but I wanted to push the weight of the truth off my chest. "I can't paint. That's all. It takes too much out of me. I spent a long time putting myself back together, and to be in the mental space it takes for me to do that work . . . I can't. It would break me."

A long silence. I wondered if she was rubbing her chin like she did when she was assessing her own reaction to a new artist's work.

Her voice was thoughtful when she spoke. "Success has a way of breaking some people, but it's not the same for everyone. A few people let it go to their heads, and what starts as talent becomes them echoing themselves, redoing versions of what they've already done. Buyers still fall all over themselves to worship it. But the work isn't real anymore, not like it was when the artists started. I knew you would never be in that category."

A rare hesitancy laced her tone, and I couldn't stop myself from prompting her. "You expected the success to break me another way?"

She sighed. "Yes. I hoped I was wrong. But there are some people who paint purely for the joy of it or because that's the only way to let the pain out. They don't care about the business side of things other than as a means to earn enough to let them keep painting. That was you. When success comes, some of them are fine. But some of them . . . it breaks them to have what's inside of them hung all over other people's walls, in homes and galleries where people collect you because other people collect you and not because they get what you're doing."

I was glad I was sitting down. Such a naked, dead-on look inside of me made my knees buckle. "I'm one of the weak ones who couldn't cut it, huh?"

"No. You're one of the ones smart enough to save yourself before you became the first kind of artist. But you have to understand something: I wouldn't have called you just to make a buck. You understand that, right?"

"I don't know," I said.

"Ouch."

"I'm not trying to hurt you. But . . . why else would you call me?"

"I don't need your work from a financial standpoint. This is one of those utterly bizarre situations in which I'm doing the right thing because it's the right thing."

That made me laugh. Victoria could be a shark, but she was an honest one. "I've never questioned your integrity," I said. "Your tact, maybe. But not your integrity."

"I bet you've also never questioned my healthy self-interest. And believe me, there's so much money riding on this that I'm very, very interested. But the part of me that loves art separate from business would be making this happen regardless. Or trying to. So you'll at least let me explain?"

"I'll listen."

"Mystery Man wants to commission work but something different than your other stuff."

"That makes no sense." I interrupted her even though I'd promised myself to let her finish. "If he likes me for my old work, why would he want me to do anything different?"

"He's requesting something less conceptual. Instead of your city/ mountain mash-up, he wants to see your take on a mountain landscape only. He wants a half dozen eight-foot canvases, and he's offering to pay exactly what he used to."

This conversation was making less sense to me by the minute. He wanted to commission a conceptual artist to do landscapes? Large ones that would run him in the low-to-mid six figures for a series? "It's an interesting idea in the way that insane people are fascinating, but no."

"Think about it," Victoria said, and it sounded like an order, the kind a mom gives her kid, not a boss to an underling. "His assistant says Mystery Man understands that neither of you may like the result, but he'd be interested in seeing you try. He's willing to pay you for your time on the first painting even if he doesn't buy it."

"I won't do it," I said.

"Five thousand dollars, Lia. That's what he's willing to pay for both of you to even see if it's worth your time and his money. Does waiting tables pay you enough to blow off that kind of money as a matter of principle?"

"There's not enough money in the world for me to do something that's against my principles," I said, the words sounding as hard as trail rocks. I'd seen too many people sell their souls instead of their art by compromising their vision for money in the first place. "This is about me having no idea if I could paint anything worth showing him." Something else she said sank in. "Wait a minute. How did you know I'm waiting tables?"

"Same way I got your phone number. I hired a private investigator to find you. I guessed you'd gone back to Utah. It didn't take him long once he looked for you under your maiden name. Was it supposed to be a secret?"

"It's not like I left you a forwarding address." The idea of a detective looking for me made me antsy.

"I was worried. I found out where you went within a couple months of your leaving. I didn't have a reason to bother you until now."

"I'm still weirded out."

"You think Donovan's going to find you? He'd have done it by now if he wanted to."

True. And I'd told myself the same thing a million times, but something about hearing another person say it made it easier to believe. "Thanks for caring to look."

"You're not trying to hide, are you?"

"Not really." I couldn't be around Dani and Chloe if I didn't want to be found. I took a deep breath and reminded myself that Donovan was done and had made no effort to reconcile in the three years I'd been gone. Thank goodness. He must have believed me when I'd walked out the last time and threatened to call the police if I ever heard from him again. "Victoria? Thanks for trying to get me to do this painting, but it's not what I do anymore."

"Don't say no. Say maybe, or I can't let you off the phone."

At that moment, I heard Chloe scratching at the glass as she attempted to slide the door open to join me.

"Maybe," I said into the phone, already reaching for the end button.

Victoria's triumphant "We'll talk soon" overrode my "I have to go."

I hung up and turned as Chloe pushed the door aside and raced to fling herself into my lap. I settled her down and stroked her hair while she told me about her Barbie movie. I eyed the mountains in the distance. Maybe . . .

No. I was done being crazy and giving up bits of my soul to everyone else.

Chapter 5

The scent of onion and grease washed over me like it did every time I walked in the door of T&R, but instead of smelling like comfort, it struck me with the force of a slap, the kind you give to snap a person out of being hysterical.

Mr. Benny was already hunched over a coffee mug, waiting to growl at me. I could predict how much I'd earn on this shift within ten dollars, and it was a sure bet that the money could buy me more watercolors or make a negligible dent in the Bethwell tuition, but not both. I took a deep breath and reminded myself that the scent of coffee mingled with bacon was one of my favorite ways to start the day. But then Mr. Benny glanced at me, and his wrinkly mouth tightened, and it was all I could do not to dive back into my car.

Tom nodded at me when I slipped into the kitchen to grab a clean apron and an order pad. He scooped up an omelet and slid it my way. "It's called The Widowmaker," he said. "Might want to loosen your apron. It ain't light."

I brightened and almost had the fork to my mouth, cheddar stretching all the way back to the plate, when Mr. Benny tapped his cup against the countertop and glared at us through the pass-through window. I took the bite anyway and immediately regretted it. I could already tell it would rank near the top of Tom's experiments, and knowing it was sitting there and I could only sneak bites of it between customers made me sad, like staring at puppies through pet shop windows made me sad.

After I topped off Mr. Benny's coffee, I snuck another bite and gave Tom my bossiest look. "It's a winner. I'm putting it up on the board."

His bushy eyebrows drew together, and he hunched over the grill. "It's not ready."

I waved a piece of chalk at him. "I'm sure Michelangelo said that every day about the Sistine Chapel, but there's a point at which you have to let your adoring public convince you that you've reached perfection. You'll be making a lot of widows today." The tips of his ears reddened, and I dropped my voice to a whisper. "Could you start with Mrs. Benny?" Tom waved me off with his spatula in pretend annoyance. On cue, Mr. Benny tapped his fork on his mug. I grabbed a plate of toast, knowing that was what he wanted. Unbuttered, even. Weirdo.

An hour later, I finished off my last bite of omelet, cold despite Tom's efforts to keep it warm. It was still delicious, another sign that it had been a good idea to throw it up on the daily specials board. I'd already talked three people into it, and I had a few extra dollars in tip money for my efforts. The Widowmaker would make Tom's permanent rotation, for sure.

I eyed the clock. Any minute now the high school hipsters would roll in, the kids who liked the novelty of getting diner coffee instead of Starbucks. They tipped okay, but sometimes their conversations made me want to beat them about the head and neck with a spatula. Usually, it was whining about anything they thought was too mainstream. So far, that included everything.

The bell jingled, and sure enough, the kid I thought of as Blue Beanie walked in. Instead of diving for a booth, he made his way over to me, a flat paper-wrapped package in his hands. "This is for you," he said.

"Who's it from?"

"I don't know. An old lady paid me ten bucks to bring it to you."

Tom rapped the counter. "What is it?"

I shook it and held it against my ear. "Sounds like a pony."

He scowled at me, and Blue Beanie beat a retreat. "Unless it's ticking, you should open it."

"No ticking," I said. "I'm pretty sure it's a book." A heavy one, hardback. What old lady was paying him ten bucks to give it to me? I tugged at the twine around it and carefully removed the paper.

"Tear it off," Tom said. "It's annoying when people unwrap stuff all careful."

"That's why I'm doing it," I said, slowing down even more.

He clamped his mouth shut, and I took the book out. *Wildflowers of Utah*. I held it up for Tom to see. From the corner of my eye, I caught the beanie kid straining to check out the cover. I flashed it at him, and he shrugged and settled into his booth.

"Who would send you a book on flowers at the diner?" Tom asked.

An old lady? Could it be Victoria? She was in her midfifties, but maybe that looked old to the kid. Maybe she'd actually come all the way out here to talk me into taking the commission. I leafed through the book. It was nice, but . . . this wasn't even what she wanted me to paint.

"I need more coffee," one of my regulars said.

"Be right there, Rusty." I'd have to figure out the book later. I stuck it on the kitchen shelf, where I kept my purse, and hurried back out to take care of the early-morning caffeine junkies.

Even as I stepped back into the rhythm of the breakfast shift, my mind drifted to the book. Pushing me would not get Victoria what she wanted. If a five-thousand-dollar check couldn't do it, a flower book and an invasion of my geographical space definitely wouldn't.

Aidan showed up a little before eight, and as simple as that, the book was the farthest thing from my mind.

"Another weekday visit? How did we get so lucky?" I asked, setting a menu in front of him.

He sighed. "Coming from the right person, that question would give me butterflies."

"Because you're a junior high school girl?"

"Because you make me feel like a junior high boy with my first huge crush on someone. But I don't want to be the clueless kind who can't take a hint, so I won't ask you for a date today. Or even your phone number. I'll just ask for the number twelve." He sauntered over to his usual booth while my stomach flipped.

"Where's Chief?"

"He treed a squirrel and didn't want to leave it. I'll bring him home an actual doggie bag."

"Of all the days to bring a dog you can feed under the table, number twelve day is the prime one. Do you remember what's in the twelve?"

"I'm right here," Tom hollered. "The bacon doesn't sizzle so loud that I can't hear you. I'm throwing the liver on."

Aidan grimaced. "I didn't forget. But I decided a Saturday shouldn't be ruined with liver, so I'm having it today instead."

"You got it. I'll be back with your coffee."

"And my liver."

"I'm not Hannibal Lecter. It will be *a* liver, not *your* liver."

He executed a rim shot with his fork against the table. He was already pulling out his iPad for his news fix.

I stuck his ticket in the window for Tom, who didn't even glance at it. No one at any of my other tables had empty plates or a needy look in their eyes, so I ducked into the bathroom and checked my reflection, cursing myself for being a sucker enough to do it. I wished I'd put some lip gloss on. I settled for refastening my low ponytail and went back out, the minutes until I could swing past and check on Aidan ticking past as slowly as if the clock hand were dragging itself through tar.

When I finally stopped by his table, he didn't look up. So much for his "huge crush." Even the sound of water filling his glass didn't get his attention. I stole a glance at his iPad screen to see what he found so fascinating. It looked like another news article. "Anything interesting happening in the world today?" I asked like an idiot.

He looked up, startled, and collected himself. "No. The whole world is boring today. Must be hard for the news people when that happens."

"You looked pretty into that article. Can't be that boring."

"Not to me, but probably to anyone else."

That was a definite brush off. My eyebrows rose in surprise before I could stop myself. Not too long ago, if Aidan had wanted to keep to himself, I would have considered him new and improved. It was stupid for his distraction to hurt my pride now, but my pride was stupid too and got hurt anyway. I rearranged my expression to make my neutral what-can-I-get-you face. Too late. He'd seen my reaction, and he winced.

"Sorry. I have an extremely bad habit of getting so focused on something I forget the rules of being human. Smile, blink, be polite." He blinked and smiled, and the usual Aidan reappeared like magic. "This is an article about my brother. I don't know if it'd be too interesting to any non-siblings."

A piece of information to file away: his brother was important enough to be in the *New York Times*. I felt a Google search coming on. "He's in the paper? Is he robbing banks or running for office?"

"What's the difference?" Aidan asked, and I grinned.

"Does that count as a laugh?" he asked. "Is the juice on you today?"

A plate of liver plunked down in the pass-through, and I walked over to scoop it up and deliver it to him. "The juice is on me because you deserve something to wash this down with."

"It's that bad?"

Extra loud griddle-smacking sounded at that question. I ignored Tom, giving Aidan the answer I would have anyway without Tom's eavesdropping.

"Nope. The taste is pretty good. The texture is even all right. My problem is that I can't get past the idea that it's liver. The trick is to tell yourself you're eating something else."

Aidan stared down at the dish. "Pâté it is."

Pâté—another throwback to the New York days, when pâté and caviar were a regular thing. I'd gone from awed by the fact that I was eating something so decadent to resenting that I had to eat fatty goose liver and raw fish eggs when I'd much rather be eating grilled cheese and potato chips. Part of working in a diner was my rebellion against the endless round of catered soirées Donovan had dragged me to.

Aidan interrupted my thoughts. "My brother's a doctor."

I stared at him in confusion.

"The one in the newspaper? I didn't want you thinking he was some kind of criminal or something."

"I didn't assume anything," I said, but I knew the words were untrue as soon as I spoke them. I'd assumed lots of things about Aidan, for example. Like that a construction worker wouldn't know what pâté was or have a brother who was a doctor. How had their two paths diverged so widely that one had gone to medical school and the other had ended up in manual labor? Something about the mixture of pride and frustration in his face forced a question out of me before I could stop it. "Does it bother you that he's a doctor and you're just a construction worker?"

He tilted his head, and my face flamed as the rudeness of what I'd asked him sank in. I waved my hand like I could brush the question out of the air. "Ignore me. I had a brain-mouth disconnect. I'll go get your juice."

"Does it bother you that you're just a waitress in a diner?" His voice was level. I couldn't tell if he was amused or angry.

"Touché. But no." I'd lived a life people couldn't imagine. I was happier now being a wage slave and an honorary parent to Chloe.

He picked up his fork to poke at the liver. "Honest work is honest work. I work as hard as I need to so I can meet my obligations. If I have to work harder or do more, I do. And I've found my place. So I don't mind that my brother is a doctor. That's an article about his work with Doctors Without Borders. I'll be getting a call later from my mother asking me when I'm going to contribute more to society. I do it my way. My brother does it his. If it weren't for those phone calls, I wouldn't even think about the differences."

"Fair enough. Sorry I said that."

"You can make it up to me with a date."

"And here we go," I said, walking away. "You almost made it through a whole meal without hitting on me." But as I crossed the floor to refresh coffee cups, a grin snuck out of me. It was funny how that little part of our routine did more to start my day right than anything except for a Chloe hug.

Chapter 6

The Bethwell Academy was the prettiest school I'd ever seen. It looked more like a fancy house than an institution. Ivy covered its brick walls, and a brass sign spelled out the school name near the front door. I'd expected a place in such high demand with all the affluent mommies to look stuffy, but it had a welcoming charm before we'd even walked through the door.

"Good morning," the receptionist said. "You must be Miss Carswell and Chloe. Dr. Bray will be with you in a moment. Feel free to look around while you wait."

"Thank you," I said, glancing around at the walls exploding with photos and student work.

The receptionist followed my look. "I know, it's overwhelming, but we're at the end of the school year, and there's been so much great work to display. Enjoy it."

I squeezed Chloe's hand. She pulled me toward the nearest wall covered in tissue paper mosaics. Self-portraits, apparently. Chloe's eyes shone at all the bright colors. "We make dat?"

"Sure, sweet pea. We'll make that."

She tugged me over to the next wall and a photo collage of the kids in a million different activities. They were costumed for a play or holding the edges of a multicolor parachute for some game or sitting and listening to a teacher wearing a Little Bo Peep outfit read a story.

By the third wall, this one full of paper-plate hats dripping ribbon and shiny with glitter, I was ready to enroll myself.

"Good morning."

Chloe suddenly threw her arms around my legs and buried her face to hide, and I turned to find a tiny woman with friendly eyes standing behind us. She wore a bright blue dress and a long chain of colorful charms around her neck. "I'm Dr. Bray. Are you ready for a look around?"

I looked down at Chloe, whose big eyes met mine with a look torn between fear and amazement, as if she couldn't believe her luck in getting to see more of the school, but she didn't know if she could talk to this new adult. I knelt and hugged her. "You don't have to talk today, Chloe. The grown-ups will talk, and you can look at things. Can you do that?"

She'd tucked her face into the crook of my neck, and when she nodded, stray strands of her hair tickled my nose, and I sneezed, making her hold on to me tighter, but I could feel her lips curve up against my skin. I looked up at Dr. Bray and nodded. "We're having a brave day. We can do this."

Dr. Bray took us to see six classrooms, half of them full of three-year-olds, the other half of four-year-olds. Each only had about a dozen kids and at least two adults, sometimes three. The walls bloomed with pictures and posters and life and color. We heard singing, saw dancing, and even listened to a story about a mouse who ate a cookie. That one kind of frustrated me, but Chloe sat entranced all the way through it, even giggling once.

Dr. Bray met us at the door as the story ended. "Are you enjoying Bethwell?"

Chloe nodded like a bobblehead, and Dr. Bray laughed. "I'm so glad." A classroom door opened behind her, and a line of three-year-olds filed out. "It's time for creative play. Chloe, if it's okay with your aunt, you can go play with them in the arts center while she and I talk."

Chloe turned pleading eyes on me. I squeezed her hand. "Thanks, but we like to hang out. She can stay with me."

Instead of answering, Dr. Bray knelt down in front of Chloe, waiting quietly until Chloe met her eye. "There's a beautiful art center in there, my friend. Would you like to make something for your aunt? The other kids will let you work by yourself if you want some quiet."

Chloe's hold on my hand tightened for a moment, and she grew as still as one of her bugs freshly dug from the dirt and startled.

"We have every color of crayon you can imagine," Dr. Bray said. "I'll show you my favorite. It's called Pink Peony. What do you say? Would you like to go see?"

Chloe looked up at me, her eyes asking if she had to go. Dr. Bray caught the look and touched Chloe's arm to get her attention. "I'll tell you what. You don't have to go play with anyone. But will you come sit over here and talk to me for a bit?"

I knelt and looked Chloe in the eye. "You are a brave girl," I whispered. "I will stay right here in this room, but I think you should go talk to her."

Chloe threw her arms around my neck and trembled. The tiny tremor was almost enough for me to squeeze her and tell her never mind, she could stay by me or Dani forever, but she sniffed and lifted her head to nod.

Dr. Bray winked at me and held a hand out to Chloe, who took it and followed her to a nearby table. They talked for five minutes. At first it was mostly Dr. Bray, but then Chloe began to nod, and soon she smiled, and by the end of their conversation, she'd said a few things too. I couldn't quite hear them, but Dr. Bray had the air of a Buddha about her, a calm that made it easy for me to sit and watch them together without needing to step in or understand every piece of their chat.

Dr. Bray stood and brought Chloe back to me. "Go ahead and ask, Chloe. Your aunt needs to know this is what you want."

"Wia, I want to go draw."

I nodded despite the lump in my throat that always formed on the rare occasions I got to see an adult invest in Chloe the way Dani and I did. "You should draw, baby girl. I'll come find you in a few minutes."

Once Dr. Bray got Chloe settled in with a ream of paper and a truly spectacular tub of crayons, she led me to her office, a cheerful yellow space with overstuffed gingham chairs. "Were you pleased with your visit?" she asked when we sat.

"Beyond pleased," I said. "I really want Chloe to come here. How do I sign her up?"

Worry crossed her face. "I think I told you we're full for the fall already, didn't I?"

I nodded.

Dr. Bray sighed. "I wish there were a way to enroll her. She's delightful. But we've had those slots filled for months. All I can offer you is our waiting list."

The chest fist squeezed. "Why did you let us come visit? I'm not asking to be rude; I'm so new to how all this works, and I'm trying to understand."

"There's a small chance we would have something available the following year. We're always willing to let people on the wait list."

"How long is the list?"

"Long enough that the chances are nonexistent for this fall and slim for the one following."

Chloe needed to be here. I knew it the way I knew exactly which yellow to choose for the daffodils, an instinct I had learned to trust. But I stared at the tiny woman in front of me and knew I might as well try lifting a boulder the size of Bethwell as try to get around the rules with her. The plan I'd been so sure would work crumbled. There was no chance she would go for the deal I'd intended to offer her. "Dr. Bray, Chloe needs this. She's not coming in with the advantages these kids have, and I've read all the articles about how she needs to start right, even this young. So what do I do?"

"We do offer three scholarships for children in need," she said, but when she saw the sudden hope I didn't even try to keep off my face, she shook her head. "The waiting list for those is even longer. And we offset their cost with a higher tuition for our other students. Bethwell is expensive."

"I couldn't find your rates on the website. What does it cost?"

"Twelve hundred dollars a month."

I flinched, and she saw it. Her eyes softened. "There are plenty of good programs around if Bethwell Academy doesn't work for you. Please try not to stress. Chloe is clearly a bright girl, and she'll be fine in any program."

She might as well have punched me in the heart. I could only offer a silent prayer of thanks that I hadn't told Dani I was coming here today. I was living her worst nightmare of watching Chloe lose out on something amazing because even if there were space for her, there was no money for it. She shouldn't have to settle for any old program and hope her natural intelligence offset any lack in the school.

I managed a nod. Words would have choked me. All that would have come out was "It's not fair," but I hated stating the obvious.

Dr. Bray glanced at the clock. "I'd be glad to put Chloe on our waiting list, but you should keep all your options open. Creative play is winding up. Let me walk you over to her."

I followed her down a bright blue hallway with framed prints of Dr. Seuss pictures. I stopped and studied one more closely. "This is a signed lithograph," I said. Those were expensive. Owned-by-people-in-mansions expensive.

"Yes," she said. "We're fortunate to have generous parents supporting Bethwell. Here's the center."

Maybe . . . maybe there was a chance after all. I'd have to think hard before I took the risk.

She opened the door to a spacious room we'd breezed past earlier. Kids were putting away their supplies, removing smocks, or organizing paints while they chattered. Chloe sat by herself at a table in the corner, her tongue poking out as she colored. The chest fist squeezed. I hated seeing her isolated from the other kids. It reminded me too much of the many recesses and lunches I'd spent alone with my sketchpad. Most of the time I'd liked the quiet to work, but every now and then I'd realized that when I didn't want to draw, there wasn't anyone to play or eat with. And that was sad.

"Chloe?" I said. Her head shot up, and a huge grin broke over her face.

"Wia!" She snatched up her paper and raced toward me.

I crouched down to gather her into a hug, resolved to stop projecting my sense of childhood alienation onto her. "Did you have fun?"

Her head bounced like the rubber ball on a paddleball board. I hugged her again. "Good."

"We're glad you came to see us today, Chloe," Dr. Bray said with a gentle stroke of Chloe's hair.

"I made you this," Chloe said, holding out her drawing. "Tank you for wetting me play." She slipped behind me and held onto my leg, peeking out at Dr. Bray.

Dr. Bray's eyes widened in surprise, and she crouched down to Chloe's level and accepted the drawing. "You're so thoughtful," she said, studying the picture, her eyes widening even further.

Chloe had drawn herself next to a fairy in a blue dress with a sparkly crown.

"Dat's you," she said. "I love your school." She let go of me and scurried over to give the still-crouching director a hug. Dr. Bray smiled at me and patted Chloe's back.

"I didn't tell her to do that," I said.

"I know. I can always tell when kids are coached. This one's pure sweetness, isn't she?" Dr. Bray held Chloe by the shoulders and gave her a serious look. "This is a wonderful drawing, sweetie. Did you do that all by yourself?"

Chloe nodded.

"Did you know you draw as well as many five-year-olds and maybe even better than some of them? How do you do that?"

Chloe looked confused. "I know zactly how it look, and I color it."

"You worked hard on it, and it shows."

Chloe gave her a shy smile and retreated behind me to hide again. "We'd better go," I said. "Unfortunately, I have to look into back-up plans." I smiled to soften the words, but Dr. Bray's return smile still held a tinge of apology. "I'm wondering if special circumstances can move a child up on the waiting list."

Dr. Bray's forehead crinkled. "What do you mean?"

I took a deep breath and exhaled, trying to push out the anxiety holding me hostage from making the play that might change things for Chloe. "I mean this." I stooped down and scribbled something on a piece of construction paper before tearing it off and handing it to her. "If you'd be willing to let Chloe in as a full-tuition student, I'd be willing to teach here, as a volunteer, even. I'm good. Google that," I said, nodding at the ragged paper she held.

Her expression changed to one of curiosity, but she asked no further questions and escorted us to the door with a pleasant good-bye.

"What you gave her?" Chloe asked in the car.

"My name," I said. My old name, the one signed on several dozen extremely expensive canvases sprinkled throughout the world, paintings like the ones Daddy Warbucks had bought and that he wanted to buy again. And now I had to consider his commission. My name might be enough to get Chloe into the school, but it would take my art to pay for it.

I shifted in the driver's seat, trying to find a way to get comfortable with the idea of producing work for Daddy Warbucks. I'd once stood next to a man studying my work at a gallery opening, and he didn't know I was the artist. The painting showed a mountain merged with a skyscraper on a scale that would dwarf even the Empire State Building. It was the idea of roots and the idea that we come from earth, all of it carved out by an unseen hand, and then we build these amazing buildings, and yet none of them can touch what God made billions of years before. In a way, it was a more spiritual meditation than anything I'd done before as I'd tried to capture what would happen if humans tried to merge with a greater creative power than themselves.

The man had said, "I guess I'll take this one. Should fit in the study at the beach house."

I'd gotten used to the wealth that came with the circles people like the Beckmans moved in, but that had shocked me. "It's thirty-five thousand dollars," I said.

He'd grunted. "Wife's been bugging me to get something from this artist. Says all her friends have her stuff. So as long as it fits over the fireplace where I need it, might as well be this picture."

That was probably the point at which the successful artist daydream for me began to unravel. I'd had visions of people connecting to my work in a way that I hadn't been able to connect to them in real life. Someone buying my stuff to keep up with their neighbors and fill in wall space at their spare home—that had been a slap. A sharp, stinging slap.

At least Daddy Warbucks had loved what I did just because. That was what his purchases hinted at, anyway. The pieces I'd loved the best were always the ones he ended up buying. But the new commission still didn't sit well with me. At all. My annoyance made no sense, and I knew it: I only wanted to sell to someone who loved my work, which Daddy Warbucks did, but this was a Beckman-style move, to buy something that wasn't for sale just because he could. I resented the fact that he could write a check to get whatever he wanted, that he thought he could summon me out of anonymity with cold, hard cash.

But he very well may have.

I didn't want to give him the satisfaction. He was the face of so much of what I'd turned my back on. Except that he actually liked my work.

But I hated his assumption that my talent was his for cash.

Gah, this was stupid. Chloe had to go to Bethwell. Had to. I couldn't be bought, but I'd sell my work to help her.

Once we were on the road, Chloe talked about nothing but Bethwell for ten minutes straight before she interrupted herself. "Dis is not how you go home."

"I know. We're going to look at another preschool. Does that sound fun?"

She nodded and went back to narrating our visit. I hoped it wasn't a tactical error to take her somewhere else on the same day. There was a danger that anywhere else might suffer by comparison for Chloe, but the days I could do this without Dani knowing what I was up to were few and far between. Besides, Chloe was bound to tell her mom all about our visit to Bethwell this afternoon, and Dani would place an explicit ban on my doing any more school research. Better to get it all in today.

Two hours later, I pulled into my own driveway, shell-shocked and wishing I could fall into sleep like Chloe, who was cashed out in her car seat. I'd taken her to the two schools nearest Dani's work, the ones she could get some subsidies to help pay for. At the first one, the kids had all been sitting in front of a TV watching *Sesame Street*. I hadn't even seen a TV screen in Bethwell Academy. This other school had kid art on its walls too, but it had looked old and faded, like the same pictures had occupied those spaces for far longer than the current students had even been alive.

The second school had been both better and worse. Each of the four classrooms we'd visited had been loud and busy—so busy that I could see Chloe shutting down as she peeked out from around me. It was clear from the decorated walls that they had lots of projects and activities like Bethwell, but it lacked the serenity we'd felt the second we'd walked into the private preschool. The exhausted-looking director had offered a weak smile and explained that the group was unusually high-spirited. A dinginess had clung to the other three rooms, one I couldn't put my finger on. It wasn't only that everything had been old—it was that none of it had looked cared for.

I'd hustled Chloe out of both places, not wanting her to spend an extra second in either preschool. I'd homeschool her before I'd abandon her to that, and Dani would have to deal with it. I'd find other ways for Chloe to socialize with kids.

I settled Chloe into her own bed to finish her nap and sat on the sofa to Google homeschool curriculum. I'd been at it an hour when my phone rang with the Bethwell number in the ID, and I snatched it up so it wouldn't wake Chloe.

"This is Dr. Bray. I was thinking about your visit. Chloe is . . . special."

"Thank you. We think so."

"May I ask why her mother didn't bring her?"

"She's finishing a nursing degree and working full-time. She's done a lot of her own research, but I think she knew Bethwell was so far out of reach for her that she didn't want to torture herself with a tour."

"About that. Forgive me for prying, but if finances are so tight, why did you come look?"

"Because I thought I had a way to make it work," I said. I must have been right, or else why would she call? "Did you get a chance to look me up?"

"I did." She was quiet, and I didn't want to risk breaking the mood by talking. "You have an impressive background."

"Thank you. Do you think it could benefit the Bethwell program?"

"Of course it would. More importantly, I think it would encourage some of our donors to give generously enough for us to add another staff member and justify even more scholarships."

"So you're telling me there's an opening for Chloe?" My pulse accelerated at the possibility. *Please let her say yes.*

"Not exactly. We're strict about our student-to-teacher ratio, and I can't displace someone who's already been accepted. But . . . I believe I mentioned a waiting list for fall?"

"Of next year. Don't get me wrong, if space opens up even next year, we'll take it, but I still have to figure something out for this one."

"We don't tell people their exact placement on the waiting lists for a reason. It gives me latitude in making some executive decisions. I'm willing to put Chloe at the top of the list for this fall. It improves her odds greatly of getting in. Almost every year we have a last-minute dropout, usually because the family moves. I haven't received official word yet, but I believe one of our four-year-old's fathers, who has a second child slated to start this fall, is being transferred to Houston. I'm almost positive Chloe has a lock on the spot. Especially if you teach a weekly enrichment for us."

I couldn't answer for a minute, my brain too busy trying to wrap around her words to form a response of my own.

"Miss Carswell? Are you there?"

"Yes," I said. "Sorry. I'm in shock, I think. Yes. Yes, I'll do it."

"We'll need to talk first about your teaching experience. Watching you with Chloe gives me a fair sense of your demeanor with little ones, but I'll need to dig deeper, if you don't mind. Your talent isn't the question. It's a matter of how you'll use it with the children."

"I totally understand," I said, feeling subdued again.

She must have heard it in my voice, because I heard reassurance in hers when she responded. "We have a wonderful school community here, but there's no question that you would bring an incredible amount of prestige with you even if you only came to teach them how to mix colors or draw stick people. There's value in that for me too, so don't think of it as an interview you need to pass. It's more making sure you and the kids will have a good experience together. And remember, as much as I wish it were, this is not a guarantee you'll get in, but I'm optimistic."

"Thank you. Thank you so much!"

I could sense the warmth in her laugh, even over the phone. "Let's save that until there's a reason for it. Besides, part of my motivation is selfish."

"I'll make the art lessons worth it, I promise."

She laughed again. "I was referring to Chloe. I want her here. She has an exceptional gift with visual art. I could see it in that one picture. My entire professional life is about early childhood development, and I worry about how Chloe would be nurtured in another preschool center. If we can get her in here, I'd love to have her." She hesitated. "It's not only that. She's from a single-parent home, and I think your sister is at a place in her life where she could use some village help in raising Chloe. I'd like to offer that. I have some sense of how we can help your niece break through the anxiety she exhibits."

I pressed my fingers to my eyes to keep any tears from leaking out. It was relief coming on the heels of massive stress, I knew, but I didn't want Dr. Bray to hear me and think she was taking on Chloe *and* an emotionally unstable aunt. "Thank you so much," I repeated, keeping my voice as even as I could.

"Don't thank me yet. I can only offer you the opportunity. I can't offer you the funding. As tight as your finances might be, the scholarships we give out go to kids in far more dire circumstances than Chloe's. You'll still have the full tuition to handle. And this may be worse news: we do require a thousand-dollar deposit. I'll let you know as soon as a spot officially opens, but we'll need the money shortly after that. I'm so sorry I can't do more to ease the financial burden."

"Don't apologize. We'll make it happen," I said.

Dr. Bray hung up after promising to be in touch as soon as she had news, and I sat back against the sofa and tilted my head to stare up at the ceiling. It was white, devoid of texture, and utterly blank. Like a canvas. I picked up my phone again and retrieved a number.

"Victoria? Yeah, it's Lia. I want to talk about the Daddy Warbucks job again."

Chapter 7

Victoria's sigh of relief made me smile. "I almost believed you weren't going to do it."

"I wasn't until five minutes ago. Things change. Nice try with the bribe though."

"Which bribe?"

"The flower book. So thoughtful. I would have expected a pashmina or something from you."

"I didn't send you a book."

Her confusion sounded genuine, but I would have believed her anyway. Victoria never let a chance to take credit for something pass her by. Who had sent it, then? Griff came to mind, but I had enough humility to realize that was me projecting what I wished onto him rather than reality.

It would be great to think he'd sent me an anonymous gift because he'd seen my daffodil painting, but we'd lived next door to each other for over a year, and he'd never made a move. Then again, that might be exactly why he'd sent it anonymously. He had some serious shyness happening. It had taken months for us to have a conversation, and it wasn't until he saw my painting that I could say we'd had more than a chat.

The more I thought about it, the more sense it made that the book had come from him. It wouldn't have been Tom. Or Dani. The only other possibility was Aidan, but he lacked subtlety, and this was a subtle gift. And for another thing, if he'd managed to think of something so nuanced, he would for sure take credit for it. All part of his charm offensive. Or his offensive charm.

"So you'll do the paintings?" Victoria broke in. "When can you start?"

"I'll do a painting—singular—to see how it goes. And we need to go over the details again. What does he want? My stuff but different from my stuff?"

Victoria's warm laugh bubbled out. "Yes, exactly. He wants mountain-scapes but not as they look. He wants them as you experience them, with your unique flavor and point of view. Does that make sense to you?"

"Yes. I don't know what I have to offer this time around though, Victoria. I might not come up with anything good."

"What you have to offer is what any artist has: yourself. And that's invaluable. Whatever you produce will be impossibly good. I'll be in touch when I have the money for you."

We hung up, and I got up to pace. I didn't want to be here, standing at the edge of an insane cliff, wondering if I should jump. And that was what delving back into huge oils would mean: a head-first plunge into a part of my brain I'd ignored for three years now.

But it would also mean a fat fee that could make all the difference in Chloe's life for the next two years if I could pay for Bethwell.

I stopped pacing. There was no choice; there was only the right thing to do.

I had an hour before Dani got home, and I had to make my case about why Chloe should go to Bethwell and why Dani had to let me pay for it. It would take fast talking and a few minor threats, but I knew I'd wear her down. No, not true. I knew Chloe would wear her down when she chattered on and on about her adventures there. I had to come up with a way to make it okay for Dani to say yes.

When Dani came in from her shift, Chloe was sitting at the kitchen table making a mosaic self-portrait like the tissue ones we'd seen at Bethwell. Dani dropped a kiss on her head. "What have you got there, baby girl?"

"I a big girl. I make a picture of me," she said, tearing up some blue to get the right size for her eyes. "Wia, dis good as the school's?"

"Better," I said and meant it. Her attention to detail amazed me.

"School?" Dani repeated. "What school?"

"Beffwell," Chloe answered, still intent on her mosaic. "Nice school."

Dani straightened and narrowed her eyes at me. "What were you doing at Bethwell?"

I cleared my throat. "Getting her in."

Hope flashed in Dani's eyes for a second before they shuttered and frustrated lines appeared at the corner of her mouth. "It's ridiculously expensive. You should have asked me before you took her there. She's going to hate any other schools she sees now." She crossed over to the kitchen counter to set down her purse and get a glass of water.

"She already does," I said. "We checked out the two closest to your work, and she's not going there."

Dani whirled to face me, her face flat-out angry now. "What do you mean you took her there?"

"You told me their names the other night, remember? I thought we should check out all the options. And you're right—she hated them. She can't go there, Dani. Dr. Bray mentioned the word *anxiety* today. That's not simple shyness."

"Can I talk to you outside?" Dani asked, her voice tight. She nodded toward Chloe, who was watching us, her gaze moving between us as worry furrowed her little brow. Dani softened her voice for her daughter. "Lia and I are going to go on the deck for a few minutes. I love your self-portrait. Will you let me know when you finish the dress on it so I can see it all together?"

Chloe stared at her for a long moment before nodding and turning back to her work. I followed Dani out.

"Every tiny difference we see in kids isn't something that has to be fixed or treated," Dani said as soon as I slid the door closed behind me, and my heart clenched at how hard she was working to convince herself that she was wrong about Chloe's social delays. "She'll grow out of it. Kids grow out of stuff like that all the time."

Her words were angry, but my heart broke the tiniest bit at the fear in her eyes. Dani loved Chloe with a deep, fierce love, and I weighed the next words I said to her, wanting to make sure each one was exactly the right shape and texture. "I thought she was like me, that she preferred her own company, but I wonder if there's more to it. Dr. Bray seemed to, I don't know, *sense* something right away with Chloe. She needs to be with someone who can unlock her a little from her shyness."

Dani took a deep breath, a sure sign that she was trying not to kill me, but I caught the glint of tears in her eyes before she turned away to stare out at the mountains. "I would give anything I had to get her into a place that can help her. But everything I have isn't enough, and it's killing me. Bethwell is totally out of reach, Lia. You shouldn't have taken her there."

"But I did, and I got her admitted." Or almost. I'd do whatever it took to make it happen. I couldn't stop pushing until Chloe was in.

"I can't pay for it," Dani said, her voice rising.

"I can."

She whirled to face me. "What? How?"

"I got a commission."

She fell silent, studying me. "No," she said and turned back to stare out at the mountains.

"I love her. I love you. This is not a big deal to me."

"Really?" she said, her tone lifeless. "That's why you haven't painted in years? Because it's not a big deal to you?"

"I didn't have a reason to before. I do now."

"Lia," she said, her voice soft. "I know you love her. And I'll never be able to thank you enough for everything you do for us. But it's already too much. I'm not letting you give up more time or money for us."

"Wait here a second," I said, ducking into the house and returning with my laptop. "I want to show you something." I turned the screen around so she could see over a dozen open tabs in my browser. One by one, I clicked them. "If you don't do Bethwell, I'm teaching her myself. Here's all the different curricula I'm looking at. And if Chloe were any other kid, I'd say this was a great option. But you're right; she needs to connect to other children. And she's going to be overwhelmed by Bethwell, but I think they can help her. At those other schools? She'll get lost. And you said before that it adds a lot of time for me to drive out to get her there instead of sending her around here. So you can either cost me time in commuting, or you can cost me time in homeschooling, or you can cost me time in letting me do my art and do the thing that will make us all happy by sending her to Bethwell. Let Dr. Bray work with her, Dani."

She rubbed her hands over face. "I want her to go to Bethwell."

I set my laptop down and hugged her. "I know. And she will."

She hugged me back. "You were never this bossy before."

"It's one of those things I've learned since New York. You'll send her to Bethwell?"

She stepped back and nodded, brushing away the tears that had escaped. "Yeah. But I'm paying you back."

"Duh." I didn't care if she never paid it back, and even if she did, I'd stick it in an account for Chloe and hand it to her for college. "Now leave me alone out here so I can think artsy thoughts."

She stopped at the sliding door. "Thank you, Lia."

"Love you. Go away."

* * *

Within two days, I had a new bank account with a fresh wire transfer from Victoria in it. The number in it should have sent me dancing around my kitchen, but it meant I was committed now. Stuck. The thought of trying to fill a series of canvases unnerved me. My art had always grown out of struggle, from the conflict that came from finding my place. At the point where my Western upbringing and my Manhattan existence crossed, paintings evolved, huge pieces designed to tackle the scale of my life and the way two places had taken equal root in my imagination.

Through my art, I'd constantly been trying to figure out which place I belonged, trying to meld the two disparate experiences together into single pieces of art that captured the dichotomy.

But now I *knew* where I belonged. And I'd tamed my life into something that made sense, with a structure and routine that stabilized the utter madness that the last two years in New York had been. I didn't need to explore that chaos anymore. It was done and over. So where were the paintings supposed to come from now?

I had the technical skill to paint anything I saw. The daffodil had proven that. But technical skill produced pleasant pictures. What I had been paid for was art, the kind that moved the viewer even if they didn't understand their own reactions. I considered Victoria's phrasing again. I wasn't supposed to paint how the mountains looked; I needed to paint how they felt.

I'd spent the last two afternoons on the deck, waiting for dusk to fall so I could study the way the fading sunlight fell on the mountains. And also on Griff. But mostly it was the light on the slopes I wanted to study.

Okay, half alpine glow and half Griff.

But Griff didn't make an appearance, probably due to work at the restaurant, and I had plenty of attention to give the problem of sunsets and mountain faces. Pencils were only the first step, so I'd made a trip to McGill's for pastels and thick drawing paper. This afternoon had produced a whole ream of pages where the color was right but the work still lacked soul. I shoved the pastels aside and decided to try a straightforward landscape in watercolor to see where it led me. That meant setting up more of my McGill's haul: an easel, the highest-grade paper, and a treasure trove of paint tubes.

I was deep into an attempt at capturing Mt. Olympus while Chloe chased butterflies again when Griff's back door slid open. I looked up and blinked to reorient myself. He blinked back, then smiled.

"Hi."

"Hi," I said, surprised by the wave of teenage awkwardness that washed over me. I wanted to thank him for the book, but I didn't think that was allowed since he'd given it to me anonymously. "Thought you'd be at the restaurant tonight."

"It's slowing down now that ski season is ending."

"You going to survive?"

"Oh, sure. I'm on salary, so it doesn't matter if it's slow since I don't need the tips." He winced. "Sorry. That probably sounds insensitive. Uh, how's the diner?"

I grinned. "I meant are you going to survive the end of ski season."

He laughed. "No. I'll be a shell of a man until November. But the diner is good?"

"Yeah. Mornings are always hopping. I guess they do even better in the evening because a lot of the Pine Peak construction crews stop in for dinner, but the breakfast rush is great for me."

"Can I steal a look at what you're doing?"

"Sure," I said. "It's not great though. I'm trying to paint a feeling, and it's not coming out right."

He leaned over the railing and studied the picture. "It's amazing. Is that watercolor?"

"Yeah."

"You have way more supplies out than you did last time. Is this going to be a thing now? Lia is to painting as Griff is to skiing?"

"Not exactly. I know which skis you use. I'd have to sink a few hundred more dollars to get the fancy brushes and all that stuff to be as committed to watercolor as you are to the slopes. No judgment here though. There are worse obsessions." Much worse. My mood dimmed as Donovan's bloodshot eyes peered at me from the depths of my memory. I shuddered and pushed the image away.

"You cold?" Griff asked, already unzipping the hoodie he wore like he was going to hand it over.

"Not that kind of cold," I said, finding a smile for him. "It's fine. It feels pretty good out here." In high school, Dani had had all the mad flirting skills. She'd probably have added something like, "It feels pretty good out here . . . because of you" and sell it like she meant it, but even the thought of saying something like that out loud heated my cheeks.

Griff slipped his sweatshirt back on. "Yeah, it does. I can't wait until we start getting the heat lightning though. It's pretty cool to sit out here and watch it."

I imagined it. Painting on my deck at dusk, a storm putting on a light show at a safe distance, with Griff keeping me company? I could do that.

I could *so* do that. Even without Dani's ability to navigate men, I knew if I wanted anything to happen, I'd have to let Griff know his gifts and attention and Griffness were welcome.

"I think I have an idea to help you through your ski withdrawals," I said.

"A time-share in Argentina? Their season will start soon."

"Ah, yes, my Argentinian time-share. Already gave that away. Sorry. But if you'll play about a half hour of guitar for me, I think I might be able to give you something cool at the end."

"Deal," he said, already pushing himself up from his chair.

"Wait." Second guesses had seized me as soon as I'd made the offer. "I can't promise. I can only try."

"Good enough," he said over his shoulder as he disappeared into his condo and reappeared moments later with his guitar. He sat down and tuned while I set up a fresh sheet of watercolor paper.

"Bluegrass?" I wheedled. He grinned and set his fingers to plucking while I frowned up at Mt. Olympus and tried to figure out how to capture the hundreds of times I'd snowboarded down other mountain trails with Dani in hot pursuit. The memories relaxed me, and I plucked out the tubes I needed.

Chloe ran over every now and then when she tired of an activity, dropping butterfly chasing for dolls, which she played by my feet, then abandoning those to dig in the dirt and bury plastic jewels.

I was working on creating the impression of the snow when the hum of the *Jeopardy!* theme song drifted from Griff's guitar. I grinned at him and scanned my work. Painting white is never about whiteness. It's about all the colors around it, all the color reflected in the white surface you're rendering, that create the character of white. I ran a critical eye over the painting I'd done. Not bad at all.

"Show me," he said. "And no pressure, but remember, this is supposed to save me from ski withdrawals."

I stood and turned the easel to face him. He rose and leaned his forearms on the rail as he studied my work. He reminded me of the old westerns my dad used to love, when the cowboys would hang out by a corral, leaning on the fence and watching the horses. He finally looked up at me and shook his head. "I can't believe that half an hour ago that was a blank piece of paper."

"You saw me do it. No magic tricks."

"If it's not magic, it's something like it."

"We're even, because I can't believe that you can pluck a few strings and suddenly I'm front row at a private concert."

He shook his head. "Thanks, but your painting wins. Not to be demanding, but when can I have it?" He leaned forward to peer more closely at my work.

I'd painted the way the world had blurred past me the many times I'd hurtled down a black diamond trail, my snowboard carving up the powder, the sky and trees undulating in front of me with each mogul I took. The snow was there in the flash and sparkle of light refracted through diamonds, not white but utterly and completely snow nonetheless.

He straightened. "That's exactly how it feels," he said, and his voice held a note of wonder that sent a bubble of happiness floating up from my stomach to tickle my chest.

"Thank you. But the question is if it will be enough to save you from depression when you're stuck with hot, sunny days full of barbecues and poolside lounging."

He smiled, and I returned it. I hadn't dated anyone since Donovan. This new thing with Griff felt nothing like the wild, headlong plunge that falling for Donovan had been, but I liked it. The difference might even be why I liked it. There was an easiness to it, not a lack of effort but an effortlessness as natural as painting the daffodils had been. "How about if I grill some cedar-plank salmon for us while you finish so I can distract myself and not be a lurker?"

I dragged my brush through some blue and red and waved him away. "Now I'm even more motivated to finish."

"That was my evil plan."

Within a couple of minutes, the comforting scent of grill char drifted on the air, and I painted with Chloe's laughs as a sound track. She'd gone back to chasing butterflies. She never caught them and yet the chase was enough to make her happy.

Sitting there with the smell of dinner cooking and the evening light slipping toward purple while Griff hummed to himself and kept an eye on the fish, it struck me that for the first time in years, my life felt as simple and as right as Chloe's.

Chapter 8

I headed into the diner Saturday morning almost twitchy to see Aidan. I had a question for him, and the sooner I asked it, the sooner I could quit lying to myself about *all* of the motives behind it.

He came in around eight, Chief by his side. As soon as they were settled, I tucked my pencil behind my ear and cleared my throat. "I have a favor to ask."

"Sure," he said, no hesitation. I liked that.

"First, before I ask, will you promise not to think we're friends if I give you a piece of personal information about myself?"

"Uh . . . I'm sorry. Did you say you have a favor to ask? Because this is a weird way of going about it."

"Do you promise?"

He sighed. "Yes. We are absolutely not friends just because you tell me something about yourself."

"Good. Are you on the Pine Peaks jobsite?"

"Yes, Sherlock. What gave me away?"

"Calluses, work boots, and proximity," I answered, ignoring his wry tone. "I promised my neighbor I'd paint something for him, but I need a better view than my back deck. Is there a way you can let me on to the property?"

"To paint? Like . . . paintings?"

"Yes. To paint paintings," I said, and he squeezed his eyes shut for a second when he heard how ridiculous it sounded.

"Sorry. Um, yes. I can get you in there. I like art. What kind of paintings do you do?"

I went with part of the truth. "Little watercolors. Nothing grand. But I'm guessing Pine Peaks probably has some great vistas, so I thought I'd ask."

"Is this your secret way of—"

"Before I forget," I cut him off, "could you make sure I get to paint in a spot where you aren't?" His eyes narrowed, and I smiled sweetly. "I would never want to distract you at work. That's kind of rude, right?" I asked, and that made him laugh out loud.

"Tom!" I called.

"I'm already pouring you some juice," he called back.

Aidan grinned. "I'll get you on the jobsite, and you don't have to do art near me. Happy?"

"Perfect. I'm going to get my juice."

"Great. Come up on Monday and ask for Sully. He'll decide where to put you."

* * *

Two days later I pulled into a dirt lot and parked next to a large wooden sign proclaiming I'd reached "Pine Peak: A Vanguard Development Project." Pickup trucks crowded the lot, and my compact car sat among them like a pony among Clydesdales, but that wasn't what intimidated me into staying behind the steering wheel for another five minutes, even after pulling my keys from the ignition. I stared up the long slope, where trees had been cleared to make a ski run, and I sat guessing at which were beginner slopes all the way to black diamonds. I slapped an imaginary double black diamond sign on one that twisted nastily down one of the peaks and admitted defeat when I ran out of runs to label. I'd have to march myself up the dirt path that looked like it would be the bunny slope and find a dude named Sully.

I trudged across the lot to a parked trailer that looked like an office, but it was empty. I trudged some more, up the bunny slope toward the first ski-lift stop, and cursed myself for coming up with this idea. I didn't want to look for a guy I didn't know. I didn't want to try this painting I knew I was going to blow. I turned back toward my car but got a hold of myself halfway there, when the memory of Bethwell flashed through my head.

I headed back in the direction of the ski lift, and as I got closer, I could hear the loud growl of power tools punctuated by a rat-a-tat-tat and the periodic high whine of a saw doing its work. Three men stood in a cluster over some papers, one of them pointing to the paper and then out in the distance toward the hairpin slope I'd decided to call FroYo because I liked the irony. A run down that thing would be the furthest thing from soft-serve, but it would be as twisty as frozen yogurt coiled in a cup. The terribleness of my naming skills made me wince, and it was then that the pointing guy caught sight of me and waved. Sully, I guessed, as he handed off the plans and made his way down to me.

"You're the artist?" he asked as we neared each other.

"Guilty," I said, holding my hand out.

He shook it and considered me. It looked like he'd spent a lot of time squinting in the bright sun at jobsites. "Where do you want to go? The highest stop is the only one off-limits today because they're doing some work up there that you don't want to get in the middle of, but other than that, it's all yours." His arm swept across the whole valley.

"I have some supplies to haul, so how about if we start somewhere close to the parking lot? Take me anywhere you think has an awesome view. Dramatic is good."

He scratched his balding head and considered the options. "Does noise matter?"

I shook my head. "Quiet is better, but I can work through noise if I need to."

"I've got a spot. And let me help with your stuff."

He followed me to my car and shouldered my easel. I schlepped the rest of it behind him for a ten-minute walk, wondering if it would make me look like a super obvious teenager if I tried to casually ask where Aidan was. I'd half expected to find him waiting for me when I drove up.

Sully stopped at the newly constructed lodge and led me to a flat stretch of ground behind it. "We built it here to take advantage of some of the best views around. This dirt patch will be the outdoor patio, but we won't be pouring concrete for it until the end of summer. A lot of skiers will be paying major cash to get this view next year, but you can have it for free."

Not free. A cranky and vocal part of my brain grumbled that I'd given up a bit of my soul to do this job, but I thanked him and showed him where to set the easel. He left with a promise to send people by to check on me through the afternoon in case I needed anything, and I sat in my camp chair and stared out at the quilt of evergreens and wildflowers stretching as far as I could see.

I breathed, drawing in the air as deeply as I could, like inhaling it would somehow leave its taste behind on my tongue. I listened past the distant drone of power tools for the heartbeat of the place and set up my watercolors. First I'd paint it as it *looked*. Then I'd translate it to oil and paint it as it *felt*. At least, that was the plan.

I had the vista in front of me more or less blocked in on my paper when I heard the scuff of approaching footsteps an hour later. I set my brush down and stretched my arm across my chest when the footsteps came to an abrupt halt and a happy woof sounded.

"Lia?"

I twisted at the sound of Aidan's voice. There he was, Chief panting at his side, both of them looking exactly as they did every Saturday morning at T&R's. I stood and moved in front of the painting. The idea of him looking at it made me feel like he'd caught me locked out of my house in my underwear.

"Boss!"

Aidan's head turned in the direction of the shout, and my eyes narrowed. *Boss?*

A guy a couple of years younger than us, maybe twenty-five, jogged over, his face looking like it couldn't decide between laughing or crying. "Sorry to bother you, but you're the first one I seen with a radio."

I glanced down. Sure enough, Aidan wore a small walkie-talkie on his belt.

"My wife called. She's in labor. I gotta go. Is that okay? And could you tell Sully?"

The guy was poised on the balls of his feet like he was about to launch himself toward the parking lot in an Olympic qualifying run.

Aidan clapped him on the back. "Congratulations. That's great, man. Tell me your name, and I'll let Sully know."

"Mike Siegel, carpentry. Thanks, Mist—"

Aidan cut him off with a wave and an even bigger grin. "Go have a kid."

Mike took off, rocketing down the hill, and Aidan's soft laugh raised goose bumps on my arms. It was laced with genuine happiness, not the teasing undertone he usually directed at me. He relayed the news to Sully and holstered the radio.

"Can I see what you've done so far?" he asked, stepping closer.

I hesitated. Two minutes ago, there would have been no way. But the way he'd spoken to Mike had undone me. Someone with that core of kindness wouldn't criticize my work, even if he didn't understand it. Granted, I could be wrong about what he understood and what he didn't.

I'd been assuming Aidan was a day laborer like everyone else from Pine Peaks who stopped in the diner, but if guys were coming to him for permission to do anything, he was clearly the foreman. Hidden depths again.

Before I'd broken through with my art, I'd worked under managers in restaurants in Manhattan who wouldn't have let a woman in active labor leave her shift early, much less a mere baby daddy going to support his wife. I'd always thought Aidan was flash over substance, like Donovan, a smooth talker who every now and then showed a little more charm than the other "challenge" guys who came into the diner. Maybe I was wrong.

Aidan had shoved his hands in his back pockets and was waiting for my permission to look at my painting. He reminded me of Chief, who was settled back on his haunches, alert and patiently waiting for whatever came next.

I reached out and touched his arm. Saying thank you for being nice to Mike would sound odd, since I had no connection to Mike myself, but I hoped he understood what the touch meant. Aidan's eyes darkened, and I didn't know what to read into that. When his gaze fell to my hand, I realized I was still touching him, and I let go and took a small step to the side so he could see the watercolor.

"It won't look much like the final piece, but it's a start."

He didn't say anything. He only studied the painting and then glanced up at the vista I had drawn it from and back to the canvas. "I think I've seen this move in movies," he said, stepping back six feet to study the painting with his head cocked, then stepping forward again but to the side to look from a different angle.

"That's pretty good," I said. "What movie?"

"*The Thomas Crown Affair*," he said. "You seen it?"

"I've seen it. I have this weird thing for heist movies. Should I be worried you're going to steal this now?" I joked, but it was a poorly veiled attempt at assessing his response to my work.

"If I was ever going to steal art, I would for sure steal this," he said. "I don't know what you plan to do differently than this because it's pretty amazing. Any other secret talents you want to confess to? Are you also a blues singer by night or a secret prize-winning novelist too?"

"I cap out at painting and coffee refills. What about you? You're an artist and a builder. Anything else?"

"I'm not an artist," he said, his tone confused.

"You're a pickup artist."

"Ha," he said, and Chief barked an echoing laugh. Aidan nudged him with his foot, but the dog only panted. "I can cook," he said.

"So you come to T&R's because . . . ?"

A slow smile spread across his face, and mine heated at the implication. When he didn't say anything, just kept watching me, a twitchiness seized me, the need to move and be less visible. I couldn't keep my hands from drifting up to redo my ponytail, using it as an excuse to break eye contact so I could stare at the ground while I pulled my hair back in place.

His look bothered me. Over the last couple of weeks, I'd relaxed with him, falling into an easy routine of jokes and a genuine belief that he enjoyed seeing me when he dropped by the diner. But the expression on his face now, the determination around his eyes that lent them a calculating gleam, the smile that stretched to a predetermined point for maximum effect, all resembled the man who'd first come into the diner three months before, full of charm that hid the empty space beneath it with a thin veneer.

"You think I'm a pickup artist?" he asked, his voice low and controlled.

I tossed my ponytail back and lifted my chin. "Yeah. Emphasis on the *artist*. You've got this down."

He closed the gap between us. "There's only one way to find out. If I'm that good, I won't get slapped for doing this." He leaned down and slid his hand around the base of my neck, leaning forward slowly. He was giving me time to escape, but the challenge glinting in his eyes kept me rooted to the spot as if I'd grown there. He was expecting me to flinch, and when he realized I wasn't going to move, the challenge quickly became surprise, then almost anger as his lips touched mine.

The anger didn't translate to his kiss. It was soft but sure, and rather than pulling away, I leaned into it. I wanted it. It had been way too long since I'd been kissed, and I was in the mood for it, to be reminded of what all the fuss was about and to be reminded by someone who looked as good in jeans as Aidan did.

He did more than remind me. As he increased the pressure and slid his other hand up to cradle my head, I wasn't sure I'd ever been kissed this well.

It was breathtaking. Literally. When he lifted his head, I had to think through the steps of inhaling and exhaling. He stepped back and hitched his thumbs in his belt loops, waiting for me to say something. His posture suggested a casual cool, but his eyes didn't fool me. They were bright and studying me closely.

I pressed the back of my wrist against my mouth, the heightened throb of my pulse thrumming against my lips. I dropped my hand when I realized what I was doing and cleared my throat, throwing out words that bought me the distance I needed. Badly. "I knew it. You're a pickup artist."

The brightness disappeared behind a shadow. There was the cool detachment. "If that's what it gets me, then I'll admit it all day long."

"I'm more concerned with what it got me," I said.

"Which is?"

"The satisfaction of being right. You're a player."

His thumbs left his belt loops, and his arms crossed his chest, his biceps flexing beneath his black T-shirt sleeves. Calculation? Or genuine lack of awareness about what biceps like that could do to a girl's intentions to keep a distance? "Glad my kiss made you feel better."

I gritted my teeth at that. "That's not what I said."

"It's what I heard."

I stepped back toward my painting. "I'm keeping you from work. I should let you go."

"It's all right. They won't miss me for a while."

I picked up my paintbrush as a more direct hint. He didn't move. I waved it at him. "I need to get back to work because I need to go home and babysit soon. You don't mind, do you?"

"If you babysit? No. But exactly how many jobs do you have?"

"That one isn't a job. It's a privilege." I waved the paintbrush again. "I need to paint? So . . ." I made a shooing motion as if it could brush him away as easily as it laid color down on my paper. This time it worked.

He jerked his head at Chief, and they started on the path. "Good seeing you," he said over his shoulder. "Let me know if you need to come back. I'm sure I can pull some strings or something. I don't think you're in the way of any of Sully's crews here."

I shrugged and turned back to my painting, swirling the brush in water for forever before I risked a look to make sure Aidan was out of sight. He was. I grinned. I couldn't help it. I kind of wanted to be mad. I kind of *was* mad. But that had been a stellar kiss. Despite the confusing play of emotions that had flickered over his face, all that had come through in that kiss was heat. Now *that* was how you broke a dry spell.

Not that I'd planned to do it that way. Or maybe ever. I scowled.

There's no way I'd be doing it again, but it was good to have it out of the way—that first post-Donovan kiss, even though he and Aidan shared a lot of qualities. The confidence, the charm, the brashness Aidan showed in reaching out and taking a kiss he wanted. But chemistry with Donovan had led to a string of poor decisions, an embezzled bank account, and my broken heart. It would end badly with Aidan too. That was the problem when it was all spark and no substance. That's how Dani had ended up with Chloe and no baby daddy.

The big difference between Donovan and Aidan was that Donovan had looked down on the whole world from his huge pile of money. But even before and after he'd flamed out of his job, he'd had his parents' money to fall back on; there was no real need to prove himself financially, because there were no consequences if he failed. He wouldn't understand someone like Aidan, who had the same confidence from the small corner of a mountain where he was the foreman. Aidan's calloused palm had brushed my cheek as he'd slipped it into my hair, so I guessed he worked right alongside his crew. I respected that, but I didn't like his swagger no matter if he was a wage slave or a Wall Street wunderkind.

Still, while I never would have so much as hinted at getting a kiss, Aidan had done me a favor—just not the one he was probably strutting around the jobsite thinking he'd done me. When I'd fled Donovan and the Beckman tentacles, I'd sworn off men forever. They confused me. I had one boyfriend in high school, a moody guy who'd edited the school literary magazine, but I think he mostly hung out with me because I wore a lot of black and he thought that meant I got him. Really, my clothes had been about what would show fewer stains from all my artwork.

In art school, there'd been a few more guys, but we'd had intense conversations about our work and then run out of things to say. Donovan had come out of left field and swept me up. I'd never understood why. Still didn't get it. Maybe I was another thing to collect. Model—check. Lawyer—check. Med student—check. Artist—check.

It had been way too easy to ignore guys altogether after convincing Dani to move in with me and let me help her. I didn't want guys coming to our house with Chloe around. And even if I'd ever had the insane desire to date, I didn't meet any guys at work. I mean, I met guys all day long at work. Just not a lot of single ones. Or even young ones.

That was probably how Aidan had caught my eye so easily. His being hot probably helped too. And funny. And he'd already shown more depth than Donovan. But not enough.

I owed Aidan a thank you though. His next OJ would be my treat without having to make me laugh first. He could assume whatever he wanted when I plopped it down in front of him, but the truth was that his kiss meant I was out of my rut. I wouldn't be stocking up on push-up bras or vixen lipstick while I cruised dating websites or anything, but I'd make myself more open to possibilities.

Not to Aidan though. He and the Donovans of the world were impossibilities. Let them be someone else's headache.

Griff was a different story. It had taken him forever to say hello to Dani or me. He still hardly ever talked to Dani, but I didn't know if that was shyness or the fact that their schedules almost never had them home at the same time. All I knew was that, somehow, very recently, I'd begun looking forward to seeing him on his deck.

I considered the paintbrush in my hand and laid it down on my easel. It was a magic wand I had waved and opened up some hidden part of me. Now everything was escaping. I sat down and drew my knees to my chest, wrapping my arms around them and closing myself into a safe knot of Lia-ness. It was exactly what I'd been scared of, this inability to close myself off once I opened up to paint. I stared out at the crest of the nearest peak and the way the sun struck it. My fingers twitched toward my brush again, and I wondered if I had any choice about any of this anymore.

No. Art had never been a choice. I'd lied to myself for more than three years about that. But I had to make sure the wildness it loosed in me didn't spill out anywhere but on the canvas.

Chapter 9

The third time I got yelled at for Mr. Benny's coffee, it was Tom, not Mr. Benny. I hurried to refill it and mumbled an apology, but it wasn't like it was going to rescue the nonexistent tip I got from him even on the days when I gave him perfect counter service.

"Sorry," I repeated to Tom as I dropped off a ticket for the special, a Spam omelet.

"What's with you today?" he asked. "Chloe keep you awake?"

"No. It's nothing. I'm distracted, that's all." I'd been up late but not because of Chloe. I'd spent two hours rearranging my garage to create a space to paint. It wasn't great. It was below our townhouse, so we could access it from the kitchen by a flight of stairs, but it only had three tiny windows to let light in. I'd roll up the door as often as I could during daylight, but it still wasn't ideal. And I'd had to carve out a comfortable space to entice Chloe to play while I worked. Once I got the canvas prepped and started, it couldn't leave the garage. I'd have to convince her that she wanted to spend a few hours at a time hanging out there instead of the yard.

"Lia? You here?" Tom snapped his fingers, and I blinked. "You keep doing that—disappearing. I realize this isn't the most intellectually stimulating job you could be doing, but you still gotta use at least half your brain for it."

I winced. "Sorry. I'll focus."

"You better, or I'm not putting extra bacon in your lunch scramble."

I widened my eyes. "That's distressing. Beyond distressing."

"Then pay attention."

I scooped up a plate of hash browns and hot cakes for Flannel Guy, who had earned his name by wearing the same red shirt every Tuesday and Thursday when he stopped in. It always looked clean, so I didn't want to judge, but every time he came in, I had to fight the urge to ask him if it was his only red flannel or if he'd bought a bunch of the same one. My dad used to do that with shirts he liked. He'd buy one of every color, but maybe Flannel Guy was taking it to the next level.

The diner's door opened to admit a scruffy snowboarder. Even in the off-season, you could almost always peg them by their shaggy hair. He stood blinking at everyone inside like we were a Rubik's Cube he'd been handed but didn't know what came next. I stopped short when I saw the brown paper package tied with twine in his hand. "Is that for me?"

"You Lia?"

"Yeah."

He thrust it at me and turned back toward the door.

"Wait. Who asked you to bring me this?"

"Some mom lady said she'd give me ten bucks if I walked it in here."

"Do you know her name or anything?"

"Nah. It didn't look like it could be anything too illegal so I took the ten bucks, and she drove off."

"Thanks." I let him go without any more questions. I doubted he could tell me anything that would dig up clues about who was behind the gifts, but from the feel of the contents through the paper, I didn't need any. It had to be Griff.

"Well, open it up," Mr. Benny said, his voice gruff. "Might as well get it over with so you can go back to pouring coffee."

I narrowed my eyes, but Tom waved his spatula at me in warning, and I walked back to the grill to join him.

"What is it this time?" he asked.

I untied the string, answering before I even had the paper off. "Paintbrushes." Sure enough, the fibers were sable, the best watercolor brushes on the market.

"Well?" Mr. Benny demanded through the pass-through. "What was it?"

"Paintbrushes." I set them down and walked back out with a fresh pot of coffee.

"Paintbrushes? No wonder you don't sound too excited," he said as he eyed his cup and watched it fill. "Who sent them to you?"

"There's no note," Tom said. "Our Lia here has a secret admirer."

My cheeks heated as a few catcalls sounded from the other diners. "Shut up, all of you."

They didn't. Of course.

"What kind of admirer is that?" Mr. Benny demanded. "Everyone knows you're supposed to send flowers."

"He kind of did," I said under my breath, thinking about the flower guide Chloe had taken over. She'd made Dani promise to buy her the seeds for at least ten different varieties so far. But all that got lost in the weirdness of thinking about Mr. Benny even being on the ball enough to think about sending flowers to a lady. I eyed his wedding ring and wondered not for the first time who had gotten stuck with its match.

"Why would someone send you paintbrushes?" Tom asked. "Is it a clue? Are you supposed to add up all the stuff you get and come up with some kind of message or something? What's a flower book plus paintbrushes mean?"

"Isn't there a flower called a paintbrush?" Red Hat asked. "Maybe it's got something to do with them."

"Those are Indian paintbrushes, and no, that's not it," I said.

Mr. Benny snorted. "Idiots. She's a painter."

I looked at him in surprise. "How'd you know that?"

Tom looked at me in surprise. "You are? Yeah, Mr. Benny. How'd you know that?"

"She smells like linseed oil, and she's got paint under her fingernails."

He was right. I'd gotten up early to mess with the canvas I'd bought the night before. I'd only meant to position it, but I'd snatched up a tube of burnt sienna before I thought too hard about it, and suddenly, an hour later, I'd been late for work and rubbing at my hands like crazy with baby oil, then soap and water to get the paint off of them. I stared down at the spots I'd missed in my rush and wondered how he knew what linseed oil smelled like.

I topped off his coffee and moved on to the other customers, ignoring some ribbing from a few of the guys.

"How come you don't look happy about your presents?" one of them asked. "Are you a diamonds-and-fur kind of girl?"

Tom scoffed loudly from the back. "No. Mind your business."

I was glad he said it since my tongue had frozen. The customer grinned and went back to his biscuits and gravy.

I wasn't happy about the brushes at all. They were incredibly expensive for someone already trying to swing a mortgage on a pricey resort-adjacent condo like Griff's. I had no idea how much money he made; managing a nice restaurant had bought him nice skis but only an older SUV to put them on. And if I was wrong and he could afford an impulse buy like the brushes, he still shouldn't have dropped this kind of cash on me, especially since I was switching to oils and needed different brushes. It doubled my guilt that I couldn't even put them to good use. I'd take one of his private concerts over this any day.

And yet . . . there was something sweet about the idea of Griff walking into McGill's and asking for the best paintbrushes they had. It was incredibly thoughtful. I wished I were more certain on the protocol for showing my appreciation. If he didn't want me to know it was him, how was I supposed to thank him? Or did he *want* me to guess it was him?

I'd have to ask Dani. Somewhere in her dating past, there must have been a shy guy or two she could use to explain to me how to handle Griff. Leaving a "thank you" unspoken kept the words sitting heavy on my tongue, but I didn't want to scare him away either. I didn't know when I had begun looking forward to hearing his glass door slide open, but it was becoming the best part of my day when it happened. There was an easiness about him, about being around him, and I didn't want to mess it up.

By the time I got home and tag-teamed Dani on her way out the door, I'd decided to thank Griff without actual words, an actions-speak-louder kind of strategy. I scooped Chloe up into a hug, and after negotiating which princess dress she would wear, we headed to the grocery store for supplies. Two hours later, we had sugar cookies in star and daisy shapes, and Chloe was outside traumatizing them with food glitter while I studied the watercolor I'd done at Pine Peak.

Griff's door slid open, and I looked up and smiled, glad he was actually home so we wouldn't have to leave the cookies on his deck with a note.

"We make you cookies, Gwiff!" Chloe said before I could say hi.

His eyes brightened. "I love cookies."

"I make them sparkle kind," she said, holding a star up by the corner. It broke and fell to the ground. Her eyes widened, and she scrambled off her chair to pick it up and dust it off. After peering at it closely, she plucked off a stray piece of grass and bit that part out before handing the rest of it to Griff. "I eat the dirty part."

I snagged it before he could take it and try to figure out what to do with it. "It's okay. We have plenty of others."

He looked worried. "But are those the sparkle kind too? Because those are the best ones."

Chloe grabbed two more glitter disasters and brought them to him. "No bites," she said. "I not drop them."

He accepted them. "Still warm? This is how it's going to be in heaven." And he ate the first cookie in ten seconds flat. "Delicious. It tasted as good as it looked. Chloe, you think you could come cook at the restaurant for me? The chef doesn't make cookies."

Chloe tilted her head as if the decision weighed on her so heavily she couldn't keep her head upright. "No," she said. "I'm not a grown-up. Maybe Aunt Wia will go."

His eyebrows lifted. "Aunt Lia? You going to come bake cookies at the lodge?"

I shook my head. "So sorry. Without Chloe's glitter magic, these are regular old Pillsbury knock-offs."

"Bye!" Chloe said before clambering down the steps to the yard.

"Butterfly?" he asked.

"Butterfly," I agreed as I watched her jump and dive.

"So what did I do to deserve cookies?" he asked, and a faint knowing flickered through his eyes before he schooled his face into an inquisitive expression.

"Oh, you know." I would see where that got us. An admission, maybe? It would be much easier to take a cue from that.

"Why don't you tell me?"

Was that a dare? Or was he trying to figure out if his cover was blown? I wanted to say, "For the book and the brushes," but only the thought that it might not be him stopped me. That would be supremely embarrassing. I decided on the safe route. "We're giving them to you on account of general awesomeness."

"I accept. But now I should earn them. I got something for Chloe. You mind if I give these to her?" He held up a packet of seeds. "She was showing me a picture of bluebells in the flower book the other day. I thought she might like them."

Seriously? Was there no limit to this guy's thoughtfulness?

"She'll love them." I called her over and laughed as she danced in excitement when Griff explained that she could grow her own flowers. Looked like a trip to the garden department would be in our near future. I watched Griff and Chloe, Chloe having climbed onto a deck chair so they could discuss the seeds over the rail. I cleared my throat. "Griff? Would you like to come over here? You could actually pull up a chair while you guys plan how to pull up my yard."

He looked surprised for a moment, then grinned. "Sounds good." He vaulted himself over and landed lightly on our side. His grace surprised me. All in all, it was an oddly sexy move.

What? *Dear self, engage the brakes.*

One hot guy kisses me, and suddenly the whole world is full of sexy men? No, absolutely not. Not going there. I liked the idea of Griff, but a week ago, he was just some guy next door. Yes, he'd shown a thoughtfulness that charmed me, but I hadn't decided how I felt about that yet. For right now, I could handle making a new friend. And if it drifted into something else, okay. But only drifting, not barreling headlong down some crazy attraction roller coaster like the one Aidan was trying to drag me down.

Chloe ran in to fetch the flower guide, and I looked back at Griff. "You're patient with her. Thanks."

"No problem. I've got nieces. I'm used to them."

"I can spring you if you want out. Hop back over, and I'll tell her you had to do some grown-up errand or something."

"I'm fine. Unless I'm bothering you," he said, half rising from his chair as if he'd realized I might be hinting.

"No! It's fine. Stay. Will I bother you if I work?" I asked, gesturing at my easel.

"Not unless it bothers you if I watch."

"Nope." In fact, I wanted him to so he could see me using the brushes he'd given me. I turned to my painting and experimented with some purple, seeing what it did to carve out the face of the mountain. I heard Chloe come back out, but she and Griff had their heads bent over the flower book pages, so I focused on getting my picture right. It was almost there, but I wasn't happy with it.

I didn't realize how quiet it had gotten until I heard a happy shriek from the yard and glanced up to find Chloe sitting in the grass and waving a worm at me.

I turned to catch Griff staring at my painting with a small smile playing around his lips. I set my brush down where he would be sure to see it and smiled back.

"Sorry. Didn't realize you guys were done with flowers. How long have I been boring you?"

"Not long," he said, then flushed. "I mean, you're not boring me. It's interesting to watch you paint."

"There should be a 'watching paint dry' joke in there somewhere."

"No jokes," he said. "This is cool to watch, period."

"Thanks." I gathered my supplies, ready to put caps back on tubes and rinse the brushes.

"Oh, sorry," he said, shooting to his feet. "I must be cramping your style."

"You're not. I promise. They're the problem," I said, stabbing a paint-brush at the horizon. He stared at me blankly. "The mountains," I clarified. "They're not cooperating. I think I'm going to have to paint on-site again."

"Not an outdoors kind of person?" he asked.

I realized how annoyed I must have sounded. "Definitely an outdoors person. It's not an ideal circumstance, that's all." That had more to do with Aidan being around than the painting though. "Plus, I wish I had this right already. I'm almost there, almost have the answer. But it's not coming to me yet."

"I don't know much about art, but I know what I like. And that's amazing."

"Don't lie," I said, grinning. "You're picturing my mountainside covered with snow so you can ski it."

He laughed. "I'm not. I promise."

We stayed outside for another hour, goofing off as the light faded toward evening. I was laughing at a ridiculous story he was telling me about narrowly escaping an avalanche he'd caused when the door opened and Dani stepped out to join us.

She wore her tiredness like a veil. It muted her features and dimmed the sparkle in her eyes, but as soon as she spotted Griff, it lifted, and she found a smile somewhere to paste on. "Hi, Griff."

"Hi."

Silence fell.

"Uh, I thought you weren't coming home until nine," I said.

"Professor didn't show. I love it when that happens."

"Cool. Chloe will be excited." I shouted for her, and as soon as she saw her mom, she gave a happy shout and came tearing toward the deck. I moved out of the way so she could throw herself at Dani, who grabbed her up in a huge hug.

"I'm so glad I get to put you to bed tonight, baby girl," she said. "You ready for a bath?"

"Yes!"

"Tell everyone good night."

I got a tight squeeze, and Griff got a pat on the arm before Dani shepherded her daughter back into the house. The tiredness settled back into the tiny grooves around her eyes as she turned away from us. I frowned.

"I better go," Griff said, standing and stretching.

"You don't have to. Chloe's room is in the front of the house so our talking won't bother her."

"Yeah, but if I overstay my welcome, you won't invite me back." He pretended to do a runner's stretch. "Gotta limber up for my trip back over the rail." He flashed me a smile and vaulted back to his side, then ducked into his place with a small wave.

Awesome.

Chapter 10

I parked by the construction trailer and poked my head in. The guy in the office radioed Sully to let him know I was there and gave me the okay to set up behind the lodge again. I wondered if Aidan would hear the call go out and come find me. I hoped . . . not?

No, I absolutely hoped not. He hadn't shown up at the diner this morning, and I was sorry but only because I'd rather have seen him there for the first time post-kiss than here. There I could have acted like everything was normal, taken his order, given him some attitude, and plunked his plate down. Boom, done. Back on our same footing just like that.

But here the rules were different. It was his turf, and I'd have to fight to stand my ground—literally, if he tried kissing me again, being as my knees had buckled when he did it before. But there would be no kissing and no weak knees this time. If I even saw him. Which I didn't want to.

I set up my easel and paints, not sure what I was trying to accomplish, wishing I could work with my oils out here, but it was impractical. Capturing the sense of the place in watercolor was a step up from pencil, at least. My palette stared at me, unblinking, and I stifled a sigh that no one was there to hear. A creeping sense of futility wafted toward me like tendrils of B-movie fog the longer I stared out at the horizon. The fog was boxing me into the same corner the first painting I'd done up here had. It might have been technically good, but I'd get it home and lose the feeling I needed, which was the whole point of the commission.

An hour later, out of sheer frustration, I knocked the easel down and glared at it. It gave me the same petty satisfaction as slowing my car to a crawl for a tailgater.

"Whoa!"

I whirled at the sound of the shout and could make out Aidan's and Chief's silhouettes on the slope behind me.

Great. I didn't look *at all* insane.

Aidan picked up his pace and jogged down. "Everything okay?"

"Yeah. The wind blew it over."

"Hate it when that happens," he said, and I awarded him points for not pointing out the total lack of wind. He leaned down and picked the easel up, setting the still-blank watercolor paper on it. "What's the painter's version of writer's block called?"

"Futility. The formal name is 'an exercise in futility.' I quit."

He did a if-that's-what-you-want face and touched the paints. "Is this usually fun?"

Fun? No. "It's more like scratching an itch. Except it's the itchiest itch and the best scratch ever." I wrinkled my nose. "That was a terrible analogy. I guess I have writer's block too."

He didn't say anything, but he looked like he was waiting for more. I sighed and tried again. "It's not fun like a picnic or hiking or anything. It's more like making something inside of you quiet for once. Have you ever felt really restless? I don't mean for a few minutes until you get comfortable on your sofa. I mean restlessness that goes on for days. Longer, maybe."

The corner of his mouth turned up, and I lost my train of thought for a second.

"I have, yeah." A real breeze kicked up for a moment and ruffled his hair. "This probably sounds weird, but every fall when I was a kid, my neighbors would rake their leaves and burn them. There was something about the smell of that smoke that made me want to go on adventures. Pirate adventures, mostly."

Oh geez, that was adorable. I imagined a little Aidan all decked out to conquer imaginary seas, a tiny version of the confident guy standing in front of me with thumbs through his belt loops, ready to take on the world. I grinned before I could stop myself. "I remember the exact same feeling; that fall smell was in the air, and suddenly, anything seemed possible. What is that? Is it because of Halloween? Or school starting?"

"I have no idea. But is that the kind of restlessness you're talking about?"

"Yes and no." I brushed a hand over my blank paper. "Sometimes I need to be somewhere else. Anywhere else. And I get in the car, and I go there. For an hour or a day, even if it's a drive down to Bryce to soak it in for an hour or two before I turn around. But nothing is right until I get there, and then . . . it is. That's what painting is like. Something wants to come out, and I don't feel right until it does."

"And it's not coming out right now." He said it like he understood.

"No. It's been a long time since I did this. I'm trying to figure out how I used to get it out before."

"All this for a picture for your neighbor, huh? Lucky neighbor."

I didn't respond to his obvious fishing. Not correcting him wasn't even a lie of omission because I probably would give this to Griff if I could get it to work out. I owed him for the brushes. And besides, I liked him having my work because of the way he'd hurried to hang the first painting I'd done for him when the paint was barely dry. Why had that one been so easy and this one was so impossible?

Aidan abandoned his fishing expedition with a shrug. "This might sound weird, but I worked with this architect once who got stuck trying to work something out. So instead of redrafting it, he got out toothpicks and did it old school. Did you ever have to build a toothpick bridge when you were a kid? It was like that. Anyway, I don't know what it was, maybe working with his hands or concentrating on the details or using a different kind of creativity, but he came up with this brilliant solution that ended up making his original vision even better."

"I wish I could paint something different, and yet I don't. I need to do these."

I scrubbed my hands through my hair. "That's a lie. I could do any mountains. But I want to do *these* mountains. I can't not do them. They're *my* mountains. But I keep trying, and they . . . It's not working. And I need it to. I need to paint." My refusal to work after leaving New York had its roots in a lot of things: hurt, anger at Donovan and his parents, disdain for the collectors who had blindly followed their lead. But staring at the blank paper in front of me, the one where I had to put something real and not an easy daffodil for Chloe's entertainment, I realized the blank white space represented fear.

What if I couldn't do this? I couldn't say that to someone like Dani or Griff or Aidan. They'd look at the watercolor of the slope I'd painted for Griff and see that it was so far beyond what they could do that it must be good art. And I couldn't say it to Victoria because she would point to my three very successful shows in her gallery and the very large checks she'd written me, and say that all of those things proved I could.

But the people who had collected my work had done it largely because of the Beckman stamp of approval. If Donovan's parents wanted my stuff and said it was good, every friend who had a neighboring vacation home in the Hamptons jumped to own a piece of me too. They bought what other people said to buy and then complimented each other on their excellent taste. Stocks, cars, wives, art. Didn't matter.

"I could help you try the paint-something-else theory if you want," he said.

"What are you thinking I should paint?" I asked to humor him. "Chief? A portrait of you?"

"I'd love to see your interpretation of me. Let me guess, a rugged manual laborer swinging a giant sledgehammer John Henry style in a salute to the idealized Western male?"

I blinked at him. "Who's John Henry?"

He shook his head. "Never mind. The 'something else' I thought you could paint would also get you on a hike, and I'll split my lunch with you so you have a picnic too. You said picnics and hikes are fun, right? Put all three together and maybe painting will actually be fun."

"Yes to the hike, no thanks to the sandwich."

"It's about a mile, mostly up, but it'll be worth it. You could leave your stuff, and no one will bother it."

"I pack light to paint outdoors. I'll leave the easel, if you don't mind." He shook his head, and I shouldered my backpack and hitched my thumbs underneath the straps. "You were going to revive my dead muse?"

He laughed and led the way across the meadow. "Is your muse really dead? That sounds like a problem."

"No, it isn't dead. I've got lots of ideas of what to paint. I just can't figure out how to paint them."

"Keep climbing. Perspective is a thing in art, right? We'll change yours and see what happens."

We went on for another half hour, steadily ascending. I was glad I had a lot of trail conditioning and a light pack since Aidan was treating the incline like a Sunday stroll. As we hiked what turned out to be the double black diamond run, he explained some of the building challenges they'd run into, his face lighting up as he spoke, and there was a realness in his expression that usually hid behind a flirtatious mask.

At one point, he stopped and pointed to a stump. "That tree didn't even need to come down, but the rest of them ticked me off so much when we were trying to remove them that I cut it down to make an example of it to the other trees."

He looked so annoyed that I laughed. He shot me a glare, but that only made it worse. "Sorry," I said. "But come on. You've cut a ton of trees down. You win. Taking that guy out was unsportsmanlike conduct."

"Sportsmanship . . . Good word. Because I turned it into a trophy."

"Explain?" I asked, imagining a bronzed tree somewhere over the next crest, captured and frozen like the White Witch's marble garden in Narnia.

"This resort is about being in the middle of the mountains and soaking it all in. Everything about it should reflect the setting, should feel like being a part of this place and not like we came in and put a human fingerprint all over it. So I took that tree out, but then we found someone to turn it into a super rustic dining table in the main lodge. And three coffee tables in the lounge."

I watched him closely, noticing the way his intensity changed his face. If I sculpted, this is what I would want to capture, the hard planes and angles his cheeks and chin took on in his determination, coupled with the excitement in the tiny crinkles fanning from his eyes that turned his face from a study in austerity to a portrait of barely leashed energy.

He caught me staring, and he brushed his hands through his hair. "Sorry. I get carried away sometimes."

"You love what you do. Don't apologize. But . . . exactly what's your job here?"

"I oversee stuff."

"You can use technical terms like 'foreman' and 'contractor' if you want. I know I was guilty of assuming you were kind of entry level, and I'm sorry."

"Why? Would there have been anything wrong with that?" His voice was tight again.

"Yes and no. Someone who is entry level and always stays that way is someone who doesn't love their job. And I don't relate. If you love your job, I think you rise through ranks no matter what. It's not about being ambitious; it's about caring about what you do. I can relate better to someone like that than I can to someone who shows up to punch a clock."

"Fair enough," he said. "I can understand that. And I'm not using technical terms because there isn't one for what I do. It's pretty fluid. So to say I oversee things is the most accurate way to explain it."

"Like which parts though? You seem to know a lot about all of it. The slopes, the lodge, the interiors."

"Yeah, I kind of get shuffled all over the place. It's good. Keeps me from getting bored." He paused and stared up the slope. "Have you looked behind us yet? Don't," he said when I started to turn my head. He put his hand across the small of my back to keep me still. If anything, the instant heat made me want to jump out of my skin. "We're almost to the point I want to show you, and I want you to be surprised."

"Then I'll keep my eyes straight ahead, captain." It was a pretty view too, with more of the ski run stretching in front of us, lined by the trees that had survived Aidan's wrath.

"Smart aleck."

"Guilty."

He dropped his hand, and we climbed a bit farther while he entertained me with the saga of Chief's losing battle with the local chipmunk population, who had formed a united front to taunt the dog. Finally, Aidan glanced over his shoulder and touched my arm to stop me. Heat again, a flare straight up to my shoulder.

"This should do it. But before you look, can we try something? It's this goofy game my niece plays with me, but maybe it could help."

"I keep telling you, I'm not a game player," I said, deadpan. "You've got the wrong girl."

"Hilarious. You want help or not?"

"Sure." I doubted he'd come up with anything that would make a difference, but it could be entertaining.

He moved in front of me, and I took a step back so the navy T-shirt stretched across his broad chest didn't fill my whole view. "No laughing, or I push you down the mountain."

I rolled my eyes. "Fine. Go ahead. Break my creative block."

"Close your eyes."

"No way."

"I gave you an order, soldier."

"It's a stupid order. Or rather, it's an order you'd only give to me if you thought I was stupid."

"Why would you think that?"

I crossed my arms. "This is a dumb idea for two reasons. First, painting is a visual medium. How does closing my *eyes* solve the problem?"

"You're going to have to trust me."

"Ha!"

"You said you weren't going to laugh," he said, his eyebrows rising.

"I said I wouldn't laugh at your game. I can laugh all I want at the idea of trusting you."

He sighed. "Maybe I'm going to throw you down the mountain anyway."

"Very trustworthy."

"What reason have I given you to think I'm not trustworthy?"

"For one, I don't know you."

"You've known me for months. You know Sully even less, but I'd bet you say he's trustworthy."

"Yeah, but—"

He cut me off by clicking on his radio. "Sully? It's Aidan. Would you say I'm a trustworthy guy?"

A long pause met that, and he held up his finger to keep me from breaking in. The radio crackled. "I'd say that all day long, b—"

He released the radio button. "See?"

"But Sully hasn't tried to kiss me. Call it paranoia, but I think if I close my eyes, you will."

He blinked at me and did his slow smile, his devilish, knee-weakening slow smile. "You think I go around *stealing* kisses? This isn't seventh grade. I don't take anything that isn't freely given. But tell yourself whatever makes you feel better about how that all went down last time."

Heat climbed up my neck, and I prayed it didn't show too obviously in my cheeks. No, he wouldn't need to steal anyone's kisses. "I never lie to myself. I know what happened last time. I own that. I'm more concerned about what will happen this time."

"This time you're going to close your eyes, and I'm going to ask you some ridiculous questions, and they might help you, or they might make both of us feel stupid. But you can trust that the stupid part would not be on purpose. So you ready to give this a shot?"

I set my bag on the ground. "Tell me what I'm doing again."

"Close your eyes."

I gave him one last challenging stare before I did as he asked. Nothing happened for several seconds except that his work boots scuffed over the graded slope, paused, and scuffed back.

I didn't like the silence. "Is this the thing I'm supposed to be doing? Standing here?"

"Yeah. But now think of a couple things that aren't what they should be. Like, for example, I'm going to hold a flower under your nose. Tell me what it smells like."

A petal brushed my nose, making me twitch, but I sniffed and exhaled. "It smells sweet, I guess?"

"Yes. Now what does it sound like?"

"Excuse me?"

"You heard me. What does the flower sound like?"

I frowned, and he cleared his throat. "When my niece made me play this, I figured out that stars sound like breaking glass and the sound of a violin tastes like dark chocolate."

I frowned harder. "That's ridiculous. Cello sounds taste like dark chocolate. Violins are gourmet butterscotch."

A soft laugh met that. "So you get the point here?"

"I get the point."

"Good. Now what sound does this flower make?"

I squeezed my eyes even tighter, concentrating on how to translate the smell to a different sense. "It sounds like . . . when little kids do an orchestra and someone's in charge of the triangle and you get this one semi-random bright note."

"Open your eyes."

He stood a couple feet away with a cluster of white blossoms in his hand. "This is a mock orange. Were you right?"

I laughed. "Yes. Mock oranges definitely sound like amateur triangle players."

"Ready for another one?"

I nodded.

"Close your eyes."

I did and heard the boot scuffing again, but this time he stayed close. A moment later he picked up my hand and turned it over to place a large pebble in it. "What does this taste like?"

"I guess you don't want me to lick it."

"Nope. Tell me what your imagination says it tastes like."

I turned it over, letting its flattest part rest on my palm while I explored it with the fingers on my other hand. It wasn't perfectly symmetrical, but it was smooth, except for small dips and rises. Sun-warm and dense, it reassured me. There was something about the solidness of it, the thereness that stabilized my insides for the first time since Aidan had called down the slope to me. "This would taste like a roasted beet salad."

"That's a good thing?"

"That's a perfect thing."

"Look at it."

I did and found a rock in my hand that looked exactly like what I had imagined. "I think I might be getting the point now."

His expression changed from watchful to pleased. "Good. Then let's try the big one. Close your eyes again and do a half turn around, but then listen and smell for a long time. No looking, okay?"

I did as he asked and channeled my inner ballroom dancer as his hand touched my elbow to balance me on the uneven ground. Heat. Again. I followed his lead, and he kept his hand in place until he was sure I was firmly planted and facing the new direction.

"You good?" he asked. I nodded. "Then I'm not going to say anything for a while. When you've done whatever sensual things you need to do, you tell me. And by sensual, I mean using your senses. Like sniffing the wind."

Laughter lurked in his voice, and I refrained from punching him only because I didn't want to look stupid flailing at him with my eyes closed.

A breeze kicked up and blew my annoyance away as simply as that. I let it wash over me and breathed deeply, taking it all in. When the wind stilled, I listened to what it left behind, in no rush to finish the experiment. Water shushed nearby, glacier runoff in a creek I hadn't realized was there. Birds sang. Much smaller things than Aidan's boots scurried over the grass. Something buzzed by near enough for me to hear it but not close enough for me to flinch when I recognized the hum of a bee. Wherever we were, it was full of sounds. But it was the first moment of true quiet I'd found in myself since I'd gotten the itch to paint the daffodils.

"I've got it." I spoke like I might in a chapel. It demanded reverence somehow.

"Okay. How does the wind taste?"

"Like root beer. The kind with licorice in it."

"And what color is the sound of the stream?"

I thought about it, about how the noise felt and what color also felt that way. "Yellow."

"And when it freezes?"

"Silver."

He asked me a few more, and each time, I found the answer easily. The sound of the birdcalls tasted like Skittles, and the brush of the breeze smelled like Zest bar soap. That one made him laugh, and that sound, right next to me, would have tasted like caramel.

I frowned at him. "I'm a painter, not a writer."

"I laughed because as soon as you said it, it sounded exactly right."

"Can I look yet?"

"Almost. One more."

Before I could ask what it was, a touch softer than the mock orange's petals brushed against my lips, but the current that shot through me, the warmth radiating from Aidan's sudden nearness, told me he'd done what he promised not to. The force of the urge to lean in farther to his air-light kiss and drink up more of him startled me, and I jerked back, my eyes flying open. "You said you wouldn't do that."

"No, I didn't. I asked you if you thought I was the type who would. It's not my fault you assumed the wrong thing."

He gave up trying to keep a straight face, inviting me to share his amusement, but my insides quaked like the aspens bouncing behind him in the breeze. Someone else might have said they looked cheerful. I thought they looked disturbed. I didn't like that kind of intangible upset happening in my chest and guts. I pivoted and scooped up my bag.

"Whoa. Where are you going?"

"Back. I have to work."

"Don't let me scare you off. You haven't even had a chance to check the view."

The accuracy of that irritated me. He *was* scaring me off, but I was smart enough to know when flight made way more sense than fight. Last time standing my ground had gotten me a much bigger kiss, and I had no room in my brain to store another one to obsess over and deconstruct.

"You didn't scare me off," I said in a bold-faced lie. "You ticked me off. And now I'm leaving."

He grabbed my elbow to stop me as I walked away, and I whirled and glared at his hand. He dropped it like I'd electrocuted it. His eyes widened. Of course. Of course it would shock him that not everyone in the whole world was dying for his attention. It had shocked Donovan too when he'd first come around, and it had only made him pursue me harder. In the end, he'd won, and I'd lost . . . so, so badly.

But I wasn't a naïve transplant newly arrived in New York this time. I was clear eyed and battle hardened, and Aidan could take my rejection of him as a challenge if he wanted to, but I hadn't issued a challenge. I was making my way to an exit as fast as I could, and if that was straight down the mountain and into my waiting car, that was fine with me. I sped up, going as fast as I could without letting gravity take over and send me down the mountain head first. I gritted my teeth at the realization that it would mean only hurried snatches of the view I'd climbed all this way to find, but I would retreat all day long if it kept me at a safe distance from Aidan.

But Aidan was right there, not daring to reach out and physically stop me again, his voice saying my name quietly. "Lia, wait up. Please."

He was just one of the challenge guys underneath. I paused and turned, steeling myself to meet his eyes and the predatory gleam I'd learned to recognize too late in Donovan's, the look that meant he couldn't accept anyone not falling for his charms.

It wasn't there. Instead, Aidan's eyes had creased in concern, narrowing to study me, trying to read my face.

"What?" I asked, torn between pushing my bangs out of the way so I could see him clearly and hiding behind them.

"I'm sorry," he said. "I misread you. I wasn't trying to upset you."

"I'm not upset."

"You look like you are. I know I've been teasing you, but I promise I'm harmless."

"I'm annoyed. Not scared."

"Annoyed," he repeated. Now the predatory gleam appeared. "Prove you're not scared."

"Are you kidding me? Reverse psychology? This isn't eighth grade."

"I'm ridiculously aware of that. But I'm going to worry about you until I have proof that I shouldn't. It's going to eat me up if I know you're out there terrified of me."

I clapped my hands to my cheeks in frustration. "Does this ever work? Really?"

"You say that like you think I'm playing an angle." He was, and his grin underscored the fact that he wasn't trying hard to hide it.

"I already told you I don't play games at all. So bye now."

I turned and headed down the trail, trying to focus on the view but too irritated to soak it in.

"Stop."

I kept walking.

"Please."

I turned.

"Don't leave because of me. Take as long as you need to look around, sketch, draw, whatever. I'll wait for you farther down the hill." He pointed to his lunch box. "I'll leave that here. Eat whatever you want, and when you're ready, come find me, and I'll walk you back."

That sounded genuine. And I really did want a chance to look out at the valley from a different perspective. And I couldn't stay mad at someone offering to give me lunch. And space. Especially not when he had more of a right to both the food and the mountainside than I did.

"It's okay," I said, but I couldn't make my voice sound convincing. "You can stay if you want. And I'm not going to take your lunch. Just sit there and eat it, and give me a buffer to work." I pointed off the trail a ways. "I want to look from there."

He held up his hands in a gesture of peace. "I'm still going to go down the slope a bit because it would be stupid for me to hang out here in the same way that it's stupid for pyromaniacs to play with matches. But I won't be far if you need me. And you should keep the lunch. I made it myself, and you earned it. You hike like a boss."

He started off with Chief loping after him, but Aidan crouched and scratched behind Chief's ears. "Stay here, buddy. Watch Lia, okay?" Chief bounded back up to me and sat, his head cocked. I scratched his ears too. Aidan waved and kept going down the slope.

"Can you draw?" I asked Chief. "Because that would help."

He scratched himself instead.

"All right. You're on chipmunk patrol."

I wandered to the spot I wanted and soaked in the view the same way Mrs. Beckman liked to wallow in her favorite Hamptons spa. But her thousand-dollar spa treatments couldn't touch this. It was everything I had smelled and tasted and heard with my eyes closed. Seeing it added not just a new layer but a whole dimension, like all the images flooding in through my eyes were melding into this thing, this feeling bigger than the sum of its parts.

It filled me so fast this time that I couldn't breathe because there was no room inside of me with the bigness of the peaks taking up all the space. I wanted to fly down the slope and spill it all out onto a canvas right then, but I forced myself to stay put, to look at it all and see it with more than my eyes. I cataloged every smell, every sound, every shade of blue and green.

If I tried to sit here in a few months when the leaves morphed into flame-bright tree feathers, I wouldn't survive it. I couldn't stretch big enough to fit it all. I couldn't take it anymore, the sitting and looking without doing. I pulled out my paints and paper and worked on a small study of everything flowing in through my senses.

Chief nosed over after a while with an inquisitive whine. My stomach growled, and he sniffed at it like he was trying to figure out the sound.

I reached for Aidan's lunch box. Stealing his lunch was fair payback for him stealing kisses. I opened it to find a turkey sandwich on artisan bread, and when I bit into it, I detected a sweet trace of fig jam. What kind of self-respecting construction worker ate gourmet sandwiches? I'd expected a cheesesteak and Fritos. Instead, he'd included pita chips and hummus. It begged the question again: why would a guy who packed himself lunches like that be slumming at T&R? Granted, Tom made the best omelets anywhere, but they weren't exactly full of Cremini mushrooms and gouda.

I finished the sandwich and packed everything away. My stomach was satisfied, but inside, I was still hungry, the kind of hungry that would only go away by getting things out, not taking things in. I needed to paint. I both loathed and welcomed the restlessness as I rose to my feet. The last three years had been much simpler without it, but for the first time since leaving New York, I stood real, whole, and solid in a way that only falling asleep with Chloe tucked against me had come close to making me feel until now.

I headed back down the mountain, already knowing I was different from the person who had climbed it.

Chapter 11

I stopped at McGill's and spent an hour picking up tube after tube of oil paints, coveting the ones I wanted but didn't need and picking up the best paints I could afford to match the feeling in my head. I eyed my favorite Kolinsky brushes locked behind glass but picked up some less-expensive mongoose brushes. If this painting came out like I thought it would, I could afford the Kolinskys soon enough. For now, it was enough to fill my basket with every paint I needed.

At home, I parked in the driveway now that the garage was fully a studio/playroom, one side littered with toys and the other dominated by a single blank canvas. It had cost almost a thousand dollars by itself, and the manager had had to special order it.

I went in through the garage door and plunked my bags down in front of the canvas, desperate to throw myself at it but all too aware that I needed to wait until Chloe was in bed before I lost myself in painting. And I would lose myself. But I'd find myself at the same time too. The prospect turned my stomach, but I couldn't decide if it was fear or pleasure churning in there.

The door leading to the tiny utility room opened, and Dani poked her head out. "Hey. You got a package."

I frowned. "I haven't ordered anything."

"I don't think it was shipped. Someone left it on the front porch in brown paper and—"

"Twine?" I finished for her.

"Yep. Is it your secret admirer?"

"Sounds like it." I followed her back in and stopped in surprise at the size of the box on the table. It wasn't huge, but it was much bigger than the book or the paintbrushes, more the size of two shoe boxes stacked on top of each other.

"Guess it proves your Griff theory," Dani said. "There's no delivery info on here, and he does know your address."

I untied the string and set it aside. It would join the twine ball I had started. I opened the paper carefully too. I didn't want to tear it. I'd flattened and saved the paper from the first two gifts as well. I wasn't sure yet what I wanted to do with it all, but the vague idea of a collage had taken shape somewhere in the outer reaches of my imagination. It would come forward if it was ever ready, and I wanted the packaging set aside just in case.

I gasped when I opened the paper enough to see inside.

"What?" Dani demanded. "Please say it's something wildly inappropriate. I'd love to know that Good Boy Griff has a bad side." It was extra snarky, even for her. Griff came off like a regular guy to me, not a good boy—not that there was anything wrong with that if he was, but I let it drop because I'd opened the box.

I shook my head, void of words. I held up a jar of Marcona almonds in one hand and a wedge of sheep's milk cheese in the other. Dani's eyes widened in appreciation, and she sorted through the rest of the contents. Smoked figs, two more cheeses, aged balsamic vinegar, and *two* bars of Vosges chocolates. Two!

"Whoa. I've seen some of this at the wine shop next to my store. This stuff is crazy expensive."

"I know," I said, coming out of my daze. I'd indulged in a lot of these foods at the parties the Beckmans had thrown. I waved the chocolate at her. "These are seven-dollar candy bars. Each."

"So? What do you think?" Dani asked. "I know you're not a foodie, but I think you like everything in here."

"I'm not sure about a few of the things, but yeah. I like most of it. But I think . . . I think I can't accept this. This had to cost major bank." This was more than an "I like you" gesture. This was . . . it was more. Did Griff understand that? I couldn't let it go unanswered, but I didn't know what to say.

"I can't accept these," I repeated. "They're too much."

"He probably brought stuff home from Leifson's."

I could live with that. "Convince me, because if you do, I'll keep it."

"Of course he got it from there. Now you have to hope Good Boy didn't steal it."

"Stop calling him that." I didn't like the edge in her voice. "That's not even an insult."

She picked up one of the chocolate bars and studied the label. "Keep it. What message does it send if you give it back? Are you ready to shut him down completely? Because that's what's going to happen."

"What message does it send if I accept a two-hundred-dollar gift?"

"We knew Griff was nice. Be careful about misinterpreting his generosity. And besides, I told you, it probably didn't cost him that much if it's stuff from his restaurant."

"You don't think he's trying to tell me something with these gifts?"

"Of course he is," she snapped, and I drew my head back like she'd swatted at me. "Sorry," she said, noticing. She softened her tone. "But do you know enough about him to know whether it just makes him happy to do the nice things? Have you noticed that he has kind of expensive taste?"

I shook my head. "Not really."

"He does. He doesn't seem to have a lot of stuff, but everything he does have is top of the line."

"Not his car. It's nothing fancy."

"No, but it's practical. His watch is crazy expensive, but he always has the same one on when I see him. His clothes are all high-end brands. I bet if we looked up his guitar, it would be expensive too."

"How do you even notice all this stuff? And you make him sound like he's a high roller or something. He wears the same sweatshirt and flip-flops every day."

"Yeah, but it's an expensive sweatshirt and expensive flip-flops. I'm just saying, maybe don't freak out too much that he's secretly in love with you. I sell to customers like him all the time. I think it's part of their MO that if they're going to buy something, they invest in the top of the line."

I scrubbed my hands over my face. "I don't know what to do next. I have to say something."

"No, you don't. He didn't leave a note. He doesn't want you to say anything."

"But he's not exactly trying to hide who it's from. He delivered it to my doorstep. I can't not say thank you."

I stepped out onto the deck, and Dani said behind me, "I think that's a bad idea!"

I ignored her and slipped over the rail, landing with a small thump and the sense that I'd stepped through Alice's looking glass. I'd never been in Griff's space before, and it was only about to get weirder. I knocked on his sliding door. It felt more right than going to his front door.

It took a minute before he stepped into view. He was almost dressed for work. His button-down shirt hung halfway open, untucked over his slacks, and he was toweling off his wet hair. He paused when he saw me, then hurried to slide the door open.

"Hi," he said, his warm smile replacing his surprise.

"Hi. So . . . thank you."

The surprise reappeared. I guess Dani was right. He hadn't expected me to call him out. "You're welcome. For what?"

"Um." I didn't know the rules here. "For . . . being a good neighbor." I questioned it as soon as I said it. Would he think I was trying to put us back on friend footing?

"You're welcome. And now I'm going to be the world's worst neighbor, because I want to hang out and talk about . . . neighborliness, but I'm running late for work."

"Oh! Sorry," I said, stepping back and toward my side of the rail again. "Have fun."

"I won't. Remember I said it's slow?"

"It's a forty-dollar-steak kind of place. It's hard to believe it ever gets busy with prices like that. I guess I'm a burger kind of girl."

"You're missing out. Are you watching Chloe tonight?"

"Yeah."

"You guys should come eat. My treat. I get a discount."

"Not a big enough discount," I mumbled, thinking about the basket he'd given me.

"Free is a pretty good discount. Seriously, come by tonight."

"You've fed us enough." There. That was a bold hint.

"I like doing it. I mean it. Come."

"You've seen Chloe in action. You want to inflict that on Leifson's?"

He laughed. "She's a good girl. And it'll be fine. We'll be half full at most, and I'll make sure you guys get a quiet corner and a patient waiter."

I climbed back over to my side. "We'll see how she does this afternoon. Maybe we will. Dress code?"

"Clothes."

"Ha."

"I'm serious. Don't stress. And come by, okay?"

Instead of answering, I waved and slipped back inside. Dani looked up from the table, where she was writing out Chloe's name for Chloe to practice copying. "What did he say?"

"He said Chloe and I should stop by his restaurant for dinner tonight."

"But what about the gift? What did you say to him?"

"I said thanks."

"And he said come on over and buy an expensive steak to show your appreciation?"

"No, he said come on over and he'd give us an expensive steak for free."

Dani leaned back in her chair. "You're kidding. He didn't admit it? I don't understand that guy at all."

"What's not to understand? You said it yourself: he's generous. He really does like to do nice things for people."

"For you. He's barely even talked to me, and I've been his neighbor as long as you have."

"You're not home as much. And he only started coming out on the deck when the weather changed. It's not like we've been hanging out all winter."

"You don't have to defend him. I'm not mad about it. I just don't get it."

"You shouldn't be mad about it. He's so good with Chloe."

She snorted. "I know. I hear all about it."

"Don't you have to go learn something? Or earn some money?"

"I have my pathology class tonight. We'll see what actually sticks." She stood and smoothed her hair into a ponytail. Her blunt-cut bangs made it look chic.

My ponytails looked like I didn't want to do my hair, because I didn't. I laughed.

"What?"

"We're both wearing T-shirts and jeans, but you look amazing, and I look like I need an intervention."

"Duh," she said, tossing her ponytail. "You could upgrade with zero effort and a tiny bit of thought. It's the accessories, dummy." Her T-shirt was black and fitted, and she wore a yellow beaded necklace and turquoise ballet flats. My T-shirt said "Arches National Park" and had a grease stain that had never washed completely out after I did an emergency repair on my mountain bike on the trail one hot, miserable afternoon.

I stared down at it and frowned. "I guess I should have changed before I went over to Griff's."

"You need to drop by Leifson's for dinner now, and you need to get something decent out of my closet before you go."

Dani didn't have a lot of clothes, but like Griff, she picked quality pieces with her store discount and kept it all fresh with inexpensive but interesting jewelry. She was the queen of the statement necklace.

"I'll take you up on that."

"Good." She studied me for a minute. "You like him?"

"I . . . yeah. I do. And I like him more every time we hang out. He may be the nicest guy I've ever met."

"I admit I'm impressed he stepped his game up for you. He's always seemed so shy; I can't believe he got up the guts to ask you to dinner."

"He surprises me every time we talk now, with the stuff he knows and the stuff he notices. I mean, he's nailed these gifts, and it's all based on what he sees and pays attention to. It's pretty amazing."

"The big question is when he's going to make a big move. Is he going to wine and dine you tonight so he can lay one on you? You could use some kissing."

I busied myself rinsing dishes in the sink so my expression wouldn't give away that I'd already been doing an excessive amount of kissing lately. "Me? What about you? You can't hide behind school and work forever. At some point, you'll have to pay attention to the guys who pay attention to you."

"You mean all the guys in my nursing program? Oh wait, there are none. I think Griff is the only single guy left in the greater Salt Lake area, and he hasn't looked my way once."

Something about the way she said that caught my attention. "Are you saying you wanted him to?"

"I'm saying that I might know how to put an outfit together, but you're still way more interesting. And I'm saying I'm not at all surprised you caught his attention because you're awesome."

"But y—"

"Don't go reading into anything. It's been fun watching this unfold, but it's made me wish I had time or space in my life for something like this."

"When the right person comes along, you will, no matter what else you have going on."

"Thanks, Dr. Phil. And now I have to go." She found Chloe and swept her into a hug before heading out to work.

As soon as the door shut behind Dani, Chloe's intense stare lasered in on me. "Auntie Wia? We do mac and cheese, yes? I get the box."

I grinned. Dani hated for Chloe to have any packaged foods, but I'd taught Chloe my great love for mac and cheese from a box, mixed with hamburger, and slapped on a bun in my twisted version of a sloppy joe. It was gross and awesome, and Dani would kill me if she knew how often we snuck them. Gourmet foods had their place, but not much could top a sloppy mac. "I have something even better, cute thing. How about if we dress up and go to Griff's restaurant?"

Her brow crinkled as she processed the idea of a new place and new people. I crouched down and hugged her. "Griff is going to take good care of us and give us a quiet table all by ourselves, with no one to bother us." Her face relaxed, but guilt niggled at me. She shouldn't be so crowd averse so young, should she?

An hour later we headed out to Leifson's in our nicest jeans, with a sparkle shirt for Chloe and a tailored jacket and boots for me, pilfered from Dani.

At the restaurant, confusion tinged the hostess's greeting when I explained we weren't waiting for anyone else in our party. It was as if she couldn't figure out why I was bringing a toddler out for an expensive steak dinner for two. I took pity on her. "Is Griff around? He invited us."

Her face cleared. "Sure, wait a second, and I'll get him for you."

A minute later he appeared, looking completely pulled together, tucked in, and fully buttoned. Which was kind of a shame.

"Ladies, good to see you. I saved a special table for you in case you decided to show up." He led us to a corner in the unused half of the dining room. "See? Nothing to worry about."

I helped Chloe into her seat, and Griff pulled out my chair for me. Nice. Was that a thing he'd learned from working in a fancy restaurant or simply plain good manners?

"I'll get a booster," he said before I could ask, and again, I appreciated his thoughtfulness.

He strolled off toward the kitchen area, and I squeezed Chloe's hand. "Are you excited?"

She looked around, her eyes big. They'd probably be bigger if she could understand the quality of the linens and heavy silverware on the table in front of us. "Pwetty," she said, touching the crystal water goblet in front of her.

"Very pretty. We have to be careful about everything we touch, okay, sweet pea? It all breaks easily." She frowned, and I rushed to explain. "This is a princess restaurant, where royalty eat. Princesses would never break a glass or knock something on the table over, so we can't either if we want to fool them into thinking we're princesses."

"Pwincess?" Chloe repeated. She looked intrigued now.

"Of course. Why do you think I dressed you in a sparkle shirt? Princesses need sparkles."

Griff reappeared, not only with a booster seat but also with a sturdy glass tumbler that would normally hold whiskey. "Harder to break," he mouthed as he swapped it out for Chloe's goblet. "I hope you're ready for the royal treatment," he said aloud, and Chloe's eyes widened.

Man, Griff was developing a talent for saying exactly the right thing. I gave Chloe a "See, I told you so" wink.

He held a menu in front of him. "You're welcome to look through this, but I'm kind of an expert on the food here, and if you trust me, I think I can order you up a pretty perfect dinner."

"Yes, pwease."

I nodded to back up Chloe. "We'd love that."

He disappeared for a few minutes while I kept Chloe busy with some I Spy. When Griff reappeared, he circulated through the rest of the diners first, stopping at a table here and there to chat before he rejoined us, pulling up a chair this time.

"I'm glad you guys came," he said, and the warmth in his words kindled an answering warmth in my abdomen that spread up and out, coloring my cheeks.

"Me too. Us too," I amended with a glance at Chloe, who was busy trying to dress her spoon with her cloth napkin. "Most people don't treat their most annoying neighbors to four-star restaurants as a thanks for the hassle."

"You guys aren't a hassle," he said. "All of you are great. Chloe cracks me up, I could watch you paint all day, and your sister hasn't said fifty words to me since I moved in. An artist, a mute, and a cool little kid—so what's the hassle?"

I laughed. "If you think Dani's a mute, you haven't been paying attention."

"She doesn't talk to me."

"Lucky. She talks to me too much. I'm the oldest. It's my job to have an opinion on everything she does, not the other way around."

"If you say so," he said. "We've never had a conversation, so I'll have to take your word for it."

"You were pretty quiet with me for a long time. Have you tried talking to her?"

He shifted in his chair. "Sure, I guess."

I eyed him. "I don't know exactly what that means, but to be honest, she's been overwhelmed by her schedule. She's doing a pretty stellar job of hanging in there."

He smiled at Chloe. "I can't argue if Chloe is the evidence."

A waiter approached with our meal, and Griff stood up again. "Hope you like it," he said.

The server put a plate down in front of each of us, Chloe's a perfectly miniature version of mine: mashed potatoes, mac and cheese, potato chips, french fries, corn on the cob, and a filet mignon, only Chloe's was already cut into small pieces for her.

"If I'd known this was what on the Leifson's menu, I'd have come in a lot sooner."

Griff laughed. "Let's just say it's the secret menu."

"Whoever's in charge of the secret menu has been paying attention to our eating habits."

"Don't be too impressed. If it's potato in any form, you guys will eat it. Does that sound about right? Enjoy," he said. "I have to check in on the kitchen, but let me know if you need anything else."

"I'm sure we'll be fine," I said, waving good-bye despite a twinge of disappointment in my stomach that he was leaving. I ate some perfectly crisped french fries to smother it. I'd hoped Griff would stay with us, but that was stupid when I thought about it. I couldn't bring him to T&R's even on a slow shift and sit and visit with him the whole time, but I watched him circulate among the guests again and wished he could stay anyway.

After following up the ridiculously good dinner with ice cream and cookies that I suspected were also from the secret menu, Griff walked us to the exit.

"Thanks for coming in," he said.

"Thank you for da food," Chloe answered and then threw herself at his legs to wrap him in a hug.

He grinned, and I disentangled her, my heart squeezing to see her share that kind of affection with someone besides Dani and me. "What Chloe said," I said. "This was so great. I'm not sure I'd be repaying the favor by inviting you to the diner, but you're welcome any time."

"I'll have to take you up on that," he said. And this time my stomach twinged like I was sailing on a swing next to Chloe to the highest point.

"Great," I said. Chloe was now attached to my leg and was yanking on it, trying to hustle me to the parking lot. "I better go."

"Catch you later."

I tried to figure the night out on the way home. He'd invited us to come, gone out of his way to prepare our favorite foods, but spent relatively little time with us, which I understood. As the boss, he couldn't suddenly act all super casual in front of his employees.

But even when we'd talked, it had stayed at the friendly conversation level, not even kind of flirtatious. But . . . then I went back to the food he'd picked. It said more than flirting.

For the first time, I wished he was more like Aidan: happy to take credit for anything and everything and bold with his interest. It would be a lot less confusing. With Aidan, I'd kissed him only long enough to remember why it was incredibly stupid to get caught up in his act and push him away. But with Griff, if anything, I was thinking I wanted to pull him closer.

When it came right down to it, I liked that Griff was leaving me a lot of options. Too many, maybe, but it was better than Aidan, who didn't leave me enough.

Chapter 12

I put Chloe down for the night and fished out her old baby monitor so I could listen for her from the "studio."

In the garage, I sat on the cold cement and stared up at the canvas. It loomed from that perspective as if I was in one of those movies where the character gets shrunk down, like in *Epic*, which Chloe watched on repeat. But I wanted that. I wanted the scope of the white space to overwhelm me so I could be sure that all the things bubbling up inside me would have somewhere to go. I closed my eyes, waiting to see what rose to the surface, waiting for the sensory overload I'd carried down with me from the mountain to coalesce into something—an image, an emotion. I closed my eyes and remembered everything I had felt rather than seen while standing on the mountain. And then I opened my eyes and reached for a brush.

I painted, and not-mountains that were somehow utterly mountains appeared. The verge of summer emerged without shape, as pure motion. And then the awareness that had stirred inside me when I had stood on the slope sensing everything growing and *being* showed up, and I stepped back. The colors on the canvas didn't look like anything, but the whole thing together began to feel like exactly what that moment had been.

And the artist part of me that had withered, that had drawn into itself like an arthritic hand crippled before its time, opened and stretched and flexed. And worked. And became right.

I threw open the garage door to let the paint smell out and the night air in and painted until my shoulders ached, spreading the color further and further. By the time I heard someone clear their throat behind me, the canvas had become the feeling of looking out from a ski slope and seeing nothing made by humans except the single path the viewer stood on.

I turned, and Griff was there, his hands in his pockets and his jaw nearly slack as he studied the canvas.

I wiped the excess paint from the brush and set it in a jar of solvent until I could get to it to rinse it out. "Hi."

"Am I messing you up? Because I can go home and let you get back to being a genius."

"It's okay." I stretched my neck and rubbed at a crick in it. It hurt. If it'd been Aidan standing in front of me, he would have sauntered right over and rubbed at it like I'd been hinting at a massage. I wasn't, and I wondered what Griff would do. He stayed put, tearing his eyes away from the painting to survey the garage. It was odd to have him there, but long before I'd broken out big enough to have my own studio, I'd had to paint in any space I could find, often where all kinds of people had drifted through. Griff's presence was far less distracting than any of them had been.

"Can I offer you something to eat?" I asked, and when his eyebrows shot up, I laughed. "That's a dumb question to ask someone who barely came from working in a restaurant, isn't it?"

"No, actually. I get tired of the same old, same old."

"Then I might be the wrong person to feed you, considering where I got the gift basket I'm going to share."

"Bring it on."

"Grab a seat and make yourself comfortable," I said, pointing at the floor. "I'll be back in a second."

When I came back out with the box of food he'd given me, he was coming back up my driveway carrying two deck chairs. "So you're feeding *and* furnishing me?"

He looked as if I'd asked him to solve a quadratic equation. "I'm not feeding you. You're feeding me."

I patted the box. "I meant this. And the brushes. And the book. It was crazy generous of you. It takes talent to put together a gourmet gift that doesn't have gross stuff in it. You nailed it, so the least I can do is share it."

This time he stared at me like I'd asked him to solve the quadratic equation using the color purple and a toothbrush. "I don't know what you're talking about."

Nausea washed over me, the kind where excruciating embarrassment struck me with such force, flooding all of my systems, that the one thing that would make it better was the only thing that could make the situation worse: puking. Every single not-so-subtle hint I'd dropped about my gratitude to him flashed like neon signs in my mind's eye, all of them illuminating my total stupidity. And I saw him remember them all and make sense of them in the same instant.

The urge to puke grew. He would figure out quickly that me thanking him for gifts he hadn't given me meant that I'd wanted him to be the one who was sending them. Which meant that I'd been taking all of his friendly neighbor gestures way beyond what he'd ever intended them to be, and it was a shame we both had to figure that out at once. Especially the part where I had to figure that out with him standing right there.

Suddenly, my fingers needed something to do, something that would let me turn my back on him now until I could sell the condo and move away and keep my back turned to him forever. I set the box on the ground, plucked a brush from the jar, and turned to the canvas. "Sorry," I said, pretending to study what I'd done so far. "I think I was confused. But there's some good stuff in there. Help yourself to cheese or whatever." I fought a cringe. I lost.

A long silence met that, and I touched the brush to the canvas. There was no paint on it, and even if there was, I wouldn't have been able to fix on a clear image with the rapid-fire highlight reel of conversations I'd had with Griff reframing themselves in my head and crucifying me with the utter wrongness I'd read him with.

I was as bad at men as I'd ever been with Donovan, and it had become obvious with Donovan that I'd never be as bad at anything as I'd been at reading him. The truth had always been there—the narcissism, the entitlement, the addictive behaviors. But I'd been blind to it. With Griff, I'd looked so hard I'd obviously seen way past the truth into things that weren't there.

It was my turn to clear my throat, and I pretended to dab at something else on the canvas. "So I should probably get back to this."

"Lia?"

I didn't answer, only smooshed the brush in harder to an area I could easily touch up when he left.

"Lia? I would have given you all those things if I'd thought of them."

That stopped me, and I dared a quarter turn to study him from the corner of my eye. "Sorry. I shouldn't have assumed. I just . . . I don't know why anyone would give me these things, but there's no real reason you should have either."

He took a step toward me. "I'm serious. The only reason I didn't is that I didn't think of it."

But if he hadn't given those things to me, who had?

Aidan's face immediately flashed through my mind, but he had no idea where I lived. Only Tom would be able to give him that information, and there was no way he'd do it without first letting me know he was passing it along.

So who had been paying close enough attention to me to know exactly what to send me and where to find me?

The only possibilities that even kind of worked made me shiver. Now I had even more reasons to wish it had been Griff and not whoever was behind these gifts.

Griff still stood there, and I turned further to face him.

"Sorry. I kind of put you on the spot by assuming. Don't worry about it. I was trying to play Sherlock, but I guess I'm more of a Clouseau." His shyness really had been shyness. He was a watercolor, and I'd tried to complicate him into an abstract oil.

"Clouseau?"

"The idiot detective on *Pink Panther* who can't get anything right?"

"Sure," he said, his face clearing. "Quit beating yourself up. I like it when getting it wrong means someone thought I was a much better guy than I am."

He stood there for another moment, and I didn't want to shut him out by turning back to the canvas, but at the same time, I couldn't think of anything else to say.

As if he sensed that, he took a step back through the open garage door. "I should let you get back to work."

"Thanks."

"Lia? I was wondering, would you want to hang out some time? Somewhere that isn't here, I mean?"

Ten minutes before, I would have said yes, but what if this was about pity now? I looked down at the brush and ran my fingers over the bristles, forcing the excess thinner out. "I don't know," I said, looking up. If I'd seen relief in his eyes, that would have become a permanent "Never." But I caught disappointment, like I'd yanked away his steak after one good bite. And that changed my answer. "Okay, yeah. Let's do something sometime."

"Cool." With a small wave, he retreated to his house.

It wasn't sealed with a kiss or anything, but it felt good anyway. No more guessing games. With him, at least. We were going on an actual date, calling it a date, and doing it because we both wanted to.

I stooped down and fished out a Vosges bar. There was a whole new guessing game to play now.

* * *

When I rolled into the diner the next morning, Tom took one look at me and frowned. "You look like someone dragged you through the canyon by your hair. What happened?"

I touched the messy top knot I'd wrangled after stumbling out of bed. "Nothing. I didn't sleep much."

"Chloe?"

"No." Oils. And canvas. And ideas. And I'd worked until two in the morning, alive with the feeling that I could never have enough paint or time to get everything out. Six a.m. came extra early after a late night. "I was working on a project. Lost track of time."

"Lost track of your comb is more like it," he said, and I had to grin.

"Shut up and flip some more hash browns. I'll get my work done."

"Yeah, but I think you might make some people lose their appetites looking like that."

"There has to be a rule against you harassing me about my appearance. I'm telling Ramona."

He snorted. "She'd shove you in the bathroom with a hairbrush and lipstick. Good luck."

I grabbed the coffeepot and stuck my tongue out at him before making my first round of the tables. By early afternoon, I had to admit that the late orders and unfilled mugs customers had complained about hadn't been my finest work, but it hadn't been due to lack of sleep. My mind kept wandering to the painting, and my whole body wanted to walk out and throw myself at it, to explore what using sap green and viridian for the facing mountain would look like.

When I finally shoved my apron in the laundry bin, Tom was frowning at me. "You gonna be okay tomorrow? Because you were not fantastic today."

"I like that you can scold me and fuss over me in the same breath."

"I don't mind people having a bad day. I do like to know how many I should expect."

"I started painting again, that's all. And sometimes it gets hold of me, and I lose track of other things. I'm almost done with the painting. I'll be more on the ball tomorrow and back to normal when it's done."

"When is that going to be?"

I brushed a hand through my hair and thought about the canvases at home. "Don't know. Maybe four or five days. This one's coming fast."

"Would it come faster if you had more time to work on it? You could take a day or two off. You've earned a vacation at this point."

True. I'd taken only a handful of days off in the whole three years I'd worked there, and that was pretty much only when Dani had been called in unexpectedly to her work and needed me with Chloe. I hadn't taken time off for me mainly because no work meant no pay. But the painting was paid work. "Are you trying to tell me you don't want me to come back while I'm scatterbrained?"

"I'm straight up telling you that you should go paint. You look happy. We'll survive for a couple of days if it'll help you finish your paint stuff."

I couldn't pass that up. The painting was good, better than anything I'd done in New York, and I had no doubt Daddy Warbucks would cough up my old prices for it. Victoria would be ecstatic with her commission, and it would pay for missing a few days at T&R a hundred times over.

"I think that would be good," I said. "You sure it won't leave you in a tough spot?"

"How often have you covered for the other girls or Caden when they needed time off?"

Fair enough. "Great. I'll be out until Friday."

He nodded. "Go make yourself some nice pictures."

"They're not nice, exactly."

"Then make some pictures that make you happy, and I'll see you in a few days."

I blew an air kiss at him and scurried out while he hollered after me, "I'm telling Ramona!"

But my mind was too far into the painting to spare any thought for his empty threat. Ramona would only laugh, anyway.

Chapter 13

The next day when I explained to Dani that I'd taken time off work to finish the painting, she grinned. "It'll be confusing to be in the house with you at the same time during the day for more than an hour, but I guess I can handle it. Chloe and I are going to get up to no good. Have fun painting."

The satisfaction written all over her face that I was deep inside my art again reminded me of cats and canaries, and it made me wonder if after years of pushing, Dani had decided to push me over the verge I'd teetered on by secretly giving me the supplies, like the brushes.

It wasn't a totally crazy thought. She'd know what I needed from back in the day when our playroom had become my "studio" at home as we outgrew toys. She'd seen my art stuff everywhere until the day I left for college, had watched me scrimp to buy the exact brushes that someone had sent me. It wouldn't be that hard for her to remember them. But it would be incredibly hard for her to pay for them.

Then again, I'd never heard pennies scream as loud as the ones she pinched, but even with her ruthless control over her budget, there was no way she could have afforded a set like that. I asked anyway. "Did you send me the stuff, Dani? Like, as a way to get me to paint again?"

She laughed. "I'm a good sister, but I'm not a rich one. And why would I send you a basket of food? I'm sure it was Griff. He was trying to tip you off to his secret benefactor status with that fancy steak dinner. Chloe can't stop talking about it. Sounds like a fun night." Her voice was wistful, and the familiar pang of wishing I could take her bullets but knowing I couldn't pulsed through my chest. I wasn't sure whether the touch of sadness in her face was about her wanting to give Chloe fancy restaurant experiences herself or about the mere fact that she was missing out on any of Chloe's experiences. Probably both.

"It's not Griff," I said.

"Can't be anyone else."

"It has to be someone else. Let me tell you a sad, sad story."

Her eyes widened as I explained how wrong I'd gotten it, and then they flashed with a look I couldn't decipher. Before I could ask her about it, her eyebrows lowered in a sure sign that she was thinking hard, and she asked the question I'd been puzzling over since Griff had left. "Then who is it?"

"I only have one theory, but it freaks me out a little. Could Daddy Warbucks be behind this?"

"It's not even pocket change to him, probably. But there are too many other variables. Like why would he be taking the time to send you this stuff? And why would he send you a flower book? Or watercolor brushes when he wants you to work in oils? And more importantly, how would he know where to find you? I mean, is he sending couriers to drop things at our house now? It's creepy. Call Victoria. See what she thinks."

"Yeah. I have to talk to her about shipping my painting anyway."

"So it's done?"

"It's close."

"Can I see it?"

"Come on down." I led her to the garage so she could look.

She walked in and stopped stock still, as if absorbing the size of the canvas for the first time. "Whoa."

She shifted so she was directly in front of the painting but as far back as she could get, and then she said nothing, only stared. I let her look while I tidied my paints, but her silence wore on me after a couple of minutes. The piece was different from anything I'd done but was still so clearly me. Did she dislike the change so much that she couldn't find words to say something nice?

When I couldn't invent any other busywork, I braced myself for the expression she wore when she didn't want you to know what she was thinking, but I'd had our whole lives to figure out that it meant she was holding back something big, heavy, or deep.

The expression on her face was wide open, and she reached up to wipe away a tear when she caught me staring at her. "I'm so going to kill you," she said.

"What?" Definitely not any of the top ten reactions I'd expected.

"I didn't know, Lia. I didn't know you could do this, and now I'm so mad that you haven't been. And how could you not be? How could you not be doing this every minute of your life? This is amazing."

My eyes stung. "I didn't want to until now. I didn't know this was all in there."

She ran over to me and hugged me, squeezing so hard I had to wiggle to create space to breathe. She leaned back but kept her hands on my shoulders so I couldn't duck away from her hard glare. "You should be doing this and only this and never anything else. I'm dropping my classes to a half load so you don't have to babysit as much, and you should call the diner and tell them they're never, ever going to see you again because I'm chaining you to your easel."

I pulled her hands from my shoulders but kept a firm grip on her wrists. "Drop your classes and I'll be the one doing the murdering. If you don't want your daughter raised by her eccentric artist aunt and eating food out of boxes until her growth is stunted and her skin glows cheesy mac orange, you'd better keep your classes as they are."

She opened her mouth to argue, and I squeezed her wrists in warning, jerking my head toward the painting behind me. "If I do one more of those, I don't have to work for the rest of the year. Warbucks will pay thirty thousand for it, and once he sees it, he'll pay more for the rest. And I'm doing seven more. So stop stressing. If I can get a second painting out, I'll know I can handle the commission, and I promise I'll quit T&R. But you will not under any circumstances drop any of your classes. Do you understand?"

Her mouth had dropped open at the price tag on the painting, but she snapped it closed and nodded. "I understand, all right. What I just heard is that Redbox is your treat forever now, Moneybags."

I let go of her and sighed. "You're always so high maintenance."

A grin split her face, a pure happiness untinged by exhaustion for the first time in months. "My sister's a genius, and I get to see it all happen."

"I'm so uncomfortable with this gushiness. Go somewhere else."

She laughed and headed back into the house to get Chloe, who darted into the garage to hug me a few minutes later before they set off for the children's museum.

I picked up the phone and dialed Victoria's number. "It's almost done," I said when she answered.

"Can you text me a picture when it's finished?"

"You don't trust me?"

"Of course I do. It's just been so long since I've seen a Leandra original, and I'm parched for it like a fish in the desert."

"I'll send it. But it's time to talk about shipping."

"I've already checked in with a friend who owns a gallery in Park City and arranged everything. He's going to send his guys to handle it if you let me pass on your address."

"Speaking of addresses, did you give Daddy Warbucks my address for some reason? Or give it to his secretary for billing reasons?"

"No," she said, her voice alert to the worry in mine. "Why do you ask?"

"Because those anonymous gifts keep coming. I wondered if he was behind it somehow, but he doesn't know where I am."

"He's got resources. I found you fairly fast. It would be even easier for him."

The idea of him sending gifts to me at my work and at my home made me shiver. It smacked too much of Dr. Evil, secretly monitoring me from his lair, but I reined in my imagination. He might be the only person with the actual resources and some kind of passing interest in encouraging my art for his own purposes, but it still didn't explain the gift of the food. It wasn't him.

"I think trying to figure this out might make me crazy."

"As long as you channel the craziness into your art, that's fine with me."

"You have a one-track mind, Victoria."

"It's what makes me spectacularly good at what I do."

I laughed and hung up on that bit of brashness, but my smile faded as I put the phone away and eyed the paints again. Who was behind the gifts?

Chapter 14

When I showed up for work on Friday, Tom met me with an expectant look. "Well? Get all this art out of your system so you're ready for hash slinging?"

"Yeah, I've repented of art. I live to serve."

"All right, your royal fanciness, you can start with Mr. Benny. He's been asking for you."

"You're kidding."

"Nope. And he's not the only one. Dog Guy has been in here every day you've been gone, acting like he's not looking for you. Not fooling me though. Asked me on the first day where you were, and I said you were taking some time off. He tried to be all casual and ask until when, but I'm not in the habit of enabling stalkers."

I wanted to hug him for his gruff concern, but I patted his arm instead so he wouldn't bluster. "I don't think he's a stalker, but it's kind of weird he's been in here every day. I'll handle it." By which I meant I'd stay out of sight as much as possible when he showed up. His help had unlocked a new direction in my painting, yes, but now that I'd figured out which direction to go, I didn't need him spinning me in a thousand other directions instead with stolen kisses or stares so intense they would make Tom blush.

Even the possibility that Aidan might come put me on heightened alert through the morning. Every time the door swished open, the muscles in my arms and neck tightened until I saw someone else step into the diner.

"It's nice to have all of you here," Tom said. "You work better when your brain shows up too."

"Tell that to Mr. Benny," I said. He'd already complained about my tardy refills twice.

"Ignore him. Glad you're back."

A tiny bit of guilt gnawed at me. It wasn't dedication to my job that was keeping me focused; it was lack of anything else to distract me. If I'd had a new canvas to fill at home, I couldn't have given my customers the same attention. But I didn't have a new painting. The inspiration that had burst out to get the first piece done had dried up just as fast. I'd been so sure my creative flow had been set to full blast, but when I'd looked over my preliminary sketches for my second piece, apathy had yawned open inside of me like one of those bizarre Florida sinkholes that ate whole houses.

When Aidan walked in, I didn't see him so much as sense him. A low-level electricity charged the air and announced it was him the second the door opened. Tom puttered at the grill, same as always, but it was there—almost like static.

Aidan made his way to his booth—when had it become *his* booth?—and sat, waiting. I hefted the coffeepot and made sure to stop and top off a few mugs before his. He watched me, the side of his mouth quirked up ever so slightly like he thought he was on to me.

It wasn't an act. I didn't want to see him, didn't want to try to sort through the complicated thoughts that knotted together worse than my twine ball every time I thought about Aidan and kissing and Aidan. I liked kissing him. But I didn't like losing track of everything else, even for a few moments when it happened. Losing track of reality was fine when I was painting, not when I was kissing. I'd lost too much of myself when I'd drowned in Donovan. Aidan had the same magnetic pull, and I hated that even though I could see it clearly this time, it was hard to resist the tug.

"What number are we on today?" I asked when I reached him.

"Thirteen."

My eyes flew to his. "Tom said you've been in the last few days. You should be past that."

"Nope. I've been eating the specials, waiting for you to show up so I could move down the menu. Did Tom tell you I've been asking for you?"

"He mentioned it." I busied myself with fishing my order pad from my apron pocket, a distraction as transparent as the window next to Aidan.

"Ask me why," he said.

"No."

"Why not?"

"Because you told me to. And last time I checked, Tom was my boss, not you."

"She doesn't even listen to me," Tom barked from the grill, and I heard a rusty chuckle from Mr. Benny.

Aidan pursed his lips and studied me for a moment. I nudged his menu at him, an unsubtle reminder to give me his official order. He pushed it aside. "Will you ask me why I was asking for you?" He made the request sound very polite.

I nudged the menu back.

"Please?" he added, sounding like he was trying not to laugh.

"Aidan, why were you asking for me?"

"Because I wanted to see you."

I blinked at him. "That's it?"

He blinked back. "Yes. Isn't that a good reason?"

"I thought with the dramatic buildup that you were going to tell me you wanted to return a million dollars that fell out of my pocket at Pine Peak or maybe ask me for a kidney. But you just wanted to see me?"

He looked taken aback. He must be used to women treating his interest in them as equivalent to getting a million dollars. I tried not to roll my eyes, and behind the grill, Tom flat out laughed at Aidan's expression.

"Men come to see me all day long, Aidan." I waved the pot in front of them. "I've got their coffee."

That prompted a few more laughs from the other guys, who gave up acting like they weren't listening, but I reddened when I realized I had their attention. I braced for what Donovan would have done at being publicly embarrassed—lashed out with an insult or turned dark and brooding. But Aidan didn't look upset at all. Instead, he became still like Chief had right before he'd tried to pounce on a chipmunk at Aidan's jobsite the other day. Then Aidan smiled, and his eyes gleamed in a way that I immediately knew was more dangerous than Donovan's quicksilver temper. It was a thoughtful gleam, like he was puzzling something out and had finally found a corner piece.

"Better men than you have tried, mister. She don't pay attention to none of 'em," Mr. Benny muttered.

I turned to him in surprise. "Thank you, Mr. Benny."

He scowled at me. "Not sure why they're trying so hard. Your coffee's not that good."

This time I did roll my eyes before I headed back toward the grill.

"What does he want?" Tom asked, his voice lowered.

"Attention, I think. I'm not up to it right now, so I'm going to run some evasive maneuvers while he's here, if you don't mind."

"I do not. But why don't I just throw him out?"

"It's okay," I said. "Maybe let's wait to see if he takes a hint, and throw him out if he doesn't." I gave him a "no big deal" look and headed back out, scooping up a couple of orders from the window on my way. They were for customers on the other side of the diner from Aidan, but his eyes followed me like a physical touch. I tried hard to act like nothing was wrong, but the weight of his stare gave me a heightened sense of my own movements.

When his order appeared in the window, I dropped it at his table, along with the entire coffeepot and an apology for being too rushed to come back to check on him more regularly. "Just short my tip for making you do self-serve refills," I said as I walked away.

"I wouldn't short you," he said, his voice raised slightly so I could hear him as I returned to the kitchen.

I waved in acknowledgment but didn't turn around. Thanks to it being our peak time, I had plenty of reasons not to spend time at his table, but when he left with a 30 percent tip in his wake, I breathed out like I'd surfaced from a deep-sea dive and served the rest of my customers that day with real smiles.

Tom shooed me out an hour early, saying there was no point in wiping down empty tables when I had art to do, and I left him with the threat of a hug if he kept being so nice to me.

At home, I ducked my head in to let Dani know I was back early, but the house was empty. Voices drifted in from the open sliding door. I walked out to find Griff on his deck, and my stomach clenched—the good kind like right before a couple is going to kiss for the first time in a movie. He didn't notice me at first, and I realized that he was listening to Dani, who was telling him about a ridiculous customer she'd had. He smiled at her impersonation of the woman demanding a full refund on the ketchup-stained jeans she'd "never worn," and relief that the two could actually talk and carry on a conversation warmed me like a Chloe hug.

"Hey," I said.

Dani turned to smile at me, and Griff looked startled to see me standing there. "Whoa. Hey. Are you a waitress/artist/ninja? I didn't even hear you come out."

"Ha," Dani said. "You've never heard her trying to sneak around to get ready in the morning."

If it were Aidan, he'd have made a crack about earning his way into waking up at my house in the morning, but Griff said nothing and laughed at Dani's lame joke.

I flicked her shoulder. "Nice. I'm going down to paint. Holler at me when you need me to take over."

"Sure."

"You working on something new?" Griff asked.

"I hope so." But I wasn't at all sure. My ideas were a laundromat dryer, where I was trying to fish out a specific piece of clothing but kept coming up with other good-but-not-right pieces instead. I was working blind, and I wondered if I needed to go paint with all the colors of the wind again.

The thought stopped me cold in the middle of the garage, and I burst into giggles. I suddenly reimagined the scene on the mountain with Aidan singing me the *Pocahontas* song. In fact, I wondered if that was where he'd gotten the idea for helping me feel Pine Peak instead of see it in the first place—watching Disney movies with his niece and then trying to play off the idea as some game she had made him do. The possibility made me like him a little better.

Which was no good.

I needed distance, not more liking. I reminded myself of his habit of kissing me whenever he felt like it. It didn't create the distance I was looking for. If anything, it almost evaporated the distance I'd already fought to create.

I pictured his expectant eyes when he'd sat in his booth that morning, waiting for my excitement at seeing him there. So cocky.

That did the trick.

When Dani poked her head into the garage an hour later to tell me she was leaving, I was on the floor, still staring at a blank canvas. At this rate, Tom would never have to worry about me spacing out at work because of my art. I was trying to fill my mind with images, but they all slid out without sticking, and I wanted to throw my brush at the canvas with enough force for the handle to pierce it and communicate my real feelings about being blocked *again.*

I put everything away, which took no time at all since nothing needed cleaning, and went in to play with Chloe until bedtime. At least I still had enough creativity left to make elaborate plots for her Barbies to enact.

The next morning I got to work well rested but frustrated. I eased into the morning routine. Mr. Benny showed up at seven thirty; Red Hat was in at eight. My nerves spooled up, ready to explode like a jack-in-the-box around the time Aidan would walk in, usually a few minutes after eight. But customers trickled in who never showed up until after Aidan did, and the tension eased out of me a bit at a time like the slow drip of the coffeemaker.

By the midmorning lull, I was rubbing at spots on the clean glasses as if they were personally responsible for my creative block.

"Now what's wrong?" Tom asked.

I looked up from a stubborn spot that wouldn't come off. "If I can't be good at painting, I'm going to be good at spot removal."

"Uh-huh. I somehow get the feeling your artwork is even better than your spot removal."

I sighed. "Thanks. But it hasn't felt like it the last couple days."

He shrugged. "Carry on if it makes you happy."

"So happy." I worked at the spot again, and several glasses after that, before the door opened and the air crackled. "You're late," I blurted when Aidan paused in the doorway.

"Didn't know I had a reservation." He looked as if he was fighting to keep a straight face.

Shoot. I wished I could snatch my words back. "Grab your booth. You're on number fourteen." It was abrupt, but his smile grew bigger, and he sat in his booth.

Tom had already started the order, and I rose to fetch the coffee. I wouldn't be able to hide behind other customers in the empty diner, so I'd need some busywork in the back.

Aidan watched me as I filled his mug, his smile steady and unnerving. "Good morning," he said.

"It's closer to lunchtime."

"How's your painting going?"

"Going? Fantastic," I said. In a literal sense, at least one of them was *going* well because the guys dispatched by Victoria's Park City connection had stopped by yesterday to crate up the piece I'd titled *Breathe* and load it into their van. So it was going, going, gone to Daddy Warbucks.

"Good to hear. I'm invested now. Will I get to see it?"

"Nope." The watercolor he was thinking of was already at Griff's house. "Does Chief want extra bacon?" I asked in a change of subject so clunky even the dog looked unimpressed.

"More than chipmunks."

I nodded and headed back to the kitchen, dropping my voice to barely above a whisper when I reached Tom. "I'm going to do that project in the storage room I've been meaning to get to. It might take me a really long time to count everything."

There'd never been a project in the storage room, but Tom nodded. "Probably need to alphabetize stuff in there too."

"I mean it—one of these days I'm going to hug you."

"Go count," he growled. "I'll walk his breakfast out to him."

I slipped down the short hall to the ten-by-ten storage room, where Tom kept the nonperishable foods and other supplies. I bent and dragged a big box of napkins out of the way. They were fine where they were, but they'd have to sacrifice their old location for a new one in the name of busywork.

Twenty minutes later, I'd reached the point where I'd made a huge mess in an effort to organize the closet/room when the door opened behind me. "It looks worse than it is. You need me out there?"

"Out there, in here. Whatever."

Aidan, not Tom. I jumped up to face him. "Something wrong with your food?"

"Yeah. You're not bringing it to me."

"Sorry about that. It's a bad time of morning. Have to get my side work done."

"Funny. I thought picking the slow time would make it easier to see you."

I should probably have felt trapped. And I would have if the reason I was avoiding him was that he gave me the bad kind of goose bumps. But he gave me the good kind of goose bumps, and when he shut the door behind him and leaned against it, a shiver shot down my spine. It wasn't the scared kind. "Tom's going to come looking for you."

"Tom thinks I'm in the restroom, and two other customers came in, so I think he'll be busy for a couple minutes."

"What do you want?" I asked. "I'm trying to avoid you."

"I know. And I want to know why."

"Seriously? Why do you think?"

"Because I'm a terrible kisser?"

I couldn't help it. I laughed.

He grinned. "Yes. Free orange juice." And he turned to go.

"Wait, that's it?"

"Yeah. I mean, how else was I going to get free OJ if you wouldn't come out there?"

"No, I meant . . . Never mind."

"Lia?"

I raised an eyebrow.

"It would be helpful if I could kiss you again. If I have proof that it's not as good as I remember, I can go back to trying to score free juice off of you and nothing else."

"You're saying if you kiss me again, you're sure you won't want to kiss me again?"

"Yep."

"That's original."

He straightened but tucked his hands into his front pockets as if he understood that I needed the assurance that he wasn't going to reach out and kiss me anyway. "Thanks. Do you believe me?"

"No."

"Smart woman. Here's the thing. I'm a pretty goal-oriented guy, and now my goal is that you'll *want* to kiss me without tricks. I'm on a mission to figure out how to make that happen."

"You didn't trick me the first time." I hated to admit it, but fair was fair.

"No, I did. I've been coming in here long enough to know that nothing pushes your buttons like a challenge. I figured if you had to choose between backing down and kissing me, you'd go for the kiss."

"I'd like to choke you right now."

He scrubbed his hand through his hair. "It's progress if you're having a hard time keeping your hands off me."

"And now I want to throw something at you."

"I should have stopped while I was ahead."

I fluttered my hand in the direction of the entire state. "There have to be way hotter women in the vicinity who you can bother."

"It's not about hot, which, by the way, you are. It's about interesting."

"Oh, conquest. I've seen twenty versions of this movie. You're going to toy with me until I beg for you to kiss me, right? Good luck."

"That's lame. No, I'm hoping you'll spend nonkissing time with me until you decide I'm not the devil so the next time I kiss you, you seem happy about it."

"I don't think you're the devil. I just . . . you're a smooth operator, you know? I don't like those."

"Ouch. I really have to do a better job of presenting myself. I thought for sure I'd proven I'm more than that by now."

"Why? Because I caught on to you so fast?"

"No," he said. "Because I don't think you get me at all." He closed the gap between us. I stiffened, but he only leaned down and hefted the huge bag of flour I'd been trying to drag to a new corner. "Where does this go?"

"On the bottom shelf," I said, pointing to the wire racks I'd cleared. He set it down and turned to face me.

"I problem-solve better when I'm moving. That's something you didn't know about me. The rest of the flour go there?"

I nodded and moved out of the way, but when he grunted while picking up the next bag, I couldn't stop a bubble of laughter.

"What? It's hard," he said, slinging it over his shoulder.

"It's not that. This is just so ridiculous. We're acting out an eighties Lifetime movie or something, where you're the corporate wolf type and I'm the sassy underling, and you're going to seduce me with the awesome combination of your brains and brawn because you're so manly."

"I would really, really be glad if you said yes to coming on a date with me, where I promise not to flirt with you and only talk to you like a normal human being." The last part was said with a strain in his voice as he tried to shift the flour to the floor without dropping it.

The door burst open, and Tom stood there wearing his grease-spattered apron and a scowl. "What's going on in here?"

"Aidan was moving some flour around for me. He's almost done."

Tom eyed Aidan, bent over with his hands on his knees. "Good. He can move the sugar next." He walked back out, leaving the door open.

"The sugar?" Aidan asked with a note of dread.

I pointed to the sack as big as the flour he'd moved. "We make a lot of pie," I said with no apology.

He groaned and reached for the sugar. "If I were a player, wouldn't I be making some kind of joke about this sugar? Something about sugar daddies or giving me some sugar or how you're so sweet?"

"I'm worried you even thought of those jokes."

"But I didn't *make* them, and that's the proof. I'm not a player." Another grunt followed as he lifted the bag.

"I believe you but only because a player would have done that so much more smoothly and flashed me some bicep."

He dropped the sugar in place and straightened, his face red from the effort. "Dinner? With me? No kissing. No flirting."

Could he be down-to-earth without hiding behind jokes and charm? His graceless flour-hauling hinted at maybe yes.

"Maybe yes."

"Maybe yes?" he repeated. He walked up to me, so close the heat from his body was a touch in itself. His hands came up but reached past me, stretching to reach something high, but the movement brought him even closer. I caught a whiff of his soap, something spicy but not overwhelming. He drew back and handed me a short stack of lightbulbs he'd pulled down from the tall shelf.

I took them. "What are these for?"

"Replacements," he said.

"For?"

"How do I know? I don't switch out the bulbs around here."

"I meant why did you give them to me?"

"I thought I'd clear the top shelf off so you don't have to figure out how to get it all down."

It was thoughtful. And I liked the way he smelled. So I said, "Yes."

"You're welcome."

"I meant yes, I'll go to dinner with you sometime. Saturday."

"Saturday I have a—never mind," he interrupted himself when I frowned. "Saturday. Where do you live?"

"How about you tell me where to meet you."

"Leifson's."

I almost laughed. "Don't think that's going to work for me. Could we go somewhere else?"

"Rosetti's. Do you know it?"

The most exclusive Italian restaurant in town? Blowing too much of his foreman's salary on a special-occasion restaurant wasn't the way to impress me, but I'd let him dig his own grave. "Rosetti's. Can it be after six?" I'd have to wait for Dani to get home.

He reached past me for the tall shelf again, and my pulse sped up. I swallowed against my suddenly dry mouth, but he just handed me more bulbs and reached up for the last set like he hadn't given my nerve endings an electric shock.

When the last bulbs were down, he crossed the tiny distance to the door and paused for a moment. "I'd stay and help longer, but I need to get back to the jobsite."

Wait, how had he gotten away for an hour in the middle of the morning? "No problem. Thanks for moving that stuff. I hope you don't get in trouble with Sully for being gone so long."

"Nah. I'm too valuable for him to get rid of me. I'll call it an early lunch. Either way, I don't think he'll care."

He offered a small wave, and a few minutes later, Tom eyed me over the grill. "I hope those evasive maneuvers were worth it," he said. "Because now I need you out here for the early lunch crowd, and you're still going to have to put my stockroom back in some kind of sane-person order."

"I will. Thanks," I said as I hurried out to the tables. I handled my customers, but heat flared in my cheeks when I thought about how Aidan's warmth had suffused me without ever touching me; I caught myself staring into space twice. The second time, I shook myself out of it and forced my attention elsewhere. Aidan shouldn't be filling my brain. That was where my next painting was supposed to be percolating.

Irritated, I focused on a blank canvas in my mind, tapping the sense memories of being at Pine Peak, and suddenly, there it was, the picture I needed. It squeezed Aidan right out of my head exactly like I'd hoped it would.

By the time Tom sent me home, it felt like a hive had exploded inside me and the bees were pushing hard to get out, pressing on the inside of my mind and chest, the beat of their million wings making my palms itch with the need to paint and free them. But at home, there was still Chloe to manage. I practiced patience over and over when she insisted on a trip to the park instead of playing in the garage and then again when she wanted me to do a fancy braid for her instead of sitting on the deck so I could at least experiment with some of the colors. When I finally got her down for the night—half an hour early for my own sanity—I flew to the garage and snatched up brushes and paint tubes.

It all came, the wind and the sky and the smell of the soil, the hint of pine, the sense of being a tiny speck on a huge thing, the ageless mountain that showed me my insignificance and yet connected me to something so vast it anchored me as nothing had for years. Roots. Possibility. Perspective.

I worked for hours, and when colors I didn't expect appeared—crimson and cobalt and a bright, true yellow—I paused. I'd painted the way it felt when Aidan stood next to me without touching me, and I'd found the color of yearning and put it in there too because, for me, Aidan was now bound up with the mountain.

Pain laced my right shoulder, and my neck muscles strained as I worked on the top section of the canvas, but I didn't care. It wasn't until I had to stretch a cramp in my forearm that I paused again, setting my brush down so I could work out the forming knot. The painting was far from done, but anyone could see me in it if they understood what to look for. That possibility terrified me at the same time it thrilled me.

"You're amazing."

I whirled to find Griff standing in the open garage door, his hands in his pockets as usual.

"Hi. Have you been here long?"

"Long enough," he said. "I hope you don't mind. I saw the light on when I got home, and I wanted to come say hello, but I couldn't make myself interrupt you."

I set my brush down and grabbed a rag to wipe the paint from my fingers. "It's fine. I zone out sometimes when I work. Sorry I didn't see you."

He shook his head. "That didn't seem like zoning out. You looked like I feel when I'm the first person on the slopes on a perfect powder day."

He understood. I grinned, letting out the sheer joy of having my work spill out into being so fast and freely. He smiled back, and it was good to see it and not the ironic lip quirk I got from Aidan sometimes. Griff drew his hands from his pockets and spread them, and before I could think too hard about whether it was a good idea, I flew into his arms, returning the hug and laughing because I couldn't not laugh, because even with everything flowing out of me in paint, there was still more inside, and it came out as laughter.

His arms closed around me, and his chest vibrated under my cheek with his return laughter, and I stood there giggling like that for almost a full minute before I settled down to feel what being there was like, standing wrapped up in him. It was good, and I quieted. His chest stilled too, leaving only the steady thump of his heartbeat.

I kept my head against his chest but tilted my face up to look at his, and his gaze met mine, his eyes still crinkled in the corners. But then the twinkle in them faded or maybe darkened. Aidan's eyes had darkened before he kissed me the first time, becoming a deeper blue in the moment before his lips touched mine.

Griff made no move to kiss me. A faint tickle of disappointment skittered in my stomach. Why couldn't I take the kiss I wanted like Aidan had taken two from me? I stretched up on my toes at the same time I slid one arm up to encircle his neck, and his eyes flashed again as I closed mine and pressed my mouth to his.

A tiny second passed where he did nothing, but he caught up quickly, returning the kiss and dropping his arms around my waist to pull me closer.

Heat didn't sweep up from my soles like it had the first time Aidan had kissed me. And the hairs didn't prickle at the base of my neck like they had the second time he'd kissed me. And my face didn't flush the way it had when Aidan had come too close in the storage room.

Kissing Griff felt . . . fine.

Almost as if he sensed the lack of connection at the same moment, his arms loosened at my waist, and I stepped back. His hands went back into his front pockets, and he bounced on the balls of his feet once, then settled into rocking on his heels. I was watching nervous energy trying to leave his body. It wasn't the kind of hungry, spiky energy that had come off of Aidan either. If I had to paint Griff right at that moment, he would be a human-shaped puddle of black and white static.

"Sorry," I said when the silence had grown so thick I could break it off in large, greasy chunks.

"You don't have to be sorry."

Awkwardness feathered down over the silence, sticking to it and illuminating how in a single moment I'd managed to trash the space between us so badly that nothing could clean it up. I was too afraid of saying the wrong thing to say anything.

He shifted his weight and stopped bouncing, but he didn't look any more comfortable. "I . . . think I might have sent the wrong signals," he said, sounding like he wished he could snatch back each word as he said it.

I wanted to scoop them up and put them all back in his mouth, pinching his lips together like I did Chloe's when she was talking too much.

"Maybe," I said. "Why did you suggest a date if you aren't interested?"

"I didn't mean 'hang out' like a date. I thought about it at first when I met you last summer, but you never seemed interested. And then suddenly we were talking, and I thought that was pretty cool. But, and please don't hate me for saying this, I was kind of . . ." He swallowed like he didn't want to finish this sentence.

I couldn't decide if it would kill me deader if he did or didn't. "You were kind of what?"

"Digging Dani." Something about the expression on my face made him rush on. "But she wasn't vibing my way at all, so don't worry about it."

"I'm not worried about that." Actually, when I could think of this whole mess without wanting to die, I'd probably want to explore that nugget further. I pressed the heels of my hands into my eyes, needing to shut out his embarrassed face for a moment. "I'm worried about why you kissed me back if you like my sister."

"Because you're hot."

That got my hands down.

"Sorry," he said. "I know it's kind of sexist, but you are."

"Not hot enough," I grumbled, my embarrassment shrinking with his matter-of-fact handling of all of this. "Not Dani hot." He reddened again, and I almost felt bad for him. Almost. Mostly, I felt bad for myself.

"I know it makes me a creep, but when you kissed me, I thought I'd better figure out if I'd been looking at the wrong sister." Now I wanted to kick him, and he read it plain as day on my face. He backed up a step. "I know it; it was a jerk move, and as soon as my brain kicked in, I backed off."

It was true. That kiss hadn't gone long at all. Maybe Aidan's hadn't either, but there was something about those that made time stop. I didn't want to think about that. Or I wanted to think about it all the time, and that was worse.

Remembering them only shone a light on how there had been nothing like that happening when I kissed Griff.

"I should go," he said, but he didn't look like he wanted to.

"You got something else on your mind?"

He swallowed. "You're a cool girl. Did I make everything weird with us because I'm lame?"

"You're not lame."

"I'm super lame. I like chilling with you and Chloe, but I can stay inside when you're out from now on or something as punishment for stupidity. I don't want you to be mad at me."

"I'm not mad at you. I'm mad at myself. I'm the dumb one."

"No. I wish that kiss would have—"

"Stop! Nothing you can say next is going to go well for either of us."

He nodded. "You're right. The longer we talk, the stupider I'm getting. I'll shut up now. But are we cool?"

I hugged myself and rubbed my palms up and down my arms, even though the temperature was actually perfect. "If we're not, it's on me, not you. Don't feel like you need to hide."

"If I hide it's only because I'd be afraid of you throwing something at me, which would kinda be exactly what I deserve."

"Then I'd deserve having some sense slapped into me, and I don't really want to be slapped, so I guess we'll call it even."

"I can live with that."

"All right. You're going to have to go away now so I can get back to this painting and see whether you completely crushed my creative spirit or not."

Guilt flashed across his face again, but I raised an eyebrow at him, and a grin slowly won out. "I'm going to pay for this for a while, aren't I?" he asked.

"Most definitely. And the more you reference this whole disaster directly, the longer you're going to pay."

"Disaster? I don't know what you're talking about."

"Smart guy."

"Sure . . . now."

I shooed him. "Go away."

"I'll go, but I sort of have a favor to ask. Could you not mention this to Dani? I know that's asking a lot because if you're like my sisters, you guys probably tell each other everything, but my side of the railing would be a much more chill place to be if she never knew I was digging her. I don't want her to feel weird about that or anything."

"You mean like I feel weird?"

"Yeah. Does it make you feel better that I realize it's a jerk thing to ask for, but I'm hoping one of us can come out of this unscathed, and I'm hoping it's Dani?"

"I won't say anything. You were going to go away?" I shooed him again, and with a smile and a wave, he left.

I turned to face the canvas, but I needed sleep more than I needed to paint. I had more I wanted to get out, but hitting another groove would take me into the early morning hours, and I couldn't spare the energy. I cleaned the brushes and set them aside, thinking about the revelation that Griff had been eyeing Dani. He'd been so quiet with his interest that I hadn't noticed it, but it wasn't a surprise that she'd caught his attention. On her best days, she was a Klimt, a soft glow around her, vibrant with color. Even on her most exhausted days, she was still a Modigliani, muted and beautiful. Guys checked her out no matter what.

But Dani could handle herself. She'd been on her guard ever since Chloe's dad had ghosted out of town for a job with an oil company in North Dakota. He sent checks, but that was it, and that was only to keep the courts off his back. He didn't call or ask to see his daughter, ever. And good riddance. It meant I got to be dad, kind of.

At some point, though, Dani would find someone, and I would lose my job as Parent Number Two. As long as he was a good guy, I'd be okay with it, because Dani and Chloe both deserved someone special. And Griff was a good guy. The more I thought about it—the wistfulness that we got to go to dinner at Leifson's, Dani's irritation when we'd thought it was Griff sending the gifts—the more sure I was that Dani wasn't indifferent to him. But his shyness had gotten in the way. It would take some serious convincing for Dani to even think about dating someone, and Griff playing it so laid back wasn't going to do the trick.

Maybe that was okay. I needed to decide if I wanted to do anything about it, whether this was right for Dani and Chloe, but right now, with my ego in shreds around my ankles, was not the time to figure it out.

Chapter 15

Showing up for a date with one bum cheek stinging was not the ideal way to start, but Chloe had decided to express her approval of my outfit by spanking me hard. And the fifteen-minute drive to the restaurant hadn't been enough for the sting to fade. I'd opted for a vintage lace sheath I used to wear to cocktail parties with Donovan. It was a warm vanilla color, and I paired it with ballet flats to keep it nice enough for Rosetti's without being too dressy. I rubbed my behind, took a deep breath, and pushed through the mahogany door to find Aidan already waiting for me.

"You look amazing," he said, dropping a kiss on my cheek European-style.

It startled me, not because it was weird—I'd gotten used to that doing the gallery rounds in SoHo—but because it was so natural for him, as if him slipping on nicer clothes for the high-end restaurant had come with a new suit of manners too. I liked both. He was as comfortable with himself here as he'd been at my diner table, and he looked beyond hot in his black jacket and open-collar shirt. "Thanks. You clean up nicely too."

"Thanks." He nodded at the hostess, who led us straight to a quiet booth. "I have a thing for booths."

"I've noticed. Not sure why you'd ever haunt mine with a place like this around." I inhaled the scent of garlic and baked bread. I could get high off of that.

"Tom is as good at what he does as Rosetti's is with pasta. I happen to like your booth."

"Wow. You said that without it even sounding like it had a double meaning."

"I can behave when I want to. You just make me not want to."

I was flattered for a second before annoyance at being made responsible for his feelings crept in. A retort leaped to my tongue, but he held up a hand.

"Believe me, I understand how that sounds. Me caveman," he said with a thump on his chest. I couldn't fight a smile. "I also want to behave myself so you'll keep coming out with me."

My gaze swept the room. Impressive. It was on par with many of the places Donovan had liked to go to be seen. "This isn't hanging out."

He grinned. "Shoot. You picked up on that, huh?"

I shot him a warning look and picked up my menu. "What do you recommend?" And he had suggestions. How did he know the menu so well? He wasn't the foreman at Pine Peaks if he was eating here regularly. He couldn't afford it. I revised my assumption upward. He was the contractor, at least. "Sully isn't your boss, is he?" I asked.

He looked startled for a second at the change of subject before he caught up and shook his head. "No."

"You're his boss?"

"Indirectly. Does it matter?"

"No. Except I keep realizing I'm not as smart as I think I am."

"You're pretty smart. I think it would be hard to underestimate you."

"Thank you." The unvarnished simplicity of the compliment gave me that locked-out-of-my-house-in-my-underwear feeling again. I retreated to my menu, relieved to have something to hide behind. We talked over the options until the server came to take our orders, but after she left, silence fell. I crossed my arms and leaned back.

"Uh-oh. There's a challenge written all over your face. What's up?" he asked.

"Nothing. Just wondering what you have to talk about when you're being you and not the pickup king."

"Challenge accepted. Read any good books lately?"

It was that easy. I loved to read, but it turned out that he did too, and it was hard not to swoon when he named some of his favorites. It was one of the most interesting conversations I'd had in a long time. "You have a good mind for analysis," I said. "What are you majoring in?"

Confusion crossed his face. "Majoring in?"

"You said school barely got out?" But as soon as I said the words, I realized I'd made another false assumption. He'd been discussing literature like someone who was trained to do it.

His face grew thoughtful like now I was under analysis, and he ran his finger around the rim of his glass while he considered me. "I'm not working on a degree. I already have a couple. I teach at the community college."

"Really? Like construction management?"

He shook his head. "Nope."

"I think maybe I've made a lot of wrong guesses about you."

"Probably."

"So what do you teach there?"

"Let me ask you a question instead. Why does it matter? What if it's prelaw? Or freshman English? Or art?"

"It doesn't matter, except it's interesting. I feel kind of like I do when I'm trying to do a still life. There's what I see, and there's what it is. Half of what I like about doing them is thinking about what they really are."

He searched my face, but I didn't know what he was looking for. A few seconds ticked by, and his shoulders relaxed. "You mean that. It doesn't matter what my background is."

"Not so much, no."

"Okay. There's stuff I should tell you," he said with a small smile.

"But we're not at the tell-me-all-your-secrets phase, and since I'm opposed to relationships in theory and practice, we won't ever be."

"Shut up," he said, smiling bigger, and I grinned back. "This isn't a secret. Haven't you Googled me?"

There it was, the bravado. Irritation crept in. "No."

"Why not? Isn't that kind of a standard practice now, to Google someone you're dating?"

"We're not dating. We're on a date. One. And I guess I meant to Google you, but I forgot. And also, I don't know your last name."

"Even if you had it, I wouldn't have come up unless you knew exactly what to look for."

The server returned with our food, and the aroma drifting off of it made my mouth water. "This looks incredible."

"I haven't been disappointed by anything here yet," he said, scooping a piece of bruschetta.

Yet? That sounded like he'd eaten here many times, and it brought me to the question of who and what he really was. Rosetti's was not a regular habit for guys even on a superintendent's salary. "These are my top five guesses for when I Google you: you're a CIA spy, you've had a sex-change operation, you're on the FBI's most-wanted list, you're under witness protection, you're an undercover cop investigating the black market for liver." I pulled out my cell phone and tapped the browser. "What's your full name?"

He sighed. "Knowing may or may not change things. But if it's going to, I kind of want to enjoy this for what it is at the moment. So how about instead of you Googling to find what I promise is *not* any of your guesses, which were both funny and psychotic, I'll take you on a drive and show you what you're going to find out anyway?"

"Take me on a drive," I repeated. "*I'm* a tiny bit psycho? That's the scariest thing anyone's ever asked me to do."

He grimaced. "Yeah, I heard it when I said it. What can I do to make you feel better about saying yes?"

"Tell me where we're going, I'll follow you, and I'll call at least two people to tell them where I am."

"Fine with me. How about if we finish dinner, then you can make those calls while I take care of the check?"

"Yeah. You haven't told me where we're going yet."

"Back to Pine Peak."

I put my phone down. "I'm not climbing a mountain in the dark with you."

"We're going to my house. It's well lit. And you'll have cell service if you need to be rescued."

We ate without much more talking, but only because I didn't want to stop eating the amazing food long enough to carry on a conversation. Other than raving about every third bite, I focused on the food. I caught Aidan studying me and smiling a few times when I lifted another forkful, but it was an appreciative smile, like he understood the religious experience I was having with the food and wanted to respect it by staying quiet.

I picked up my phone again, and he waved the server over, who brought a dessert tray.

"Is your house better than tiramisu?" I asked. "Because that slice looks almost impossible to beat."

"I guess you'll have to come see and decide for yourself. And I've got dessert there."

My eyebrow shot up. "You were so sure I'd say yes to coming over that you stocked dessert?"

He grinned. "No. I have a sweet tooth. I always have dessert in my house."

I blushed. *Way to jump to conclusions, dummy.* "As long as it's good," I said, trying to recover. I nodded at the tray. "That's hard to give up."

"Noted. You up for this?"

I gave him a what-the-heck shrug, and he requested the check from the server as I tapped out a text to Dani and considered the implications of

Aidan living at Pine Peak. He could live in the trailer, maybe, but I had a feeling that wasn't it.

I texted Tom too because he was as likely as Dani to tear the mountain down if I went missing.

When Aidan signed the credit card slip, he led the way back outside. He nodded when I told him where I'd parked. "Me too. I'll walk you over."

Return texts came in from Dani and Tom as we rounded the corner to the public lot down the block. Dani's was a simple "Whoohoo!" with kissy lips. Tom had more to say.

You text me as soon as you get there, every fifteen minutes after you get there, and as soon as you leave again, or I'm calling the sheriff.

I held up the phone to show Aidan. "This is from Tom, so you know I'm not being rude when you see me on the phone a billion times tonight."

He laughed. "If texting him is what it takes for Chief to keep his inside privileges at T&R, it won't bother me at all."

"Smart man."

In the parking lot, I pointed to my Subaru, and he jerked his head toward a sporty pickup truck. "That's me. See you up there."

The drive took almost twenty-five minutes, which was more than enough time to talk myself into and out of turning around a half dozen times. But every time I thought about peeling off and pointing my car toward home, curiosity kept my hand away from the turn signal.

We passed the parking lot with the construction trailer and continued another mile up the canyon before he turned off on another road, graded but not paved. He slowed way down as we crunched over the dirt, but my car handled it easily enough. I was too busy peering through the trees, trying to figure out where he was leading me, to pay attention to exactly how far we'd gone, but we traveled at least another mile of gentle switchbacks before we rounded a corner and I nearly slammed on the brakes in shock.

Chapter 16

Aidan pulled right up to the paved driveway of a well-lit lodge. Well, a lodge in the sense that Pavarotti was a nice singer or Tom Ford made pretty clothes.

It was huge. No. It was *vast*.

It was a blend of contemporary and classic, clean lines, interesting peaks and facets without being too busy or stark. It was one of the most beautiful lodges I'd ever seen. The Park City ski resorts finally had some real competition from their Salt Lake neighbors.

Lights shone from all the windows in the center, making it clear that the heavy double front door opened into a vaulted space, where a cool iron chandelier hanging. I'd have to see it closer to be sure, but it looked hand worked.

I tapped out another quick text to my virtual chaperones, describing where we'd gone and promising they had nothing to worry about.

Aidan parked and walked over to wait for me outside of my car, far enough away that I could get out without feeling crowded.

"Nice place," I said.

"Thanks. Ready for the grand tour?"

"Sure."

We walked toward the front doors, but we'd only made it five yards before I stopped short. "Wait. This is your house."

"Yeah," he said, his eyebrows raised in question. "I told you that's where I was taking you. What did you think it was?"

"One of the resort lodges," I said, dazed. I looked at it again and realized that the windows weren't spaced in a way that suggested resort-style compartmentalization of the rooms. "It's your house? This is a *house?*"

He sighed. "Remember I said I had some things to tell you? Come on in. This is probably a good place to start."

I had nothing to say to that. I followed him up the stairs and through the front door after he punched in a code on the keypad and held still for a retinal scan. It was science fictiony and kind of freaked me out. I'd been in houses like this before, but I hadn't ever expected to be in one again. The Beckmans had friends among the most powerful East Coast elite, and I'd spent three summers going to parties in Hamptons summer homes that were mini palaces like this, good for housing a village, not a family.

I'd left it all so far behind, buried as deeply in the past as I could heap the dirt, yet there I was again on the threshold of insane wealth. I still wanted to hear what Aidan had to say, but even as I stood in the foyer beneath soaring skylights and the beautiful wrought-iron chandelier, several things about him from the last few months snapped into focus. Painful focus, even.

The confidence bordering on arrogance, the assumption that he would get his way, his ease in his own skin, the way he extracted special treatment for himself that no one else would dream of asking for, like bringing Chief into the diner. All of that added up to wealth, the kind that wasn't countable because no one had the patience to go that high, the kind of wealth so massive it granted power purely because of what money like that could do when at the disposal of a single individual.

He led me down a short hall directly in front of us that opened into a huge room with floor-to-ceiling windows. I couldn't see anything in them but our own reflections, dwarfed by the windows' size.

"This is . . ." I couldn't find the words. Overwhelming? Unnerving? Nauseating despite its impeccably decorated interior?

"Do you like it?" he asked, and again, his eyes narrowed as he studied my face, the analytical glint clear inside them.

"It's stunning."

"Thank you. It took two years of back-and-forth with the architect to create what I wanted, but he did it. Can we sit?"

I nodded, too overwhelmed to do anything else, and followed him to the sofa, where I sank down and tried not to stiffen at the touch of the butter-soft leather beneath my palms. It hugged my whole body the way the handmade Italian leather boots Donovan used to buy me had encased my feet, but I still couldn't enjoy it. The couch probably cost a year of tuition for Bethwell. No, twice that.

"Is this the part where you reveal your secret identity? Because I wouldn't follow you like an idiot into a remote canyon for anything less than that."

"You're fine. Check your bars. You'll have full reception. I have a cell tower here. It looks like an actual tree, none of this artificial Christmas tree rip-off garbage."

It was a good description for the eyesores phone companies tried to dress up with green petal-shaped plastic. But none of that got to the real point here, which was that Aidan apparently had his very own cell tower. "Of course you do," I murmured. Why not? That was the thing with rich people. If they ever stopped to ask themselves about the wisdom of how they were spending their money, the only question they asked was *Why not?* And it never even crossed their minds that having a personal cell phone tower was an insane luxury.

"So you're going to spill your secrets now," I prompted him.

He took a deep breath. "My real name is Theodore Aidan Cormack. I've always gone by Aidan with my friends and family. I go by Ted for business. A consultant told me once early on that people would take me more seriously as Ted because Aidan is a trendy name, and I listened, like an idiot. I've spent the last three years wanting to punch everyone who has called me Ted."

I didn't know if that name was supposed to mean something to me.

"If you Googled it, you'd find out I was one of those guys who got lucky enough to develop and sell a social networking app for a lot of money. Go ahead and look it up. It's called Flickgram."

I was glad I was already sitting down. I'd heard of Flickgram. That was the site I'd used most in New York for keeping up with Dani's endless stream of photos. It'd helped me stay connected to her. The sale of Flickgram had made the news last year for a few days because it had been acquired by another huge company. I couldn't remember the exact amount, but it was in the hundreds of millions.

I glanced around the room again. "So this is what that kind of money buys you?"

"Yeah. Plus the actual resort."

He sounded like someone trying to get the bad news out all at once.

"You own Pine Peak?" I asked.

"Yes." A statement of fact, not pride.

I rubbed my face. "I guess this is where I make my own confession. I hate rich people."

That startled a laugh from him. "Do you hate them like I hate brussels sprouts, which is with a fiery-hot loathing, or do you hate them like I hate insomnia, which is a periodic but minor annoyance?"

"Insomnia, I guess."

"Sounds like a good story. Want to tell me?"

Go into my divorce and shambles of a life from before? Nope. "I spent too much time around wealthy people. They're very hateable. The ones I met, anyway."

He laughed. And he kept laughing. He laughed so hard he collapsed against the sofa, and he still kept laughing. It tugged an unwilling smile out of me. He finally caught his breath and grinned at me, slouched and holding his side like he'd hurt himself. "Why aren't you offended?" I asked.

"Because it's so true. And because you say it like someone who knows, not someone who hates rich people just because we're rich."

"I don't understand you at all."

"You haven't tried to up to this point." He said it matter-of-factly, but it stung because his words were as true as mine. And if I was going to be that honest with him, I had to be honest with myself: I *hadn't* tried to understand him. I'd been too busy dueling with him, keeping my guard up, to understand why he did anything he did.

I took a deep breath and held it, because when I let it out, some hard words would have to come with it. I finally released it and said, "I'm sorry. You're right."

His eyebrows rose. "Really?"

"Really."

He clasped his hands and studied his interlocked fingers before shifting that thoughtful gaze to me. "Do you want to try now, maybe a little? I might not be interesting, but at least you have a shot of disliking me for real reasons and not just because."

"I don't dislike you."

His eyebrows rose again, although this time he didn't voice his disbelief.

"I don't," I said, recognizing truth again. "I can like you and be irritated by you at the same time. I guess I mostly let you know about the irritation."

"Mostly," he agreed, humor lines appearing around his eyes. "No, only. You only let me know about the irritation."

"So why keep coming around?"

"Because I liked meeting a girl who treated me like Aidan, not Ted Cormack. I like that you give me crap for sitting in your booth because I'm just some guy, and you don't run around trying to impress me because I'm loaded. And I like that you absolutely aren't dating me for my money."

"I'm not dating you at all," I objected.

"Then I like that you're not on a date with me right now because I have money."

"I'm not going to lie. You having money doesn't make you any more attractive to me," I said, only because I already found him ridiculously hot, "but it does make you more interesting."

He laughed again. "Let me guess. You want to solve me now."

"Yeah. I'm almost itchy about not having answers."

"And now's a bad time to make a joke about scratching itches?"

My lips twitched. "Assuming you want me to stay, then, yeah."

"All right. Then ask your questions."

"Why are you living in the mountains and driving a pickup truck?"

"Because this is always who I was," he said. "I grew up in Sandy. Not rich but comfortable. My parents pushed us hard in school, so now they have a doctor, a businessman, a high school principal, and a lawyer to show for it. And when I got sick of shuttling between the venture capital firms in Seattle and the banks in New York, this is where I wanted to come back to. I can't get away from my roots. I never wanted to really, and I came back the first chance I got."

I understood it. I'd done the exact same thing.

He leaned forward and rested his elbows on his knees. "I'm answering a lot of questions. I think it's your turn. I'm beginning to think you have a deep, dark past."

"Yeah. Dead bodies rotting into skeletons in a lot of my closets."

"Then I'm sure you've got cool stories. Not that I'll be able to drag any of them out of you. Are you open to bribes?"

"I can't be bought, dude."

"Bull. I was thinking Ben & Jerry's. My massive wealth allows me to buy the name-brand stuff even when it's not on sale, and I keep my freezer stocked."

"So if I accept ice cream, I have to give you . . . what?"

"Answers. To five questions."

"How about zero?" I liked having the upper hand for once, but I kept my tone teasing.

"This is why I'm a millionaire and you're not. That's not how you negotiate."

I tilted my head as if it would give me some new perspective as I studied him. "You're pretty glib about the whole money thing."

"Sure, now that I know you don't care."

"Oh, I care. But opposite of the way you expected, I think."

"You think correctly, then. Seriously, ice cream? I have the kind with cookies in it or chocolate chips in it or both mushed together. It's yours for the price of four questions."

I pretended to think. "I'm intimidated by the fanciness. I'm a vanilla girl."

Surprise crossed his face. "You are?"

"No."

"Good. I couldn't believe my instincts about you were so wrong. Whatever ice cream you want from my freezer for the price of three questions. And I have about twelve flavors."

"Do you have a freezer just for ice cream?" I asked, laughing, and it only made me laugh harder when he looked embarrassed for the first time. "You totally do! Rich people." I shook my head in fake disgust. "Fine. You get three questions but only after I get ice cream."

"Deal." He stood and held his hand out to pull me up. I slid mine into his, excruciatingly aware of the heat that flowed through our palms and up my arm at the first touch. Dang it. It made me so uncomfortable that he could do that. But I didn't want to let go, and when he turned to lead me toward a hallway, he didn't let go either. And as simple as that, I was holding hands with Aidan Cormack.

The kitchen was only a short distance down the hall, and I was honestly surprised to step in and find that it wasn't an ode to stainless steel and chrome. The room welcomed us with warm, dark cabinets and marble that glowed like it was lit from within. It was an expensive room but in the way that Rosetti's had been, where you wanted to sink into a comfortable seat and revel in it, not freeze, afraid to touch anything.

Aidan walked over to a cabinet door that turned out to be hiding a fridge. Sure enough, the freezer side held nothing but ice cream. "What would you like?" he asked.

"Any combination of mint and chocolate."

"You have to work harder to stump me. I always have that."

"I don't want to stump you. I want to get ice cream I like."

"Why don't you sit at the bar while I do this?" He pulled some bowls down and dished up the ice cream, and it was like watching a movie scene someone had scripted wrong; in a house this size, the owner should have his own Alfred or Pepper Potts to pop out and handle these mundane details. Aidan served me a heaping bowl and took the stool next to me. "Question one."

"I changed my mind. You'll have to sue me for breach of contract." I took another bite and waited to see what he would do. I liked holding the reins too much to let go of them yet.

"You are in the mountains, alone in my house, deep in the woods. You have to do what I say."

"Or what?"

"Nothing, actually. It's a totally empty threat. But you *should* do what you said you would do."

"This is pretty good ice cream. I guess that's fair. Okay. Shoot."

"Why do you not like me?"

"I was kind of hoping for questions like what's my favorite color." Then again, that was a pretty complicated question for an artist.

"Lia . . ."

"Fine. I'll answer. I like you fine, but dating isn't my thing. Add to that a relationship with a guy who reminds me a lot of you and which exploded with debilitating injuries a few years ago . . ." I took a bite and shrugged. "I didn't feel like hopping into your truck and riding into the sunset the second you asked." I smiled, and he shook his head at me.

"I want to know more, and yet I'm pretty sure this conversation is going to go badly for me if I remind you of a catastrophic relationship fail."

"I didn't say catastrophic." I licked my spoon and thought about it. "No, it was catastrophic. But you are beginning to seem less like him. So that's good. Maybe."

"Since I'm a smart man, I'm going to change the subject and put some more distance between that guy and me. Next question: what do you do when you're not working?"

"I help take care of my niece, and I'd rather do that than anything when I'm not at the diner. Although painting is turning into a second favorite thing pretty fast."

"You're good at it. That was an amazing watercolor you did. Are you self-taught?"

"No. I went to art school."

"Cool. Where?"

"Sorry. That was three questions."

"No, it was only two."

"You asked if I'm self-taught. That was three."

His spoon clattered into his bowl. "No way! That was a follow-up. It doesn't count."

"It counts. As in one-two-three, and I don't have to answer any more questions about myself." He looked so disgruntled that I giggled before I could help it.

"There are people from coast to coast who would tell you I'm incredibly persuasive, but I'm pretty sure there's no way I'm going to convince you to give me a real third question, am I?"

"Nope."

"I give up. Our choices for conversation are either the NFL or politics."

"Or your house. I think you promised a tour. You'd better deliver, or I'll have to call you a dirty welcher."

"A dirty welcher?" he repeated. "Do you by any chance spend time watching old movies?"

"Was that another question? Because I don't think I have to answer it."

He scooped up my bowl and plopped it in the sink. I sort of loved that he didn't leave it on the counter or feel the need to put it straight into the dishwasher. It was my same level of housekeeping. Although he probably had someone who would come handle it all later. Still . . .

"Hey, Aidan?"

"Yeah?"

"I studied art in college. It was way beyond a hobby to me. I kind of *lived* it, you know?"

He nodded but said nothing, as if he were afraid that interrupting would make me clam up. It might have. But his silence let me risk even more. "I painted different stuff than what you've seen me do, but when my personal life fell apart, I couldn't paint anymore, for a lot of dramatic, artistically temperamental reasons. So I didn't. And I've been here awhile, and now I'm painting again."

He waited, but I didn't have anything more to say. "I'm fascinated. Want to tell me more about it? I'll give you another bowl of ice cream. A big one. And fill it to the top."

"No. I answered my three questions, real ones, even. I think I'm done."

"I can live with that for right now." He glanced around the kitchen like he was reorienting himself, which made me feel like he must have been paying some pretty intense attention to me. And that planted seeds of warmth in my chest that worried me but not enough to say good night. "All right, I promised a tour, so let's go," he said. "We'll start from the bottom and go up. This is where you make a crack about me trying to trick you into my basement."

"I'll go willingly on the condition that there's something cool in there."

"You'd think it was cool if you were a ten-year-old." My eyebrows lifted in question, but he only shook his head at me. "You'll see."

Chapter 17

A door off the kitchen led to some stairs, and when I stepped into the basement, my jaw dropped. It was like walking into a secret room in Disneyland or something. The space was huge and had more doors at the far end leading to who knew what, but I could barely take in what I was already seeing. It was a kid paradise full of overstuffed furniture, beanbags, a massive flat-screen with several game consoles connected to it, a wall lined with shelves full of children's books at the perfect height for little kids to browse, and a huge play space packed with bins of toys.

"This is . . . incredible," I said when I found my voice.

"Uh-huh. Before you start questioning why a single guy who's almost thirty has a giant kids' room in his bachelor pad, you should know I have eleven nieces and nephews, all under twelve years old. And since my entire family lives within two hours of me, I planned for the fact that every single holiday and family event will be here now."

"Wow," I said, and the image of him drowning under a pile of kids made me warm to him even more. This was becoming a war of attrition with him steadily gaining, and yet I couldn't bring myself to turn around and march myself back to my car even though it was the smart play.

"There's more. Prepare to hate me for all my ridiculous excess in about ten seconds." He crossed to the wall on the other side and opened the double doors in the middle to reveal a three-lane bowling alley.

"Wow."

"Yeah. Did I mention all those nieces and nephews come from my four siblings plus their spouses? I like to keep everyone happy. So I also built this," he said, nodding at a door leading off from another part of the play room. It opened to reveal a home theater large enough to seat at least thirty people.

"Uh . . ."

"I know. I'm everything that is bad about consumer America. Lay into me. I can take it."

It wasn't even the conspicuous consumption thing that bothered me most about the wealthy. If Aidan had acted as if this whole set up was in any way normal or had presented it to me as evidence of his awesomeness, I would have faked a headache and gone home. But he fidgeted ever so slightly, like he'd shared an embarrassing secret. That and the need to be unpredictable prompted my next words. "I was thinking you must be a big film buff. We could talk about that instead of politics." I'd seen enough movies on my own over the last three years.

"I like movies, but this is super convenient for watching football too. I believe I mentioned the NFL as one of our talk options already."

"Not my thing."

"Fine. But just so you know, this room is like this because my brother made me do it. Dude seriously can't be parted from his games during the holidays. Also, it's entirely possible that I watch a lot of movies and sometimes spend entire Sundays down here doing marathons."

"Like what?" I expected him to say Stephen King or maybe something reeking of testosterone, like the *Fast and the Furious* films, but he mumbled something I didn't quite catch because it sounded like *Lord of the Rings.*

"I'm sorry. Did you say you do *Lord of the Rings* marathons?"

He shifted on his feet. "Yes."

Ha. He had an inner geek. "I should sell this to the tabloids. 'Sexy businessman is a closet nerd.'"

"Sexy?" he repeated with a glint in his eye that I trusted about as much as I would a hungry coyote on a deserted running trail.

"Just trying to think of a good headline."

"So you're not saying you find me sexy."

"I did not say that, no." It was true. I hadn't said it even though it was exactly what I thought. I wanted to paint him as a streak of superheated blue, the intensity of a lightning strike, with the same tendency to disappear the second it hit its target—gone with nothing but wreckage in its wake. Singed, bewildered wreckage. I took a step back. The gleam in his eye brightened.

"Scared?" he asked, his voice quiet but not gentle. Where had the nerdy guy from half a minute ago disappeared to? Aidan stood so still I almost wanted to lean in to check his breathing; his eyes narrowed as he read me, waiting to see what I gave away.

"Not even a little scared because I'm not playing this."

A fraction of a second passed, and he relaxed, his easy smile back. "Nothing to fear from a guy who watches *Lord of the Rings* marathons. Come on. There's a lot more house to see."

We walked back toward the stairs, and his tightly coiled energy ebbed to normal as fast as it had flowed in, but there was still a charge in the air.

Back on the ground floor, he took me through the great room again before pausing at the hallway leading off the other side. "My nerd secrets are out, so I guess it's safe to show you some of my other secrets. Here's another one. I respect that you paint because I love art. I started collecting it a few years ago, and I don't have a big collection, but what I have, I love. I keep some of it in this next room, gallery style, but my favorite pieces are in other places throughout the house, part of my everyday living experience, in a way. So this is where you get to judge my taste."

I wished I could say I wouldn't judge him, but if I saw anything that looked vaguely Thomas Kinkade-y, I was going to have to never speak to him again. The thought perked me up a bit. If his art sucked, then he would be automatically less attractive. "I'll try not to judge. But fair warning, I'll be able to psychologically profile you with perfect accuracy once I see what you collect."

"Wow. No pressure, huh? What I like is pretty different from what you paint." He winced. "That sounded incredibly insensitive. I meant that you do some stellar watercolors, way better than what I see in the Park City galleries. But I tend toward collage and oils, and big pieces, that's all."

It would be interesting to see what Aidan's taste in art looked like when he could show me what he truly liked and not just say that my stuff was nice.

A squeak escaped me when Aidan flipped a switch and flooded his personal gallery. Suddenly, bright lights on the walls illuminated how much trouble my resistance to Aidan was in.

Chapter 18

I wandered into the room and tried to keep my face neutral. The paintings were all abstract: two Peruns, a Phillip Na, and three I didn't recognize, but it was clear they were from artists with a strong aesthetic point of view. They looked like pieces I'd hang in my own home if I were made of money.

I looked more closely at the room itself. It was rectangular and smallish, compared to the several I'd already seen, but it was still bigger than any room in my house. Three of the paintings hung on each of the longer walls, and two pedestals in the middle displayed abstract sculptures. There was even a bench for visitors to sit and study the pieces, like in a museum.

"Do you like them?" he asked. "Like I said, I know it's pretty different from what you do."

From the watercolors he'd seen me do, yes. But not different from my oils.

"I do like them," I said, pointing. "That's a Perun."

"Yeah," he said, his eyebrows rising. "I guess that's your New York training showing, huh?"

I ignored the question because the truth was that I'd shown with Shon Perun and would know his work anywhere. I took my time rounding the first sculpture, a swooping piece of steel with seamless contours. It looked cast, not welded, and it fascinated me.

"How do you figure people out?" I asked.

"What do you mean?"

"Like some people will judge others based on what's on their iPod or bookshelves or refrigerator. How do *you* do it?"

He nodded slowly, like he was figuring out the question. "Can't say I ever cared too much about what was on someone's fridge."

"You should. Yours worked in your favor today."

He grinned. "Bookshelves and iPods are fair game, I guess. But I think I use what people show me. I judge on actions. Behavior. I've heard it all speaks more loudly than words. Someone should make that into an expression because it sounds kind of genius."

It was my turn to smile at him. "That's the only reason I ever talked to you, you know. Because you made me laugh."

"I know. That's the only reason I talked to you either. I wanted to see if I could do it. After you made that comment about that idiot Zhaday, I had this sudden need to know what else was in there."

"Too bad I haven't cooperated, huh?"

"Doesn't matter. I've still figured out a lot, even with you stonewalling me."

"Like what?"

He walked back to the door. "Come on. I'll show you my two favorite pieces."

"Aren't you going to answer me?"

"If I laid out for you what I think I see in you, it would send you running for your car. Don't you think it would be weird to hear this in-depth analysis of yourself from someone you don't know that well? It would be even scarier than following a vague acquaintance up to his deserted cabin in the woods."

"So you're saying you're not going to answer?"

"Am I going to tell you things about yourself that you refuse to tell me about yourself? No." He mimed holding up a spoon. "Dose of your own medicine. Deal with it."

I shook my head in that you're-a-lost-cause way Chloe did to me so often. "Show me your other stupid paintings."

He stopped short in the hallway. "You think my paintings are stupid?"

"No. You actually have a great eye."

"Right answer. I don't like sharing the next ones with everybody, and you almost lost out."

"Why? What's so special about them?"

"Not everyone gets them. I don't like explaining them to people. I just want to enjoy them, so I keep them upstairs where every guest can't trip over them and ask dumb questions."

"Is this the part where you trick me and start using all your lines on me again?"

"Yes. I'm going to trick you into coming upstairs because I haven't already had at least ten opportunities to kiss you. Somehow, taking you up to the second floor will give me the chance I've been hoping for." He shook his head and started up.

I didn't know what made me say it. The way he'd been careful to respect my boundaries all evening? The fact that he loved art like I wished everyone loved art? His freezer full of ice cream?

Whatever it was, instead of following him up the stairs, I said his name. Softly, to give myself a chance to change my mind, but he heard me and stopped on the third step.

"Yes?" he asked, turning his head to look at me.

I didn't say anything, but he turned all the way and came back down the steps anyway like he knew which words were trying to come out. He didn't stop until he was a foot away and staring down at me. "Yes?" he repeated.

"You should . . ." I trailed off. Kiss me? I couldn't finish.

"You'd better say it." A steady watchfulness carved his face into stillness.

A jolt shuddered through me. Could he read me so easily?

"Lia."

I wanted to take a step back, but I couldn't back down from the dare in his tone. "Yes?"

"Say it."

No. Whoever else he might be used to ordering around, he wouldn't do it to me. I ignored his command and leaned forward instead, rising slightly on my tiptoes to set my hands on his shoulders and brush his lips with mine. "Thanks for the art walk."

I eased back down.

His hand snaked out around my waist and pulled me toward him, an inevitability, I could see now. When he had me lined up perfectly against him, his head dipped, and for a sweet instant, he returned the kiss I'd given him before it slid into something much hotter. I wrapped my arms around his neck. To hold myself up? To keep him there?

When he lifted his head after an eternity, he stared down at me.

Please don't ruin this with some flippant remark, I begged him with my eyes.

"Thank you."

They were the perfect words for him to say. I wouldn't have believed anything else that came out of his mouth.

"I'm pretty sure I'll never get you to come back if I push you any further, so how about we continue the tour?" he asked.

He was right about that too. I dropped my arms, but he captured one of my hands before it returned to my side and laced his fingers through mine, then led me back up the stairs.

"I swear I'm not taking you to my man lair," he said over his shoulder. "The second level is still community space but only for family and close friends."

The landing opened to a loft overlooking the great room below. The giant bank of windows stretched upward in front of us here too. The furniture was dark and overstuffed and inviting, but I could barely take it in when I caught sight of the two paintings mounted on opposite sides of the room. I recognized them. *Remade* and *In the Beginning*, done by an artist who had cared deeply about getting it right, about translating the kind of scenery hidden beyond Aidan's forever-tall windows into an experience so people who had only ever witnessed skyscrapers and not real mountains could understand, could *feel* what it meant to look at those peaks.

They were mine. I had painted them in my other life and sold them to Daddy Warbucks. My signature was there, Leandra Tate, my old-life name scrawled in the corner, my name from before I had turned back into Lia Carswell, the name I'd had my whole life until New York had tried to morph me.

The heat from Aidan's kiss was still muddling my mind too much for it to process anything rationally, and I could only stare in shock at my work, snippets of Aidan's words coming back to me over the pounding of blood in my ears. *Don't like sharing these with everybody. What I have I love. Favorite pieces.*

He'd meant *my* work.

It should have felt so good to see them hanging there in a place of honor. I should have turned to him and said, "I did that," and watched his eyes light up in surprise and maybe delight.

But it was the idea of the surprise that stopped me cold. He didn't see me in this work at all. He thought I did high quality quiet watercolors. And the reality was that he had no reason to see me in the giant canvases on his walls because I wasn't sure that was still me. Not knowing scared me. I'd been working out who I was on those canvases. I'd thought I'd found an answer over the last few years in leaving my painting behind me.

But his commission had changed that, had pushed me out into wide-open spaces I wasn't sure yet that I wanted to be in, and I wasn't sure because, like too many other people in the life I'd left behind, he'd written a check to get what he wanted.

He didn't know that picking up that first tube of oils had been an act of insanity as much as it had of faith. And he didn't know that my soul had stretched bigger and my doubts had yawned wider than they ever had before when I'd touched that brush to canvas. And he didn't know that accepting his commission had brought me back to myself. But I didn't owe him any thanks for it because that wasn't why he'd demanded the pictures. He'd wanted what he'd wanted, and he'd written a check, not knowing or understanding what it was doing to me, not knowing that attempting the work could have undone me totally. He'd just wanted his pictures.

I could almost hear Dani's voice inside my head telling me I wasn't being fair, but I pushed that away. I didn't have to be fair when I was standing in front of a guy who, like Donovan and a thousand wealthy guys before them, had simply opened his wallet like it was the key to the world. And exactly like I had done for three years before wising up enough to save myself, I had danced to the bidding of money.

And he had no idea that I knew he was behind it all.

"Why did you pick these?" I asked.

"An investor I was trying to sweet talk invited me to his place in the Hamptons. He had a smaller work by this artist, and I loved it, so I looked up more of her stuff. And I loved that too, so I started buying her pieces."

"The Hamptons? That seems like a strange place for a picture of mountains. Seems like it should be all paintings of sailboats or seascapes. In watercolor, like I paint."

"Good point. The piece I saw was in the guy's library. The art overpowered the room."

"But you still wanted it?"

"Yeah. It reminded me of here. This artist does a lot of pieces like this, with mountains and city kind of merged. Part of what I liked about her paintings was that I couldn't ever decide if the merge was successful, whether I believed what she had painted or not."

"Why would you buy a painting you didn't believe in?"

"Because I understood it. It looked how I always felt when I had to meet up with some big shot in New York for something or other. I was there, but I wasn't ever sure exactly how much a part of things I was. Inside I felt like a kid from suburban Salt Lake dumped out in the city and totally faking it."

His words resonated with me even though I didn't want them to. As much as I'd longed for someone to understand my work, it shook me that he did. Victoria had come closest before, but she mainly had a trained eye to value my technique and an intellectual appreciation for the concepts I explored. It hadn't reached inside her and twisted her guts like producing it had done to me.

But my work had done that for Aidan. It must have for him to pay what he did for it and to keep it in his home, where he let only a select few up to see it. I was facing something every artist dreamed of: a patron who truly got what I did, who appreciated it at a level second only to the one I had to reach to create the work.

And it scared me spitless.

Donovan, who had never understood what I did, had only valued me as a commodity other people wanted. Aidan was still a question mark.

They'd both won me over with easy charm. I'd had no defenses with Donovan, but I'd erected fortresses around myself after him. Aidan had breached them. Had I learned nothing? I wasn't so sure he and Donovan were as different as I needed them to be. Could a guy ambitious enough to become a self-made multimillionaire before age thirty step out of the fast lane and settle down to a quieter life? He hadn't exactly gone into retirement. The local news had reported pretty tirelessly on the vision Vanguard Development had for the Pine Peak resort. Aidan *was* Vanguard, and he was still pushing hard. When Pine Peak was all built and done, I couldn't see him sitting back and calling it good. He'd be tackling the next big thing.

The restlessness would take him like it had the workaholics in Donovan's crew of hard-driving friends. Aidan was wired the same way, to feed off of closing the next deal, the high of the newest idea. No matter what he said, the high of the challenge was what had kept him chasing me.

"What do you think?" he asked, slicing through the noise inside my head.

I think I'm crazy. I think I need to leave. I think this is all too much. I think this can't be real.

"You don't like it?"

I couldn't interpret his tone, a guardedness I hadn't heard in a while.

"Does it matter what I think?"

He looked up at the painting nearest us for a long moment, then back at me. "Yes."

"Why?"

"Because the world is divided into two camps, in some ways. There are people who get this, and people who don't. And I connect to the first group more than the second."

"So you're saying if I don't get this art, if I don't like it, that we're doomed? We can't be friends?"

His eyes flashed. "I've never wanted to be just friends."

"But these two paintings determine that much for you? Who you'll keep close and who you won't?"

"Sometimes. And sometimes it's taking someone to dinner and seeing how they treat the waitstaff, and sometimes it's watching how people handle my nieces and nephews or the way they talk to my employees. But right now, yes, I guess this is the test. And you haven't told me what you think."

He'd done it again—transitioned from the laid-back guy with a bowling alley in his basement to the hard-eyed businessman who was weighing and assessing. And not one part of me wanted to prove anything to him.

"I think it's work done by someone who didn't know herself yet as an artist. But don't take it personally. It's not like I'm an expert." I headed back to the stairs.

"Where are you going?" he asked, following me out. "Are you assuming you failed?"

I whirled to face him, irritated beyond reason by *his* assumption that his opinion mattered. That was straight out of the Donovan Beckman playbook, and I couldn't ever, ever forget that. "I don't care if I failed. I wasn't taking your test. I was telling you the truth." I skimmed down the stairs to the front entry, and he stayed right behind me. "Thanks for the dinner and the ice cream. I'm going to go."

I opened the door. I half expected him to slam it shut and say his piece, but he only stood behind me with his arms crossed and deep furrows carved into his forehead.

I couldn't fake a polite good-bye, so I nodded at him and walked down to my car, thankful for his round driveway that let me pull out without a backward glance.

I had no idea what this meant next. The nervous, angry energy inside me wanted to come out on canvas in wild color. But that canvas was his, bought and paid for. And that meant he had taken something significant from me. Before, I'd almost been angry that his money had forced me to face the fear of losing myself if I picked up a paintbrush again. And although I'd found myself instead, the anger was back, hot sulfur burning in the back of my throat; I couldn't put everything inside of me on canvas for him. I wouldn't be able to paint, not knowing that he would be able to see me so clearly in anything I gave him. I couldn't offer to peel my skin off and pin myself down for examination.

But what was I supposed to do with all the things inside of me pushing so hard to get out?

For the moment, all I could do was channel it into a barely controlled race back down the mountain, whipping the car through turns, hugging the sides of the road like I was skiing a black diamond. I hated that all of this was his too.

How was I supposed to take back my art? I couldn't shut off the switch I'd flipped inside.

After New York, I'd needed to quit it all. The quiet had been important. But quiet would suffocate me now. And yet I didn't want to produce anything to do with Aidan's commission or him or how he made me feel or the way he'd been able to stir up the inside of my head so much I couldn't think straight. I needed my brush, and I needed to create something free of him.

I gripped the steering wheel harder but eased off the speed. Art needed to be mine again. The mountain series I'd been working on had helped me, but I wouldn't have picked it to paint. It wasn't something I'd started for the pure love of doing it. It was a connection to my old days, and even though Aidan had bought my work without knowing me or the Beckmans, he'd still collected it at a time when there was an irrational mania around my paintings, a hype that never would have happened without Donovan's family's connections.

The only thing that could break me free completely from my doubts and Aidan's money was to do work totally on my own and sell it on its own merits, without anyone knowing about the great Leandra Tate. It would have to be the work of Lia Carswell they wanted. Lia with no history, no track record, no nauseatingly thick file of vapid reviews.

I would have to earn my way into galleries and museums all on my own. And Aidan's work would have to wait. Maybe forever. The thought broke the grip of the chest fist, and the chaos inside me organized into a single, driving need.

The colors came to me faster, snatches of imagery, memories of scents and feelings I'd cataloged for the last few years without realizing I'd filed them away. They wanted out. I could hardly wait to get down the mountain now. My vision was massive, and for the first time in years, I would be able to see whether I truly had the talent to match it.

Chapter 19

"What are you doing up?" Dani asked.

I glanced at the digital numbers glowing on the microwave. It was past one in the morning. "I could ask you the same thing."

"I'm studying for an exam on Tuesday because my work schedule isn't going to give me any other time over the next three days. But I also don't have to be at work in five hours."

"I'll survive. I'm not tired. I'll probably go straight there and come home and crash."

"And Chloe will fend for herself like a feral child while you sleep? Cool." Her tone was teasing.

"Yes. Or else she can go play at Avalon's house for a couple hours. I'm sure Tara won't mind, and if that won't work, I'll inject caffeine straight into my veins and wait for her bedtime before I crash and die."

Dani stared at me through bleary eyes. "Sounds good. Are you doing anything right now, or can you help me study?"

"Yeah, I can help."

She padded out on slippered feet and returned with the index cards she always made for quizzing herself. I flipped through them and groaned. "I don't even know what any of these words mean. You so owe me."

"For this and everything. I know it. I can repay you in sandwiches now, and if I ever win the lottery, it's all yours."

"Sandwiches are fine. I want one literally right this second though." It had been hours since I'd downed the ice cream at Aidan's house, hours fueled by nervous energy and the buzz of ideas I could barely harness.

"Turkey coming up. You didn't tell me why you're awake. Anything more specific than insomnia?"

"Oh, no reason. Reinventing myself is all."

Dani deposited the mayo on the counter and turned to face me, blinking a couple of times. It cleared the fog in her eyes, and her expression grew alert. She looked the way our mom used to when we were kids and I said something like, "I didn't break the lamp" when lamps had not until that moment been under discussion. "You had a date tonight. How did I forget that?"

"It can stay forgotten."

"Tell me what happened. Is this reinvention related?"

"Yes. But not the way you're thinking," I added when she frowned. "I'm not turning into anyone new."

"Good, because you're pretty perfect."

I drummed my fingers a few times, trying to figure out how to explain my thought process over the last few crazy hours. "I'm going back to the me I always was. The me who got hijacked a long time ago."

"You mean before . . ." She trailed off, the look on her face suggesting she didn't know if she wanted to pull the trigger on He Who Should Not Be Named.

"Donovan? Yeah."

She leaned back against the counter and studied me. "I don't even know what to ask."

"You don't have to ask anything. I'm going to paint as me, as Lia Carswell. And I'm going to paint what I like. And I'm going to see if it's good enough."

"Of course it's good enough."

"Says my sister who can't draw a stick man. But thanks for saying it." I flipped my laptop around to face her. "The Park City Arts Festival is happening in a month. I have a week and a half to produce something for the juried exhibit, and I'm going to enter. We'll see." Juried exhibits meant that the pieces were judged by people with trained eyes. Gallery owners, art teachers, other artists. I'd have to be good enough to make it in, which I was fairly sure I would. And then I'd have to be good enough to win.

I had no idea what I was going to paint yet, still not sure what to pull out of the impressions swirling inside me. I had no idea if winning was a reasonable hope, but I didn't want to be reasonable. I wanted to be wild and impulsive and *create*. And I wanted people to love it, whatever I painted, and to find an answer in it to questions they didn't know they had. And I wanted it to be all mine, to belong to me and the people who viewed it without any taint of Victoria or Aidan or the other elite who'd decided what was good in New York.

Dani looked at the home page for the festival and grinned. "You'll dominate."

"Thanks, kid. Now make me a sandwich."

An hour later, even I was groggy after running her through her note cards several times. I knew the 6:00 a.m. alarm would go off way too soon, but it would be my last day at the diner for a while, and I could grit through one more morning with Mr. Benny and Red Hat and anyone else who came in for hot coffee and bacon.

Almost anyone. The diner had better stay Aidan-free.

* * *

I threw a painter's cloth over the second Aidan piece in the garage and pushed it to the side, shifting that obligation out of the way to paint what I wanted. I set up my smaller canvas, this one only three feet across, and stared at it, at the whiteness of it, and wondered if this was how writers felt before they made the first keystroke in a new document or how mountaineers felt when they stood at the base of Everest. Exhilarated but not letting their minds wrap completely around the task ahead of them because thinking too far out would steal away the breath they couldn't afford to give up.

I didn't have to paint a mountain, much less climb one. I could choose to never think in mountain analogies again if I wanted to. And knowing I had the freedom to paint whatever I wanted made the challenge bigger still, so big I couldn't even sense the boundaries with my mind. A touch of panic crept in, but it was the top-of-the-roller-coaster panic, not fear.

I picked up a brush. The picture in my head had grown from the feeling I'd woken up with to an image so clear I could barely see past it to take care of my customers earlier at breakfast. Relief had crossed Tom's face when I'd asked for a week off.

I touched the brush to the canvas, and a smear of red appeared exactly as I wanted it. I could build a papier mâché bridge to the moon with the pages that had been written about how great art grew from conflict. Maybe. My other-life art had, for sure. But this was not a painting about that. It was a painting about the joy of a little girl who finds a butterfly to chase—about the joy of loving a little girl like that.

Every now and then, Chloe, who was playing dolls in the corner, would glance at the canvas and ask what I was painting. "Wait and see," I said each time. By the time Tara pulled up to collect Chloe for her playdate with

Avalon, the only friend Chloe would play with, the core of the painting was there. It was still days out from being done, but the soul had shown up already. Chloe ran over to hug me good-bye, and she stopped and stared at the painting. "Dat me," she said, her voice as certain as it was when she shouted the answers that Dora the Explorer demanded every morning.

"How do you know?" I wouldn't have expected a three-year-old to recognize herself in a neo-expressionist piece.

"Dat feel like me."

She had art in her for sure. Regular three-year-olds couldn't sense stuff like this. No way. Her words made me happier than anything the *New York Times* had ever printed about one of my shows. I crouched and hugged her. "I love you. Be good at Avalon's."

Tara's van door slid open, and she waved while I buckled Chloe into her car seat. "I'll drop her off before I start dinner. Thanks for letting her come play."

I used to feel bad when someone took Chloe for a couple hours, but I'd learned once her own friends came over that in a lot of ways, it was easier to have two kids to watch than one. They entertained each other and needed less of my attention. But nothing beat a solid couple hours of no-kid time every now and then. Tara and I were helping each other out, although I was getting the bigger favor, but I'd return it soon.

They pulled out of the driveway, Chloe already in a conversation with Avalon that involved lots of flailing arms, and I turned back to the canvas. I should sleep. That was the whole point of the playdate: to give me a chance to catch up on the sleep I hadn't gotten when my brain wouldn't shut down last night. But I didn't want to. The work was better than a drug. Maybe I would pay for it later, but right now, it was time to paint.

I was deep into flow when the sound of the phone ringing intruded like an especially persistent housefly. I ignored it and tried to dip back into the gap where the world stopped and art started, but after a minute, the phone rang again.

I shook my head, realizing it might be Tara and feeling stupid for not remembering that in the first place. But the caller ID said it was Bethwell. Had Chloe made it in?

"Hello, Ms. Carswell. I have good news for you," Dr. Bray said when I answered. I worried that I wouldn't hear her over the sound of the blood pounding through my temples. "We have a spot for Chloe this fall."

My heart gave a single hard thump, and I closed my eyes and mouthed a thank you to the garage roof, hoping the words would make it up and out to whichever angel had pulled that string for us. "Thank you." The words were too insubstantial to hold the weight of my gratitude, but I meant them with every one of my atoms.

"You're welcome. We look forward to having you on the faculty. I had no doubt our board would be thrilled with the arrangement."

Everything inside of me sang. I almost wished it was Christmas so I could wrap up the news with a giant bow for Dani to open while I shouted, "Ta da! It's your dream come true!"

I hung up with Dr. Bray and pressed Dani's number so fast my hand slipped and I had to try again.

"Everything okay?" she asked, answering immediately and without a hello.

"Everything is awesome," I answered. "Chloe's at Avalon's, but I got a call I think you should know about. It was Bethwell. They have a spot for Chloe!" Total silence met that. "Dani?" I asked, my heart pounding again but not with excitement this time. Had I misunderstood how much she wanted Chloe to go there?

I heard a hiccup, and I couldn't decipher it. Was she crying? When she spoke, her voice sounded flat, but there were no tears in it. "This is going to cost you too much, and I hate myself that I'm still going to say yes," she said.

My heart calmed down. "It's not going to cost me. The paintings are going well. This is going to be better than fine."

"I wasn't thinking about the dollar amount," she said. "When word gets out that you're producing work again, won't it change everything for you in a way that's going to, I don't know, wring you out?"

"I love you for thinking of that. I do. But this commission is the last thing I'm ever going to do as Leandra Tate, so it doesn't matter. If Victoria can't take no for an answer, I won't take Victoria's calls." I slumped against the wall, relief that Dani was going to let Chloe go to Bethwell flooding through me. "I'll tell you a secret if you don't tell anyone else: I'm kind of happy with painting. There are still some scary days, but there have been some mind-blowingly good ones too. I'm coming at this from a different place. I'm going to be okay."

"Yeah?"

"Yeah. So, Bethwell?"

There was a long silence and then a shriek. "Yes, yes, yes! Thank you so much! Chloe is going to die when you tell her. She hasn't stopped talking about it."

I grinned at the delighted stream of words. "You're welcome, and you tell her."

"But this is only happening because—"

"Because you had the good sense to recognize a great school when you heard about it. Tell her, or she'll never know. Got it? It should come from you."

"Thank you," she said again, her voice soft. "Seriously. I owe you."

"No. You guys saved me. I'm starting to get even, that's all."

We hung up, and I switched out my canvas for a blank one, leaning the one in progress carefully against a wall so I could come back to it— so far, it was the beginnings of joy, but full joy still needed some work before it shone from the painting.

I let my brush fly over the new canvas for a while, and my insides stretched again as I painted what it looked like to run one of my favorite trails and let every care fall away. An hour later, I stood back to study it and couldn't decide which one I liked better.

The whine of Griff's garage door opening lured me outside for a break. He backed out and stopped when he saw me waving at him, and he lowered his window to smile. "Hey, Picasso."

"More like Matisse, but hey back," I said. "I need to tell you something. It's important."

His smile faded for a more serious expression. "Sure," he said, and subtle tension stiffened his shoulders. I admired that he stayed put.

"Dani's most favorite thing in the whole world is those waxy chocolate-covered donuts and *Veronica Mars* reruns. Use that information for good, Griff."

Confusion crinkled his forehead for a minute, and then it smoothed out. "You're a good egg."

"Yes."

He grinned and backed the rest of the way onto the road, offering a good-bye wave as he drove off. I had no idea if I'd done a good thing or not, but it had felt right, and every hour I spent in my studio confirmed my instincts. I wouldn't second-guess myself on this. Instead, I ducked into the kitchen for a banana and went right back out to my work. It was better than food, anyway.

Chapter 20

It had been a long time since I'd spent so many days on a high like this, but like real drugs, the crash had to follow. It was Tom's fault this time. I'd ignored messages from Aidan, who had given up after two days. I'd ignored messages from Victoria, who had called every morning and would probably continue for infinity. And I'd ignored two messages from my boss already.

If I could have turned my phone off, I would have, but I couldn't leave Dani without a way to get in touch with me, and that meant putting up with everyone else begging for my attention too. It was Tom's text with a 911 and a panicked emoticon that finally got me to call him back, even though I wasn't due to pick up any shifts until the next week. If Tom was desperate enough to use emoticons, it was bad.

"I need you to come in," he said.

"Can't. I'm in a groove." I wished there were a better way to explain it, but I couldn't find the words. The hours I'd spent in my garage over the last week had produced almost a dozen canvases, all of them good. Two of them might have even been great, including the one of my trail run. But there wasn't a way to put it into words beyond *groove* to explain the impossibility of leaving the creative space to wipe down tables for a morning. I didn't mind the work—never had—but I couldn't stop painting now to do it.

"Good for you, but I'm in the opposite of a groove. Chaos, maybe. Charlene's girl caught something bad, meningitis, and Caden busted his ankle mountain biking on Tuesday. You gotta come in."

My stomach clenched. "Is Charlene okay?"

"I don't know; I barely got the call. Couldn't figure out why she hadn't shown up, but that's a good reason. What Charlene does is going to depend on how her girl does. They think they caught the meningitis early enough, but it's going to be a couple days before either of them is in any kind of decent shape. In the meantime, I need you."

I glanced over at the painting I was working on. I knew from past experience that there was no telling for sure when a creative streak like this would end, when the filter that sometimes stood between my mind's eye and the canvas would reappear and dam the flood pouring out of me. And there was no telling when that happened how long it would be before I found flow again. It was a sure bet that going in to work wouldn't help.

Tom's voice broke a silence I hadn't realized had fallen. "I know you're doing good with your painting, but there was a time when you needed this place way more than I needed you, and I took you in. Now it's—"

"It's okay," I said, not wanting him even for two seconds to feel like he had to beg. I knew the right thing to do. "I'll come in. I don't know how much of my brain will come with me, but I'll work my tail off until Charlene's up to it again. But I won't cover for Caden. He's a chump, and you're going to have to hire someone to replace him until he can work again."

"Fair enough," Tom said, and the relief in his voice was so palpable that a knot of guilt lodged in my stomach at the notion that he'd worried even for a second that I wouldn't help. "I have one of the evening girls covering today, but I'll need you tomorrow."

"I'll be there." We hung up, and I turned to face my paintings. In a single phone call, my time had become infinitely more precious. I had three days to submit my work, and I'd lost the luxury of playing with ideas. Maybe that was okay. I already knew which two needed to be finished, and I swapped the first of them out for the one on the easel. It was good. As good as anything I'd ever done, even on this smaller scale. But I had to make it better, and there was a hard stop to the time I could spend doing it. I pulled out the right oil colors and set them in easy reach. Then I disappeared into the painting one last time.

* * *

"I've never been so glad to see anyone in my life," Tom grumbled when I walked into the kitchen the next morning. It was still pre-sunrise gray outside, but the familiar diner smells had woken me up as soon as I stepped through the door.

"Stop it. You're going to give me a big head."

"Doubt it. Don't get me wrong. I'm in a take-what-I-can-get mode, help-wise, but out of curiosity, did your brain come in today?"

"Wish I could promise, but I'm itchy to get back to my studio. Can we leave it at 'I'll do my best?'" The front door swung open to admit a new customer, and I scooped up the coffeepot. "So it begins."

We didn't talk about anything except the steady stream of orders coming in until Mr. Benny, who had eyed me as if my presence were a personal insult to him, climbed off his stool to leave for whichever destination he liked to drive people crazy at next. I bet he sat in the public library and heckled people's book choices for amusement.

"You been jumpy," Tom noted when the door closed behind Mr. Benny.

It was getting worse as the morning wore on. "Yeah. Sorry."

"He'll come in."

I stopped and peered at him. "Who?"

"He's been in every morning."

"Asking for me?"

"No. But I'm expecting him to break down any day now and ask if you quit or went on vacation."

"Thanks for the heads-up." In a weird way, Aidan was the reason I'd been able to pay attention to my diner work. Instead of wandering back to my paintings, my senses had been tuned to warn me if he walked in. Every time the door opened, I'd freeze for a tiny fraction before turning to see who it was, knowing even before I did that it wouldn't be him because I hadn't sensed a change in the air. I grabbed a rag and headed out to do some side work while we waited for the early lunch crowd and distracted myself by trying to think of a word for the shift in the molecules that happened when he showed up. It was like the air thickened the way it did between two magnets when they sensed each other but you held them apart at that point where they wanted to pull toward each other.

I'd filled in the sweeteners on the next-to-last table when the door opened and the air changed. I looked up, glad I'd had that fraction of a second to compose my face. "Hi," I said. My voice wanted to come out as cold or awkward, but I kept it as neutral as my face. I didn't want him to read anything in it—not frustration or relief or annoyance.

He hovered inside of the door, a coil of energy. Usually he was relaxed, as if he were on the verge of stretching out and sinking into a *Times* article or clasping his hands behind his head to take in a view. Now he looked caught between moments, a hesitancy I'd never seen in him before. Instead of saying anything, he turned and walked back out.

I looked over my shoulder to see if Tom had noticed. His eyebrows arched. He'd missed nothing. He shook his head and looked back down at the grill; the scrape of steel against steel rang as he cleaned it for Aidan's order. Business as usual. Good plan.

I looked down at the tin of sweeteners in my hand. It was full, and it was the next-to-last one I had to tend to. I dumped them out and replaced them, putting each one with its corner slightly higher than the one before it so it created a pretty sunburst shape fanning out from the top. With each packet I replaced, I came up with a theory to explain Aidan's sudden retreat. *One. He only wanted to be here if I wasn't. Two. He forgot I worked here.* By number twelve (he'd misremembered my attractiveness and decided to run before he got caught), the door opened and he stood there again, this time carrying a brown package tied with twine.

Chapter 21

"I guess I've known it was you," I said, taking it from him. Seeing him with the package made me realize I'd known it for a while at some level.

"Is that a good or a bad thing?"

Both. You're so thoughtful, and you're also so many things I don't want you to be. I ignored his question and asked one of my own. "How did you get the food to my house?"

"I had someone pay Caden fifty bucks to look up your address and drop it off."

Tom growled. I wasn't sure Caden would be coming back to work ever now.

"Why did you do all this as a secret?" I asked the second-most-burning question I'd had about these packages after "Who?" It's not like he'd made his interest in me a secret at any point.

"I wanted to do something nice for you," he said. "I didn't think you'd let me."

"I'm not opposed to people doing nice things for me," I said, rubbing my hand over the brown paper. Whatever it was inside was light and cool to the touch.

"Yes, she is," Tom said.

I turned around and glared at him.

Aidan held up his hands. "Maybe you are, and maybe you aren't, but I figured for sure if you knew this stuff was coming from me, you'd think it was a gimmick or something. It's not. I wanted to, that's all." He smiled, but it showed strain, and I wondered if that was my fault. "I don't know what happened the other night. I've replayed it, and I don't think I did or said anything out of line. But the way you took off out of there, I worried that I had . . ." He swallowed like the next words pained him to say them.

"I worried that I had scared you somehow, and I wanted to say I was sorry."

I opened my mouth to reassure him that he hadn't scared me, at least not in the way he meant, but he held up his hand. "Let me finish, please. I realize if I really did scare you that coming in here in person might only make it worse, but I had to see for myself that you're okay, especially after you didn't show up for a bunch of days."

"You didn't scare me," I said. *Not physically.*

"Okay." Some of the worry left his eyes.

I shifted the package between my hands. "Couldn't you have snapped your fingers and sent a minion to check on me or something?" I didn't know if I meant it as a joke or an accusation.

He paused like he was trying to find the right answer. "I do the important jobs myself."

Wow. Yeah, that was the right answer.

The door opened to admit a couple of young guys who looked like they needed Tom's Hangover Cure, a protein-packed omelet favored by some of the partiers who came to play in the canyons. I frowned at them and then gave Aidan an apologetic look. "I'd better take care of them. I'll bring some coffee to your table in a minute."

He shook his head. "It's probably hard to believe, but it's never been my thing to stay where I'm not wanted. I don't want to stress you out. I only came to give you that and apologize," he said, nodding at the package. "Stick it in the fridge if you don't open it soon. Felt like I owed you for cheating you out of real dessert with store-bought ice cream. See you around, Lia." He shoved his hands in his pockets and walked out. I watched until his truck disappeared, but one of the hungover boys clinked his silverware, and I snapped out of it.

Tom eyed me when I set the package in the fridge. "You're not going to open that?"

"Customers," I said, reaching for the coffee.

"Those boneheads will wait. See what he got you."

He didn't need to tell me twice. I undid the paper to reveal an amazing-looking piece of tiramisu from Rosetti's. A note in strong black handwriting stuck to the top. "*I don't understand you at all, but I finally see you don't want to be figured out. It shouldn't have taken so long. Sorry.*"

Was this fresh? Did he stop in at Rosetti's every day to bring me a piece until I came back? He would have had to.

I tucked the twine in my pocket, and my hand brushed against it every time I fished my order pad out for the rest of my shift. Every time I touched it, the rough texture chafed at more than my skin. It irritated my conscience too. Aidan's gifts hadn't been wildly extravagant compared to what he could have afforded. But he'd chosen simple things that reflected what he knew about me the best he could. I'd commented on daffodils and gotten a book about wildflowers. He'd seen me painting and sent me higher quality brushes. I'd complimented his sandwich and gotten gourmet food.

And I'd glanced at a tray longingly and gotten tiramisu.

If he'd come in with a whiff of alpha male on him, I would have shut him down faster than Tom could flip a hotcake. If Aidan had brought me anything flashy, I'd have followed him out and handed it back.

But he'd brought me dessert because he thought he'd shortchanged me. This was the gesture of an apologetic man, not one still trying to score points. I slid the tiramisu into the restaurant fridge and got the boys their coffee, but I did it all mechanically while my brain looped a single question: How wrong had I been about Aidan? And should I be relieved or worried about the undertone of good-bye in his note?

* * *

I often came home from Tom's too tired to do more than plop down beside Chloe for an episode of *My Little Pony* while I recharged enough to chase her until bedtime. Today I rolled into the house on a wave of restless energy. Dani was still in sweats, which meant she didn't need to leave for a while.

"Do I have time for a run before you take off?" I asked.

"Sure. Want some before you go? You can eat and burn it off." She held out a bag of chocolate Donettes, and I grinned.

"The donut fairy bring those?"

"Griff dropped by with them. Said he had extra from a staff meeting and asked if we wanted them."

"He said he had store-bought donuts from a staff meeting he held at his high-end restaurant, where they can make anything they want from scratch?"

"Yeah." She stopped chewing. "Why would he get these? I only eat them because I'm weird. It's not like they're real food."

"Might be interesting to ask him," I said.

She stared at me like I'd suggested we take up llama farming. "That wouldn't be interesting at all."

"You're right. Watch for falling *Veronica Mars* references," I muttered on my way back to my room. I'm sure Griff would find a way to be out on the deck soon, working some Logan versus Duncan questions into the conversation. (As if there was a debate.)

I changed and headed out to the trail, my thoughts racing way ahead of my feet. Out of everything Aidan had done or said since he first began flirting with me for real, the one thing that had gotten to me most was his saying he wouldn't be coming back into T&R's. It wasn't like one of Chloe's attention-getting threats when I wouldn't comply with her sudden rule changes in Candyland and she vowed to quit. He'd said it with a tinge of discomfort, like he was facing the fact for the first time that I didn't want him around, *really* facing it.

I didn't get it. For months he'd been handing me lines, trying to make me blush. He'd been cocky when he'd moved in for that first kiss. He'd had hard, angry eyes but soft, tender lips. He was the guy in work boots who read the *Times* Arts section. He was a multimillionaire who cut down trees to build what he wanted but then turned the felled trees into something good. He was a constant contradiction, now that I thought about it.

If Aidan had been the same guy from the beginning that I'd seen this afternoon, maybe I would have said yes the first time he'd asked for a date. The guy this afternoon was humble and considerate. So which was the real Aidan? And if his player persona was only that—a persona—why? If it got him more women, was it getting him the kind he wanted?

The farther I ran, the more questions I had, and by the time I reached the last quarter mile up the street to home, I was left with the biggest question of all: Was I okay with never knowing the answers? Because that was what Aidan's good-bye meant.

No.

I wanted the answers, or Aidan would always be this puzzle I never solved, the great What If. What if guys could ruin your life, and I'd made a firm rule about not letting another guy ruin my life. Which meant there was only thing left to do.

Chapter 22

"Where we going?" Chloe asked for the millionth time as we wound up the canyon road.

"To visit my friend," I said.

"She nice?"

"He's a boy friend," I answered and winced as soon as I said it, but Chloe jumped on it before I could rephrase.

"My friend has a boyfriend. He gave her a rock."

"Not a boyfriend. A boy who is a friend." I thought about making a pun on how smart guys give rocks to their girlfriends but then decided it would lead to a way longer explanation about diamonds and carbons than I was prepared to make. Although . . . it would distract me from what I was about to do. And that was a good thing.

"You love him?"

"No!" Who loved someone after one date? I had barely even decided I liked him.

"You kiss him?"

"I think I see a mountain goat," I said, pointing out of the side window. Chloe turned to look at the goat I'd invented, but the half minute she spent searching for it was enough to distract her from questions about kissing.

"He have a dog?" Chloe asked.

"Yes. A nice dog," I said.

"How long till we get there?"

"Too soon," I said as the sign for the Pine Peak turnoff appeared. We rumbled over the gravel lot and parked. Aidan's pickup sat near the trailer office, and I took it as a good sign. I pulled my phone out and dialed his number, trying to figure out the best way to explain I'd crashed his jobsite. He didn't answer. I called again, and it went straight to voice mail.

Not good. I hadn't turned the engine off yet, and I considered throwing the car into reverse and abandoning this whole stupid plan. Except I wouldn't come back again. I knew it. I turned off the car and got Chloe out, keeping a firm grip on her hand so she didn't bolt off after a butterfly or a ground squirrel.

I poked my head into the office, but the only guy in there was someone I didn't recognize.

"Can I help you?" he asked.

"Uh, I'm looking for Aidan."

"Aidan?"

"Dat's her boyfriend," Chloe offered unhelpfully.

I squeezed her hand to shush her. "I meant Aidan Cormack. Could you radio him?" It came out in an embarrassing stammer.

"I better ask my boss first. I don't radio Mr. Cormack directly."

Right. Because one did not call up millionaire bosses and summon them. I'd sort of forgotten about that element of dealing with the rich; they often had many layers protecting them from the regular folk. But . . . Aidan wasn't like that, I didn't think.

"Boss? Mr. Cormack has a visitor asking to see him." The desk guy turned to me. "What's your name?"

"Tell him it's the artist."

"She said to say it's the artist, Sully."

He released the button, and static was followed by silence before the radio crackled to life again.

"Send her to the lodge," Aidan's voice said.

"Yes, sir."

I promised the guy I could find it, and with Chloe still firmly in hand, I wound my way up toward the spot where Aidan had first kissed me. Maybe that was why he'd picked it. Chloe chattered all the way there, trying to get away to pick a few flowers, but I didn't let her go because it would have taken forever to rein her in. "On the way back to the car, sweet pea," I had to promise her a dozen times.

I paused on the side of the lodge, bracing myself for the first glimpse I got of Aidan. Chloe tugged my hand again, and I rounded the corner to find empty space, the site of the future deck looking as vacant as the first time I'd set up my easel there.

"What we doing?" Chloe asked when I stood for almost a minute trying to decide what to do.

"Good question." Where was Aidan? And what was I supposed to do until he showed up?

When Chloe tugged on my hand again, I let her go. She ran to the edge of the meadow and crouched to inspect a bluebell. I watched for a while, mixing the colors for the flower in my mind.

"That's what you were painting the first time you came here."

Aidan's voice sent a thrill down my spine, and I whirled to see him standing in front of the lodge door. Chief's tags jangled from somewhere nearby.

"Hi," I said for lack of anywhere better to start.

"Hi. You brought company. She yours?" He nodded out at Chloe and sounded curious about the possibility, not concerned, which I had to give him credit for. I couldn't count the number of times guys had checked me out at the park only to become busy elsewhere when Chloe had run up to me with some find. It always made me want to punch them on Dani's behalf, but of course, they weren't even worth the time it would take to swing.

"She's the niece I babysit, Chloe. We get to hang out a lot."

He nodded. I waited for him to say something else. He didn't.

Right. Well, I was the one with the questions. "I was wondering something."

He pursed his lips, then said, "Okay. Shoot."

I swallowed and stuck my hands in my back pocket. Wait, that probably looked like I was trying to stick my chest out. I pulled them out and wiped my palms on my thighs instead. "You're not one thing," I said. That was a useless statement. "I mean, you change how you act sometimes. I get confused. *Got* confused," I corrected myself since I wasn't sure we would be speaking in anything other than the past tense ever again. "When you first came into the diner, we didn't talk at all. Then we had normal conversations. Then you got all . . . I don't know. Flirty. In your pickup artist way, which I don't like."

His eyebrows had lowered, a sure sign that I was making the mess I'd expected to. I eyed the path to the parking lot and wondered if I'd feel stupider for standing here and continuing the conversation or taking the long walk of shame back to my car with his eyes on me the whole way. "Sorry. I'm not explaining this very well."

"No, I understand you. And you're explaining yourself honestly, I guess."

"What I'm trying to say is that if you acted the way you did this morning all the time, I would want to hang out with you. All the time." My face flamed.

"I'm not sure what to say to that," he said after a pause so long I could have climbed up the black diamond trail and back again.

"I'm asking why," I said. "Why do you come on so strong sometimes and other times you're cool and mellow? Sometimes you seem cocky, and the first time you kissed me you even seemed almost mad. And then suddenly you're nice again, and it's a totally different kind of kiss. I don't get you."

Chief came lolling out, and Aidan crouched to give him a thorough scratch around the head and ears. I recognized that he was buying time while he figured out his answer, but I felt stupid standing there. The nearby grass rustled, and Chief lunged for it, leaving Aidan nothing to do but straighten and shove his hands into his pockets. He stared into the distance for a minute, then faced me. "I want to point out all the ways you're confusing too, like kissing me one minute and then tearing out of my house like I was chasing you with a meat cleaver. But I won't point it out because that would be avoiding your question, and it's a pretty fair one."

Chloe shouted then, a happy shout while she pounced on something, and I moved closer so she couldn't get too much of a head start if she decided to take off. Her shout caught Chief's attention, and he loped over to sniff her, making her giggle as she held her hand out to him to smell.

Aidan followed me over. "Cute kid."

"Thanks," I said, turning so I could track him and Chloe at once. "You were going to explain yourself?" I shut my eyes for a second. "Sorry. I meant that in a non-Spanish Inquisition kind of way."

"Ever wanted to be famous?"

I'd had a taste of it already. "No."

"Good. It's pretty bad. I hate to be a cynic." He stared into the distance and sighed. "Life has tried to make me one, I think. Coming back here is my way of trying to outrun it, but it's going to take time. I'm still convinced everyone who meets me wants something from me. Funding, a handout . . . something."

"I didn't," I objected. "I think I only gave you things. Like bacon."

"Yeah. Which takes me back to something you said earlier. You said we had 'normal' conversations at first. But we didn't. Do you remember the first thing we talked about that wasn't food related?"

Not really. I hadn't known I was going to have a wild almost-crush on him, or I would have tracked every interaction we'd ever had so I could analyze it. I shook my head. "Zhaday the tool, I think."

"I was reading an article on Senegal, and you glanced at it and said that one of your favorite singers was from there. And then you poured me coffee and walked away. And it was cool. Because it wasn't normal."

My face heated again. It wasn't the first time my normal had not been someone else's normal. I wished I could claim artistic eccentricity and brush off those incidents, but I knew how people perceived me, and it bothered me. Every time.

He touched my arm, bringing me out of the haze of awkward memories. "If someone tells me they like Senegalese music, they're usually trying to impress me when they've never even heard it. I haven't heard it. But you said it because it's actually true. You like it. I could tell. Things aren't usually so simple."

"They can be. You hang around rich people too much." I'd said it to make him laugh. He didn't.

"Probably. And I hang around people who want to use me to join the rich-people ranks. So it was pretty refreshing to hear someone who had no idea who I was state an opinion that was yours and yours alone about something most people don't pay any attention to. It told me a lot about you right away, and I wanted to know more. So . . ." He stopped and fidgeted, watched Chloe and Chief for a minute. "Is my face as red as yours was a minute ago?"

"No," I said. My face heated again that he'd noticed the first time.

"I guess I'd just better say this. I'm used to women who want me as a trophy."

I couldn't help it. My mouth twitched, and he caught it, even though I pressed my lips together to stop them.

"Laugh," he said. "I know how it sounds, but it's true. I know you read the *Times*. At least, you do over my shoulder." True. "I'm guessing you never read the society pages?"

I shook my head. That was the province of Hilaire Beckman, who had always pretended a mention on those pages was vulgar but who lived to see her name in conjunction with the elaborate fund-raising soirées she and Creston Beckman had regularly shelled out to attend.

"My name used to show up in those a lot. I got a reputation as a 'modelizer.' Do you even know what that is? Because that was an eye-opener for me." I nodded because I could figure out what it meant. He pushed his hand through his hair. "I had no idea when I hit a certain level of success in the business world that it was going to create so many social obligations, places I *had* to be to schmooze. I bet you think I'm an awesome schmoozer."

"Yeah," I admitted.

"I am. But I hate it. It bores me stupid. And one thing I had to figure out quick was that it was always better to bring a date of my choice so I didn't have a dozen women trying to stick to me the whole night."

"Only a half a dozen."

"Make fun, but I'm not even exaggerating. I always saw it for what it was, by the way. And it was never about me. It was about the money. It was one of the best things about selling the company and coming back here."

"To hide?"

"No. To reenter reality."

That's what I'd done. "I get that."

His eyes searched mine for a long moment. "You don't drop a lot of clues about yourself, but they're always pretty fascinating when you do."

"Don't try to figure me out," I begged. "I'm not that interesting."

"False. But I'll let that go. Anyway, I still haven't had a ton of time to date while I get this place running, but I want to. And not because I'm a party guy either," he said, his tone warning me not suggest it. "It's because I'm hanging out with my brothers and sisters and their kids, and I remembered that's how I always thought things would go for me, but I forgot how to get there. I'm not playing, Lia. And if I am, it's for keeps."

The words warmed me. I didn't think I'd ever want marriage again, and right then, Chloe was enough kid for me, but she and Dani wouldn't live with me forever, and the thought of their absence created an echoing hole inside of me. Eventually I'd want a kid or two of my own, and I was traditional enough to want to do that the old-fashioned way. And here was a beautiful guy telling me he wanted the same things. But I still had questions.

"I respect all that. But if you wanted something real, why were you so . . . not real with me sometimes? Why did Aidan, guy on the prowl, keep showing up?"

He groaned. "It's because I'm an idiot. Prowling is a habit. Before I sold the company, I'd get in these high-stakes business situations, and everything was adrenaline fueled. It's stupid. I ran at full bore all the time, and it didn't switch off when business was over and it was time to date. Even women trying to snag their trophy liked to play hard to get, and I had to win them. It's all so messed up. It's just how I was used to talking to women," he said, pressing the heels of his hands into his eyes. "I was interested in you because you were so different from other women I'd known, and I should have met real with real. I thought I was getting better at that lately."

"You're pretty Tarzan-y," I muttered, flashing back to his deliberate invasion of my personal space when he'd cornered me in the diner storeroom. And the first time he'd kissed me.

"Yeah. But I'm not always a jerk."

"What was that about?"

"We're talking about the first time I kissed you, right here?" he asked, pointing at the ground.

I nodded.

"Old habits again. You'd been standoffish, and then Mike walks up to me and suddenly you figured out that I'm not a wage slave, and you warm right up. I knew you had no idea I was Ted Cormack, but I thought you were still status-hunting on a smaller scale because you figured I was foreman or something."

"I think I might be offended," I said slowly. He'd thought I was a gold digger. It was almost—but not quite—funny how wrong he was. "I was nicer to you because you were kind to that Mike guy, and it surprised me, not because I suddenly thought you were a big shot."

"It's a reflex, and it's one that stinks. It felt like I was being used again, like you were going to be nice to me because I was suddenly worth your time if I made good money. I decided to use you back, and since I wanted a kiss, I took it instead of earning it."

I flinched. That was brutal and ugly.

"I know. When you still refused to go out with me and kicked me off the mountain so you could paint, I realized I might have it all wrong. And the way you treat Mr. Benny? That shows real kindness, and that's not something I see every day. So I decided even if you were kind of opportunistic, there was still something good and real in you that was worth putting up with."

Worth putting up with? How swoony. "I kind of want to hit you right now."

"Can't blame you."

Still, I had to give him credit. He was far more self-aware than Donovan, and I always respected honesty. I'd run away to find it again, to find the real. It spoke volumes that Aidan had done the same thing. In his own way, he was a bigger mess than I was. We'd both been damaged by the life wealth and fast-paced living could confuse people into believing was the end-all of everything. But both of us had made the conscious choice to quit letting it define us.

A breeze kicked up, and the scent of the meadow floated over to me, clearing my head and leaving me with one simple truth: Aidan was not Donovan. It was why I'd come here—the quiet parts of me had already known that. While there were a hundred things to be afraid of about getting involved with Aidan, none of them had to do with losing myself and disappearing into his world. His was defined by the same things mine was; I could see that now—hard work, family, roots.

I breathed in deeply, and the cool air filled my lungs and expanded in a more-than-physical way—it was like a tiny baptism inside, sloughing away the old hurts and fears that had nothing to do with Aidan. It filled me with possibility, and I exhaled a breath of resolve. He was telling me things about himself and his motives that I'd begun admitting to myself from the second he'd walked out of the diner earlier. I was ready to take the last step toward him.

I drew in another deep breath, this time for courage and to steady my nerves. "Okay. You were kind of an idiot, but I get why. But I've been a bigger idiot. I'm sorry I just figured that out. Let's start over." I stepped toward him and placed my hand on his arms, which he'd folded across his chest. I smiled up at him and tilted my head in a way that asked for a kiss. This moment was as perfect and balanced as my favorite Matisse painting.

He stayed still for a tiny forever, his eyes locked with mine, and then his expression closed with a flash of regret as plain as a shutter dropping into place. He took a step back, and I snatched my hand back. "It's not that easy," he said.

I dropped my gaze to the ground so he wouldn't see the tears of humiliation stinging my eyes. His words were heavy with regret. "I wish I were above my ego. I really do. But you've shut me down so many times at this point that I don't know what you want from me, and I've given you several different versions of me to choose from. The other night when I brought you to my home, I showed you the realest me there is, and that's who you walked out on."

He whistled for Chief and turned to face me again. "I'm glad you came up here today. I'm glad we talked this through and figured it all out. But your instincts seemed to be telling you all along that we're a bad fit, and I guess we both should have been listening. I'm sorry." His radio crackled something about a lift, and he turned it down. "I should go. Stay as long as you want. And Chloe can pick all the flowers she wants. I'm going to go check on some things." He gave me an uncomfortable nod and headed back toward the lodge.

There were a hundred things I wanted to say to that, but it was my actions that had shut him down, and words couldn't fix that. And as much as part of me wanted to dig a hole where I stood and bury myself in it, the part of me where paintings grew stirred, and I called out before he disappeared from earshot. "Aidan!"

He turned in the doorway.

"There's a reason I ran out of your house that night, but it's not what you think. You know that painting you saw me working on here the first day?" He nodded. "Remember it, okay?"

He hesitated like he was trying to figure out the point of the request, but he nodded again and disappeared.

Chloe wandered over with a fistful of flowers. "He go bye bye?" I stooped down to hug her and brush some pollen off her nose, staring over her head toward the lodge. "Just for now, I hope." And I meant it. I hoped it with all my whole being. I still had a shot left to take, and if it didn't work, then Aidan and I were never meant to be.

Chapter 23

Dani poked her head into the garage and wrinkled her nose. "You want the door open right now?"

A clap of thunder punctuated her question. I glanced over my shoulder to catch another flash of heat lightning. "Definitely." The charge of ozone in the air was exactly what my imagination would smell like if I could bottle the scent. I smiled at the thought of explaining it to Aidan that way.

Dani edged farther in. She was pretty careful to stay out of my space when I was on a painting jag, which I had been since the late afternoon when she'd returned home from a final. "Can I see?" she asked.

"Sure."

She rounded the canvas, coming to a sudden stop and gasping. "I think you're brilliant until I see another one of your paintings, and then I realize when I thought the last one was brilliant, I had no idea what I was talking about because the new one is pure genius."

"Wow. Thank you."

"I mean it," she said, her voice soft again. "It makes my heart hurt to look at that."

The words sounded bad, but her tone sounded like it was a very good thing. "And I mean it when I say thank you," I said. "It matters to me that you love what I do."

"I do," she said. "You know that. I haven't always understood it. But this one . . . I get this one. I feel it, I guess is the right way to say it."

"Yeah?" I watched her study the painting. "What does it feel like?"

She studied the two entwined flowers I had painted, glacier lilies I'd seen on the mountain with Aidan. "I'm sure I'm about to sound like a bad imitation of a big-shot New York art critic by talking about how I respond and not what I see, but it's the best way to explain it. So I'll start with this. I get that we're looking at two flowers. I get that, okay?"

I nodded, not sure where she was going.

"But they don't feel like two flowers. When I found out I was pregnant with Chloe, Brandon bailed. He didn't do it all at once, but over time, he disappeared utterly and completely. And there was a huge hole in my life. At first I thought I wanted him back. I was so scared about keeping Chloe and raising her by myself. I thought it would be so much easier if he were here helping me figure everything out. I wanted him back so much it was like an ache. Then Chloe was born, and I thought I would collapse under the weight of her. I mean, not her teeny self but the reality of her and this whole life that she is and how I could feel myself failing her before it all started."

I dropped my brush and pulled her into a hug as her first tear fell. "Baby girl, I'm so sorry I wasn't here for that."

She hugged me back, hard. "You were here soon enough." She pushed away from me and dashed the tears away. "But that's not what I'm trying to tell you. When Chloe was about a week old, I got up to nurse her in the middle of the night, and I was so tired I thought I would die. She wrapped her hand around my pinkie and fell asleep while she was eating, then she twitched in her sleep and squeezed my finger, and suddenly, I knew it was going to be okay, that I would tear down and rebuild the whole world for her with my bare hands if she needed me to. And that's when I realized it wasn't Brandon I was missing. It was someone who would look at my baby and love her like I did, someone who could understand that emotion I couldn't explain."

She walked closer to the painting and studied in silence for another long moment. "The way I imagine that will be, finding someone who loves me and Chloe like that? If I could paint that future *us*? That's what it would look like."

I cleared my throat once and then again so I could get words past the lump that had filled it. "You understand what I do better than any New York art critic ever did."

"Is this the one you're sending in for the festival?"

"No, those are already in." I walked over to the two paintings I'd photographed and submitted, the one Chloe had seen herself in and the one that showed the joy of a trail run. I would hear soon whether I'd made the cut, but my gut told me I had a good chance.

"I love both of those," Dani said. She stared at the pictures for another minute, then took her turn clearing her throat. "Um."

I narrowed my eyes. That was a favor-wheedling um. "Yes?"

"So Chloe's asleep."

"You need to go do something? I can keep an ear out for her. Bring the monitor down."

She reddened. "That would be good. But, uh, I won't be that far away."

My eyebrow rose. "Spit it out."

"Griff and I were talking the other day—"

"Oh, *reallllly*," I drawled, and her flush deepened.

"Shut up. We were both out on the deck. And he mentioned the *Veronica Mars* movie and how his sister is all nuts for it and how he didn't get it."

Good one, Griff. "So you're going to watch it."

It shouldn't have been possible, but she went even redder, which made her extra effort to sound casual even funnier. "I told him he should probably watch the series first before he saw it, and he asked if I had it, and I said yes and that he could borrow it sometime." Her words got faster. "Then he asked if I minded watching it with him at first in case he had any questions about it, and I said I thought that would be fine, and then just now when I was on the deck—"

"Where he happened to be too?"

"Shut up. So I was on the deck, and he suggested that maybe now would be a good time to watch the movie, and I said I'd check with you about keeping an ear out for Chloe."

"So you know he doesn't need you to explain anything to him, right?"

Her blush faded, and a small smile appeared. "Oh, I know."

And seeing that bit of happiness on her face might have made me fall in love with Griff myself if I wasn't heading down that path toward someone else. I'd spent three days trying to hide from that realization, but as I worked on this painting for Aidan, every stroke of my paintbrush uncovered more of the truth.

"Enjoy the make out. I mean, the movie."

"Oh, I will," she said, not specifying which one, which made me laugh. "I won't be gone long." She scooted for the stairs but stopped at the foot. "You sure you're okay with this?"

"Beyond okay. I'm insistent. Go."

When the door closed behind her, I grinned and only grinned bigger when it opened long enough for her to shove the baby monitor onto the landing and disappear again. Every instinct in me told me Griff was the right fit for her.

I went back to the painting. The same instincts told me I'd found the right fit too, but that wasn't going to matter if it was only *my* instincts talking. It had been a long time since I'd trusted them, but I'd never wanted to believe them as much as I did about this.

Chapter 24

The road to Aidan's house looked a lot different in the warm light of late afternoon, but I remembered seeing a clump of aspens at the turnoff to his place that I hoped would guide me right. It had been a white-knuckled drive all the way up the mountain so far, which made me think of how I'd driven away from his house the same way last time. Even though I was running to something and not from it this time, I couldn't make my hands relax. What happened next mattered too much.

I should be seeing the aspens any moment, and my stomach fluttered when the evergreens passing by my window blended into each other with no hint of a driveway. Finally, a mile past where I'd expected them and only a few minutes short of utter panic, I spotted the clump I was looking for.

I slowed and made the turn, forcing my hands to stay steady as the road rose higher to reach Aidan's house. We'd driven forever when I'd followed him up here after our dinner at Rosetti's, but this time the miles flew by, and suddenly I was there, pulling into the driveway in the falling dusk. I hoped I'd come late enough to catch Aidan home from work, but there was no way to tell from the empty driveway if he was gone or had parked in the long garage I spotted in the remaining daylight.

I could make out all the details of his house I'd missed in the dark—the natural stone and wood that joined in striking angles. I'd seen mountain homes that were so aggressively modern that the contrast to their setting was eye-jarring. Aidan's home was unapologetically contemporary yet still in harmony with the woods surrounding it.

I wondered if I'd get a chance to see what the view from his great room actually looked like, and I sat for a moment picturing it, but it was a delaying tactic, and I knew it. I squeezed the steering wheel like it was a life preserver, my last connection to safety, and let go.

The paintings slid easily enough from the back seat, but when I hefted them into my arms, I felt like an ant trying to carry a giant crumb except way less graceful. They weren't even big paintings, only three feet long each, but I'd agonized for hours over the right frame for the one that was my reason for coming here today. And now I held that one and another one wrapped in cardboard to protect them. It was impossible not to think about the situation as some kind of metaphor. *This whole relationship is in my hands, like these paintings. I have to protect this relationship like I would these paintings.* I tried pushing the cheesy thoughts out of my head, but as I climbed the steps to Aidan's front door and juggled the paintings when I couldn't see the stairs, I thought about how my package was symbolic of the figurative step I was trying to take.

Ugh. Stupid. Time to stop thinking about symbols and ring the doorbell. It was weird that there would even be a doorbell to ring. A house this size should have a doorman standing out front at all times, ready to spring into action.

Nothing happened when I pressed the bell. I waited for half a minute, trying to decide if I needed to give Aidan time to cross the house to answer or if I should ring again in case he hadn't heard it or in case the doorbell didn't work. I rang again and waited a full minute this time. If the doorbell was broken, what was I supposed to do? I remembered the alarm Aidan had disarmed the other night with its eye scanner. What would it do if I opened the door and stuck my head in to holler "Hello?" like a nosy neighbor? Drop a cage around me and trap me where I stood?

Intruder cages? I didn't need a clearer sign that my imagination was getting the better of me. I drew a cleansing breath, held it, and pressed the doorbell one more time right as the door opened and startled my cleansing breath out of me in an inelegant *whoosh*.

"Lia? What are you doing here?" Aidan asked, standing in the doorway in bare feet and jeans, his hair poking up and his eyes blinking like he was still clearing sleep from them.

Crud. There were a few marginally worse ways I could think of to have started this visit than pulling Aidan from a nap. But not many. I lifted a hand as much as I dared to offer a tiny wave without dropping the painting. "Hi. I, uh, brought something for you?"

A frown crossed his face. "I'm confused. I thought our last conversation pretty much wrapped things up."

"Maybe it should have. But I owe you an explanation for why I ran away from your house before you decide you're done with us, and this seemed like the right way to do it." I glanced down at the load wearing out my arms and shoulders. "It's not brown paper and twine, but I needed to make sure nothing happened to the canvas."

He leaned against the door and scrubbed his hand through his hair like he was trying to remove the last of the sleepiness from his brain. "I think you're going to make me crazy," he said, dropping his head against the door and closing his eyes for a moment.

The chest fist appeared, squeezing hard without any warning. His response was far from the "Come in. Let's pick up where we left off, no questions asked" I'd imagined. He straightened and jerked his head for me to follow him to the great room. "I need caffeine if we're going to do this. Can I get you anything?"

I shook my head while he made his way to a bar built into the far corner while I leaned the paintings against the sofa. I turned to the windows and gasped. It was a thousand times more intense than I'd imagined. Mountain peaks loomed in the distance, the tallest one looking snowdusted because of its permanent glacier. The yard in back encompassed a beautiful pool before stretching for at least an acre of smooth lawn broken by a stream cutting through. Small boulders lined its sides and practically begged for someone to sit on them and paint or read or dream. The lawn stretched out to meet the tree line as it sloped downward, an unbroken expanse of firs and pines as far as I could see. I pictured them with their own coat of snow and wanted to cry at the perfection.

"It's nice, isn't it?"

Aidan's voice made me jump. I hadn't heard him walk up. "Yeah. Amazing. Way better than my imagination."

Silence fell between us, an uncomfortable one. An air of waiting surrounded him, but fear choked me. He cleared his throat after another minute dragged by. "So you brought something for me? Or you were going to explain . . . something?"

I hoped his detachment was an act. Like, hoped it a lot. I wished he'd make it easier on me. A simple, "My life has been desolate without you" would have broken the ice.

Instead, he stood there, arms crossed, perfectly still, but with a tightness around his shoulders and jaw that betrayed his outward show of patience. This was nothing like the courtesy he usually showed me, and irritation flared in my stomach. It was more comfortable than the panic fluttering there, so I stoked it to settle my nerves. He had to know it wasn't easy for me to come here. "Why are you making this so hard on me?" I asked, keeping my voice even but firm like I did when Chloe was wheedling for extra TV time.

His eyebrows lifted, and I saw the first signs of life in his eyes. I wished it wasn't anger. "You are the last person who should be asking that question."

I swallowed, but it didn't push the fear down. All my insecurities flooded back to me. This wasn't about winning a verbal slap fight anymore. I wanted something totally different, something that not once in my life had I ever had the courage to ask for. I could walk away now, leaving the question unasked and the last tatters of my pride intact. Or I could do something brave instead. I closed my eyes and thought of the emotion that had poured into the second canvas I held, how it had flowed out through my paintbrush without stopping off at my brain for deconstruction. It had been wild and chaotic and the first thing that had purely made sense in a long, long time.

"Fair point." I looked at Aidan again, searching for some sign that he was softening, but I saw only frustration, and my chest fist tightened instead of loosened. "I'm sorry I ran out of here that first night. I freaked out, and it was wrong to leave without explaining."

"What happened? I thought we had it all resolved that as far as rich guys go, I'm not one of the evil ones."

"We did. You aren't. It wasn't that." The fear of his wealth upending my life flashed through me again. "That's a lie. It was that, but not for the reasons you think. I think this is where I need a drink. Or to be hit over the head with a hammer."

"I can help you with either," he said.

I waved him off. "No. What I need is truth serum and a massive tranquilizer to get me through this."

"Can't help you there." His voice was still too guarded. I missed the teasing note that was always in his tone.

I swallowed to dislodge the lump forming in my throat, wishing I could magically summon the teasing, laughing Aidan I'd gotten so used to instead of this distant, analytical version of him. "Eight years ago, I moved away from here and went to art school in New York. It was terrifying. I'd never been outside of Utah before, and it was such a different world that I wasn't sure I would ever fit in. But I loved it. I loved it as someone outside looking in." I glanced over at him to see how he was taking this so far.

"I'm surprised you've never mentioned living there before."

I nodded. "I know. It's because in some ways, I've been trying to forget. My third year of school, I was invited to participate in this guerrilla art exhibit, I guess you'd call it. Some friends were crashing an empty loft in Chelsea for a one-night-only show, and I showed some pieces. It was the weirdest crowd I'd ever been in."

"In New York, that's saying something."

I mustered a smile. "I know. But it was the oddest mix of these middle-aged portfolio managers wearing huge Rolexes and scruffy guys barely in their twenties coming to experience Art, in the capital *A* sense, as this thing that was more than paintings on the wall. There were young Wall Street guys and Brooklyn hipsters, and somewhere in all of that, I met Donovan."

It had been a wild night. Over a dozen artists had shared their work that night, but the energy in the room had all focused on three artists: a sculptor who worked with reclaimed copper, a guy who made incredible mixed media collages, and . . . me. Nothing in Utah had ever prepared me for a room full of people who responded to art like this loft full of them had. "Donovan was this interesting hybrid of the people who talked to me about my work all night. It's kind of excruciating to stand there when you're a hardwired introvert like I am. I mean, it's not as bad as having to make small talk or whatever, but person after person came by wanting me to open my brain for their examination, like I was on display too or something." It wasn't cold, but I rubbed my hands up and down my arms for warmth as I remembered standing there, exposed.

"Here, let's sit down," Aidan said, his arms uncrossing for the first time. I followed him to the sofa, and he pulled up a large armchair for himself. He leaned forward with his arms resting on his knees. "Go ahead."

"So Donovan talked to me that night. But instead of trying to dissect my brain to understand my work, he charmed me. He made me laugh, made me feel comfortable for the first time all night. He was like this oasis of normalcy in chaos. And he asked me out. And we started dating. His parents weren't thrilled at first. He's from an old New England family, and I seriously think they still operate under some caste system where they don't like their kids marrying outside of their class."

"Marrying?" Aidan interjected, his eyes sharp.

I bit at my bottom lip for a moment. When did it get so dry? Why did Aidan have to stare at me so closely? "Yeah. I'll get to that. I think Donovan got a kick out of bringing home an artist to meet his mom and dad, especially one with no East Coast roots. I have no idea if they put any direct pressure on him to drop me, but if they did, it didn't work. We kept dating. And I think"—I wiped my palms on my jeans, hating this part—"I don't know if he ever loved me or just loved how easy I was to dominate. I'd been drifting for the three years I was in New York, and suddenly, he threw out a tow rope and said, 'We're going this way.' And it felt so good to have a direction that I went."

"I can't imagine you doing that. At all," Aidan said.

"I know. I wish it weren't true. I wish I'd been a better, smarter, stronger, more sure person then. But I wasn't. And the more it bothered his parents that we were dating, the more Donovan made a point of shoving me in their faces. I mean, this is all stuff I figured out toward the end. They weren't the kind of people to be overtly rude, but once I figured out how to read them, in hindsight, it was pretty clear they couldn't stand me."

"They sound like—"

"Whatever bad word you're about to say, yes, they were that times ten. But I think they got scared that their golden child was about to marry some bohemian street artist, so they decided to do damage control. They were pretty well-respected art collectors themselves, which is how I think Donovan ended up at the guerrilla show that night. He was always trying to be like them, even when he thought he wasn't. Anyway, his parents had connections, amazing connections, and before I knew it, the Van Exel gallery had displayed a couple of my pieces."

His eyebrows shot up again. "That's big league. I've bought work from there before."

Yeah, like the two massively expensive paintings hanging on the walls a floor above us.

"It's the major leagues, yeah. And those two paintings sold fast. If Victoria puts her stamp of approval on it, people line up to buy it. Within a year, I had my own show there, and suddenly, I was this wunderkind exploding onto the art scene."

"I have several questions about this, but I'm going to start with the most distracting one. That gallery usually deals with large-scale oils, but you do watercolors."

"I do both, which I'll get to." I could already see the wheels spinning for him. He'd put this together soon if I didn't hurry and do it for him on my terms.

"Getting that first show must have been what the Beckmans needed to make me palatable or whatever, because six months after that, Donovan and I were married."

"Are you still married?" Aidan asked, the tension back in his jaw and shoulders.

"No. Smashed that all to bits a few years ago." He relaxed a fraction. Not much. "The in-between isn't important other than it took me two years of marriage to figure out that Donovan saw me as a pawn, not an equal. He treated me the way his parents treated him—as a showpiece, like I was the prize he'd won. 'Look, I married an acclaimed artist. I win.' You weren't the only trophy," I said, lacing my fingers together. The next part was easier to tell because it was the part where things finally got clear. "I saw person after person spend sick amounts on my work because they saw other people spend sick amounts of money on my work. It happened because the Beckmans made it happen. And that is never what I wanted my art to be about."

I dropped my head into my hands and stared at the carpet. "It made me sick that I'd been painting everything inside of me because of the pressure of my in-laws and the insane pace that Victoria wanted me to produce at, all to put my work in front of people who were in this weird bloodlust to own it without any interest at all in understanding it. On top of everything else, Donovan was working as an investment banker and the stress got so intense for him that he ended up with an addiction to prescription painkillers. It took me almost a year to figure out that his wild mood swings weren't about me."

"I'm so sorry," Aidan said, his voice quiet.

I didn't look up. "It's okay. I tried to get him into rehab, but I couldn't pay for it because he'd cleaned out my accounts. I tried going to his parents to get him help, but they didn't believe he had a problem. They said I was being dramatic. And after another month of trying to talk to him about it, he'd had it. He hit me."

Aidan bit out a curse, and I glanced up to see his hands tightened into fists on his thighs.

"It's okay," I said. "I mean, not that he did that. But it woke me up enough to realize I had to leave. I hated that my art had become this commodity with no soul. There was no reason for Donovan and me to be together anymore. I made his parents pay back some of what he'd stolen, and I came back here to be with my sister and help with Chloe. The money was enough to put a generous down payment on a condo and let me get away with working in the diner. I had enough to cover the basic bills and make sure one of us is always with my niece."

I straightened and scooted back against the couch, pulling my feet up and tucking them beneath me. Talking about Donovan always took so much out of me that it was all I could do not to curl up right then and close my eyes and dream it all away. Instead, I stayed still and waited for Aidan to speak.

"What name did you paint under?" he asked, his voice still quiet.

I stared down at my hands. As usual, I had paint smudged on my fingers. Now was the final step, the one I could never, ever take back. I looked up at Aidan, at his worried eyes and the tiny wrinkles beginning to fan from them that became grooves when he smiled. I loved the character they added to his face.

Instead of answering, I climbed off the sofa and crouched in front of one of the paintings I'd brought, my fingers working at the twine. Aidan stayed quiet, but the weight of his stare rested like a feather touch at the nape of my neck. I pulled the second piece of twine off and peeled back the cardboard. When I turned to face him, I kept the back of the first painting toward him. "Do you remember the watercolor you saw me doing at the lodge?"

He nodded.

"You'll be getting the larger version you commissioned soon, I guess. If you still want it. Victoria arranged the shipping several days ago."

I turned it around, and I couldn't have looked away from his face even if someone had set my hair on fire. He studied the canvas, and it took less than thirty seconds for recognition to flicker in his expression. I'd redone the watercolor as the smaller oil version of his commission piece I intended to tackle next.

He blinked, reached out like he wanted to touch it, then dropped his hand away. It was the look of someone who was registering that he'd been shoved off a cliff. Disbelief, an intellectual understanding of what had happened without fully comprehending what it meant yet.

"I have another painting to show you. I worked on this all last week. It's the truest thing I've ever done." I pushed myself up from the floor and set the second painting on the sofa, forcing myself to sit near it and keep watching his face. It was the glacier lilies that had made Dani cry. "I've done a bad job of explaining myself with words, so I gave up and did this. Every time I ever told you to go away was a lie. This is the truth."

He didn't move from where he sat, only stared at the new painting with a look I couldn't interpret. His eyes brightened and narrowed slightly in concentration, but otherwise, he showed no expression. "You're her," he said, his voice sure. "You're Leandra Tate."

"I was," I corrected him. "That's my full first name and middle name. But Lia Carswell painted this for you."

As the confirmation of who I was sank in, his gaze traveled over my face, studying it the way he had the painting, as if he was examining all the colors and angles I was made of, missing nothing. He stood and crossed to crouch in front of me.

"The first time I ever saw your work, it took my breath away," he said, and hope finally flickered to life for me. "It was like looking at the inside of my head laid out for everyone to see. I'd never felt so understood. You got it. You got what it was like to be from here and live there and try to make it all make sense."

He gathered my hands in his, carefully, like he was afraid a sudden movement would make me bolt. "I tried to buy it right on the spot, but the guy wouldn't sell. He did tell me where he got it, though, and I immediately called my assistant and told her to track down your work. She figured out that the Van Exel gallery was the exclusive dealer for your work, so I made a point of wandering through it from time to time, looking for another piece like the one in the Hamptons, a piece that reflected all the conflicts inside me." He studied me closely. "I looked you up online. I wanted to know who was behind the art. I can't believe I didn't recognize you."

"I looked different. And besides, it's not like you had any reason to make that connection." I'd grown out the severe dark brunette bob I'd thought fit so well in the artsy crowd, let it go back to its natural color and grow slightly untamed. And I used to be a scrawny, pale thing, always in my studio. All my outdoor running had still left me scrawny, but I had a peachy tone now.

He squeezed my hands. "I guess it's time for another confession. Don't hate me."

It didn't seem possible to hate him for any reason, ever.

"I always bought your work anonymously because I didn't want the price shooting up when Victoria realized I was the buyer. I feel like I need to confess that, but I want you to know I'd have paid any price to get it."

The fist in my chest unclenched, and the relief wanted to come out as laughter. "I won't hold it against you."

"Good. I love what you do," he said, and his serious eyes met mine and searched inside them for a response.

I tugged on his hands until he eased up next to me on the sofa, and then I twined my arms around his neck. I pulled his head toward mine and pressed my lips against his, but he took over, wrapping his arms around my waist to pull me closer, sending heat flaring between us. There would never be such a thing as close enough. His mouth traveled to mine for another kiss that made my insides thrum with the same energy that had surrounded us on the mountain.

For hours or maybe days, we explored that kiss, but when I finally drew back, the sun was still in the middle of setting. I rested my forehead against his and smiled. "I'm always going to be sorry I ran away from you that night," I said. "I'll never be able to get back the last two weeks where I could have been doing a lot more of this." I leaned back and brushed my hands over his face, gently tracing the planes and angles. "I'm sorry I misunderstood you. I'll be better."

He reached up and pulled my hands down but kept them between his, warm and safe. "I get why you ran. But I want you to know, I understand you. *You.* Lia. Not you as an artist. You as an everything." He turned his head slightly to look at the framed canvas of the glacier lilies, and since his forehead was still resting against mine, I turned to look too. "I understand that painting. How did you know?" he asked, his face now lit with a soft smile.

"Know what?"

"How did you know that's how it feels to be with you?"

I looked at my heart spread out on that canvas, then brought my lips up to meet his. "Because that's how it feels for me too."

And this time his kiss tasted the way happiness felt.

About the Author

Melanie Bennett Jacobson buys a lot of books and shoes. She eats a lot of chocolate and french fries and watches a lot of chick flicks. She kills a lot of houseplants. She says "a lot" a lot. She is happily married and living in Southern California with her growing family and more doomed plants. Melanie is a former English teacher, who loves to laugh and make others laugh. In her downtime (ha!), she writes romantic comedies and cracks stupid jokes on Twitter. She is the author of five previous novels from Covenant.